Born in 1922, NIGEL KNEALE is one of the most important and radical British screenwriters of the last century. Predominantly a writer of thrillers that used science-fiction and horror elements, he was best known for the creation of the character Professor Bernard Quatermass, who appeared in various television, film and radio productions written by Kneale for the BBC, Hammer Film Productions and Thames Television between 1953 and 1996. He wrote original scripts and successfully adapted works by writers such as George Orwell, John Osborne, H. G. Wells among others, and was twice nominated for the BAFTA Award for Best British Screenplay.

TOMATO CAIN
AND OTHER STORIES

NIGEL KNEALE

To My Parents

Tomato Cain and Other Stories first published in Great Britain in 1949 by Collins. 'Essence of Strawberry', 'Mrs Mancini', and 'The Patter of Tiny Feet' first published in *Tomato Cain and Other Stories* published in the US in 1950 by Knopf. 'Billy Halloran' first published in *Tattoo*, August 1946. 'It Doesn't Matter Now' first published in *Britannia and Eve*, August 1946.

A CIP catalogue record of this book is available from the British Library.

ISBN-10 1912697653
ISBN-13 9781912697656

The publisher gratefully acknowledges the support of Arts Council England

Supported by
ARTS COUNCIL
ENGLAND

Contents

CONTENTS

Introduction

IF THE QUATERMASS SERIALS of the 1950s have anything approaching a catchphrase it's the description of the troubled titular character as 'the rocket man'. After his brave space experiment 'brings something back' with horrifying consequences, the British public (perhaps helped by seeing the monstrous alien creature in Westminster Abbey) know very well who Bernard Quatermass is and the particular brand of slightly detached scientist he represents. But 'the rocket man' could equally well apply to Quatermass' creator, the brilliant, visionary, uniquely unsettling Nigel Kneale.

I first became aware of Kneale via the TV screening of the film version of his *Quatermass and the Pit* – the legendary and hugely influential tale of an ancient Martian invasion uncovered by excavation in modern day Knightsbridge. It's become something of a cliché to talk of pubs emptying upon its first transmission but the original serials had gripped the nation like nothing else and my parents had long memories. They knew how scary it was and allowed me to stay up to watch the film only under strict supervision. It was the talk of school the next day. Then, in short order, I saw the other two *Quatermass* films which, though bowdlerised for the American market, still held an extraordinary power. Then, at last, came Kneale's

ITV series *Beasts*. Aged 10 (and completely hooked on any kind of supernatural TV), this series of one-off plays all centring, in one way or another, around animals, promised to be just what I craved. I can remember watching the first play 'During Barty's Party' (a superb exercise in mounting dread and terror) in a sheen of cold sweat, and the ghastly effect of 'Baby' has never quite left me even after all these years. In 1979, there came the epic final *Quatermass* story with John Mills, by which time I was completely besotted with Kneale's work and seeking out everything I could. I found the privately printed edition of 'The Year of the Sex Olympics' (Kneale's infamous and incredibly prescient depiction of a TV-obsessed future), 'The Road' (a now-lost period ghost story with an extraordinary, chilling twist) and 'The Stone Tape' (Kneale's own searingly clever, terrifying modern day 'ghost story for Christmas'). Then the reissued *Quatermass* scripts and, after something of a (wild) hunt, 'Tomato Cain', his book of short stories which you happily hold between your hands now. Kneale's book won the prestigious Somerset Maugham Prize and brought him to the attention of the BBC and thence to Rudolph Cartier and thus to *Quatermass*. A hugely successful career in television and film sprang from this but Kneale was not to return to prose – except for the novelisation of the fourth and final *Quatermass* in 1979. This is a great shame because the stories contained here (some only featured in the American edition and two never previously collected) not only show an amazing imagination at work but the seeds of so much that was to come.

What's fascinating and revealing, reading these terrific tales again is that they fall into distinct strands. There are the ones we might say exist in 'Quatermass-land', a greyish, post-war world of housing estates and milk bars and nascent youth culture, of suspicion and a certain type of domestic unhappiness. This strand embraces everything from the startling poltergeist of 'Minuke' to the grim suburban despair of 'Essence of Strawberry', from the thumbnail of broken dreams which is 'Bini and Bettine' to the superbly chilling ghost story 'The Patter of Tiny Feet' (one of my favourites). This is Kneale as the cynic he was so often characterised as, casting a jaundiced eye on the human condition and human relationships. Yet even here, there are signs of the big heart we know him to have had. He is quite forgiving of his domestic tyrants, his disappointed lovers, his cuckolded shop-keepers.

Then there are experiments. 'Chains' is a revenge story shot through with a sense of proper anger. There's a World War Two story which reads like something from the *Arabian Nights* and a brilliantly grumpy depiction of being in a terrible matinee of a terrible play (no doubt inspired by Kneale's short career as a RADA-trained actor). And there are a couple of first person narratives, one from Ancient Egypt, one from post-war Italy which perhaps point more towards script writing and the superb ear for dialogue which became Kneale's trademark.

Then, of course, there are the island stories. Kneale, though born in Barrow-in-Furness, was a Manxman and the curious strain of superstition, isolation and magic imbued in him from birth was to stay with him throughout his long career. The Manx stories are dense with carefully observed detail and evocative names (Quilliam, Dicky-Dan, Gob Kelly). But the island also feels full of wonder. Angelic visitations and booming-voiced sea monsters vie with beautifully observed vignettes of long-forgotten outings, of Victoria's Diamond Jubilee and family feuding. The title story is a little comic gem, effortlessly transporting us back to a time when a new fruit could be looked upon with suspicion and fear. And there are wonderful and touching little stories like 'Tootie and the Cat Licenses' and 'Curphey's Follower' which could almost, you might think, have been conceived by no one else but Nigel

Kneale. It's interesting to note too, in light of the later 'Beasts' just how many animals are featured here too. There are lots of dogs, cats (with tails and without), ducks, frogs, rats... Oh yes, there are rats...

Which brings us, of course, to horror. Though Kneale very much disliked being labelled as a horror writer (and a science-fiction writer for that matter) there is a strong thread of genuine ghastliness which acts as a sort of background hum to all his work. So much so that, reading the stories as a whole, one tends to suspect the worst is going to happen even when it doesn't! 'Jeremy in the Wind' has a gripping, muted chilliness ('But Jeremy he just chuckled. As we went along, he talked to me – funny sort of voice he's got – until a pebble fell out of his mouth'). 'The Photograph' is genuinely upsetting and 'The Pond' almost like the plot of an E.C. Comic. And there's 'The Stocking', of course – as nasty a tale as Kneale (or anyone else) ever mustered.

Nigel Kneale remains a hugely important part of our popular culture; a proper visionary whose jaded eye was always inflected with a deeply felt humanity. It's both tremendously exciting and deeply reassuring to think that these stories are, in this handsome new edition, back in print after so very long. His imagination and, by extension, the reader's, soars once more – like a rocket.

Mark Gatiss
London, June 2022

Foreword
to the Original Edition

WITHIN THE LAST FEW years, readers have become less shy of the short story. That this form of fiction is also a form of art had fairly long ago been recognised; what is more important, from the point of view of popular favour, is that the high potential of entertainment in a good collection of stories may now be seen. There exists, too, a growing body of people who no longer turn to a book in search of 'escape' but are genuinely interested in writing – who value craftsmanship and react to originality. To such readers, the short story – in its present rather fascinating position half-way between tradition and experiment – must particularly appeal.

The experimental writer, lately, has in fact been given a good deal of rope: that the best use has invariably been made of this I cannot say. There has been a danger that, because of its literary privilege, the short story might fall under a certain literary blight, and become an example of too much prose draped around an insufficiently vital feeling or a trumped-up, insufficiently strong idea. The declared reaction against plot – as constraining, rigid or artificial – was once good up to a point, but possibly went too far: the fact that a story must be a story was overlooked. There are now signs of an equally strong (and, I think, healthy) reaction against plotlessness. Of this Nigel Kneale's stories are symptomatic.

Indeed, in one sense, these tales in *Tomato Cain* show a return to the great mainstream of the English story tradition – with which one associates Kipling, Wells, Saki, Somerset Maugham. When I say that Nigel Kneale's stories have plot, I mean that they make their effect by the traditional elements of invention, tension, a certain amazement and, ultimately, surprise. Like his great predecessors, he is impersonal, not using his art either for self-expression or exhibition. His art is the art of narration – the world's oldest. He knows how to rouse interest; and, which is still rarer, knows how to hold it. He is adept to giving a situation a final twist. These *Tomato Cain* stories vary in quality, as stories in any collection must; but, personally, I find the author guilty of not one single story which bogs down.

The writer of stories of this type must be bold; he disdains the shelter of ambiguity; it is essential that each of his pieces should come off. He is gambling – in an honourable sense, for are not Kipling, Wells, Saki, Somerset Maugham gamblers also? – on the originality of his imagination, on his power to grip, on the persuasiveness of his manner of story-telling. It might be too much to say that all the world's classic stories have had an element of the preposterous about them; one might safely say that any memorable story carried something which had to be put across. A part of the fascination of Nigel Kneale's story-telling is that he takes long chances; a part of the satisfaction of it is that in almost all cases he justifies the risks.

This writer is a young Manxman. He has grown up in, and infuses into his stories, an atmosphere which one can cut with a knife. He is not dependent on regionalism – not all of his work has an Isle of Man setting – but it would appear that he draws strength from it: his work at its best has the flavour, raciness, 'body' that one associates with the best of the output from Ireland, Wales, Brittany, and the more remote of the States of America. He turns for his inspiration to creeks in which life runs deep, to pockets in which life accumulates, deeply queer. Is the Talking Mongoose a sore subject with the Isle of Man? That interesting animal – of which the investigations of the late Harry Price never entirely disposed – might well be the denizen of a Nigel Kneale story. Has he not made frogs avengers; has he not made a deformed duck a tragedian?

In far-off days [he says, at the opening of 'The Tarroo-Ushtey'] before the preachers and the school-masters came, the island held a good many creatures besides people and beasts. The place swarmed with monsters.

A man would think twice before answering his cottage door on a windy night, in dread of a visit from his own ghost. The high mountain roads rang in the darkness with the thunderous tiffs of the bugganes, which had unspeakable shapes and heads bigger than houses; while a walk along the sea-shore after the sun had set was to invite the misty appearance of a tarroo-ushtey, in the likeness of a monstrous bull... At harvest-time the hairy trollman, the phynodderee, might come springing out of his elderberry tree to assist the reaping, to the farmer's dismay; for the best-intentioned of the beings were no more helpful than interfering neighbours...

This is the background atmosphere of one group of Nigel Kneale's stories; call them the local pieces. 'Tomato Cain' itself, 'The Excursion', and 'The Putting-Away of Uncle Quaggin' have (for instance) a naturalism not unworthy of Maupassant: the supernatural never raises its head, but eminent human queerness is at its height.

It is the function of every emerging writer to create, and stamp, his own universe. This Nigel Kneale has done. In his universe, love, in the sentimental or social sense, plays almost no part; but the passions stalk like those island monsters. Like the unfortunate bungalow in 'Minuke', his characters are wrenched and battered and heaved up. What is remarkable, given the themes of many of the stories, is that the writer so seldom – if; indeed, ever? – crosses the bounds into extravagance; his forte is a sort of control, restraint. His 'Quiet Mr. Evans' tale of an injured husband's revenge in a fish-and-chip shop, threatens at one point to approach in horror H. G. Wells' 'The Cone', but the last twist gives a pathetic-ironic end. It would be fair to say that his children and animal stories, with their focus on suffering (e.g. 'The Photograph', 'Oh, Mirror, Mirror', 'The Stocking', 'Flo', and the semi-fantastic 'Curphey's Follower') most dangerously approach the unbearable. It may, however, be found that Nigel Kneale knows how to relax any too great realism at the saving moment.

To the sheer *build*, to the something better than ingenuity of the best of the stories, attention should be drawn. 'Peg' and 'Bini and Bettine' would seem to me to be masterpieces in a genre particularly this writer's own. This is a first book: Nigel Kneale is at the opening of his career; he is still making a trial of his powers. To an older writer, the just not overcrowded effect of inventive richness, the suggestion of potentialities still to be explored, and of alternatives pending, cannot but be attractive. That the general reader will react to Nigel Kneale's stories, and that the perceptive reader will relish what is new in his contribution to fiction, I feel sure.

Elizabeth Bowen,
1949

Tomato Cain

WHEN PEOPLE PASSED HIS cottage they said to one another, 'That is where Eli Cain lives. He is good, and a sidesman at Ballaroddan Methodist Chapel.'

Certainly they pointed at his house with interest, for he had often seen them, as he sat at his tea and soda bread in the evenings.

On the morning of the harvest festival, Eli brushed his dark-grey Sunday suit with the long tails until every speck of dust had departed. He draped it carefully over the back of a chair while he wrote in his new hymn book 'Eli Cain,' and the date, 'September 28th, 1883.' He formed the words slowly and carefully: when he left this fine leather-backed, gold-edged volume in his will, his niece would tell her children, 'Learn to write like your Uncle Cain.' He underlined the words twice, and placed a bracket on each side for symmetry.

A flat, damp piece of peat taking care of the fire, he set out with the book held delicately to avoid fingermarks.

As he passed Mrs. Crebbin's, he raised his hat to the window, in case anyone should be looking out, but after that he kept his eyes on the path to avoid muddy pools and slippery gravel.

His face, which was seen only by the creeping things that

1

lived on the roadside, was grim, and his mouth was pressed tight so that he could not even talk things over with himself.

He did not glance to the left, where the grey mist was slowly rising on the hillside; or to the right, where sheep looked up mournfully from the stubble. There were serious thoughts in the mind of Eli Cain.

He grimaced as he picked his way between the pools at the Chapel entrance. Removing a speck of dust from his hat before hanging it on a peg in the vestibule, he could hear Jacob Skillicorn, the organist, practising softly inside:

'... For His mercies still endure,
Ever faithful, ever sure...'

Eli pushed the door open and found in the hymn book the place he had marked by the ribbon. Number 381 and number 383 were the harvest hymns for today. In good, large type. He checked them against the wooden indicator above the pulpit, deliberately keeping his eyes from straying until he had completed the routine.

'Good morning, Mr. Cain,' said little pale-haired Skillicorn, holding a note on the new American organ.

'Good day,' said Eli.

'Come early to see the vegetables, eh?' Skillicorn giggled. 'And tomatoes, would y' believe?'

Eli Cain looked at the table before the pulpit, seeing what he had feared he might. True, there were piled honest Manx harvestings – potatoes, corn, carrots, leeks, turnips, cabbages, barley. Three there were of Eli's own best swedes.

But in the centre of these, shone a little heap of scarlet fruit. The new *tomatoes* of John James Quilleash.

'So he brought them, for all!' said Eli.

Skillicorn gave a little fizz and turned again to the organ.

'Praise Him for our harvest store,
He hath filled the garner floor.'

Eli stared at the things with a cold blush of shame. Anger too. Anger that Skillicorn should be amused. Anger that Quilleash should have shown so little respect for what was fitting.

'Showin' off, he is,' whispered Eli's drawn lips, 'with his conservatory!'

For that was where the tomatoes had been grown, as all the village knew. They were not a harvest-fruit to sing hymns for, but foreign things drawn from the earth by hot glass, and then hardly ripened, even at this time of the year. These, likely, were all the miserable, misunderstood plants he had been able to produce. And hardly a creature in the Isle of Man, save John James Quilleash, had ever tasted them.

Yet he had flouted, carelessly flouted, the earnest wishes of good men; abused his high position as a trustee. Eli felt contemptuous hate for Quilleash as he laid the hymn book in the rack of his appointed pew, restraining himself to gentleness.

Neither fruit nor vegetable by nature, it appeared. Some said they were poisonous if eaten in numbers, and others that the things came from South America, whose immorality was a deep concern to all thinking men. 'Love-apples' were the tomatoes called.

'Next they'll be havin' one of those stage-dancin' women in the pulpit,' said Eli.

Skillicorn sniggered absently behind his curtain.

'Mortifyin', it is. Mortifyin' and – and wanton desecration!' Eli glared at the brilliant, unnatural redness. Trust a Quilleash to be trying to catch the public eye, by whatsoever means. But to spoil the harvest-home for self-glorification!

He should not. Eli grew stiff with resolution. The purity of the Chapel swelled high in his mind. Like a great wedding cake, shining, rich, complicated and brittle.

People were entering the outer door, mumbling pleasantries. Skillicorn was playing softly behind his curtain.

Eli stepped forward, tucked his coat up across his chest. One by one, he gathered the soft, loathsome fruit quickly into it. He hurried to the side door and out into the narrow yard, even as the first worshippers came in at the other end. Beads of sweat hung on his forehead. He stumbled in his haste on the gravelled path.

At the hedge he stopped, trembling a little in his legs. It would be enough to hide the fruit until the service was over. Then Quilleash could do as he wished with them.

Eli kicked at the flimsy hurdle that barred the way to the tea field. It fell with a rattle, and as it did so a large tomato tumbled in a red splash on the stony ground. He snatched at it, only to see another fall from his coat front, and then a third.

Desperately he ran into the field, crouching low, and deposited the things while he returned to the splotched mess on the stones and swept away the juice and pips with a tuft of grass.

In the field, close to the hedge, he tore up a great sod with his bare, hard hands. When he had scraped some earth from the place, he bundled all the tomatoes, broken and crushed as they were, into the cavity, and stamped the sod back into place.

He stood, breathing heavily; leaned against the hedge to think for a time.

The things were lost now. But no one had seen them go. And later perhaps he would explain the position to his brother officers in the vestry.

When he walked slowly round to the front entrance he was just in time to assist in closing the draughty doors. As he took his place at the back, Skillicorn was playing with gusto. Always a bit theatrical he was with his stops.

A woman in front of Eli whispered to her neighbour, 'I thought John James was bringin' some of those new tomato fruits?' The neighbour shook her head to indicate ignorance. Eli felt an inner glow.

'... And for richer food than this,
Pledge of everlasting bliss...' he sang.

The sermon was long and the preacher was dully cheerful, and Eli's gaze wandered to his three fine swedes before the pulpit. Their skins shone cleanly and smoothly, and it seemed to him that they were all a good harvest-home demanded.

Then he dozed a while, though never forgetting himself completely, so that he rose as readily as his colleague, Willie Mylroie, when the offertory came.

'As generous as possible,' recited the preacher, and Eli picked a speck of cotton from the dark-blue velvet of the collection plate, to lead off himself with a bright shilling.

People coughed and shifted themselves noisily, feeling in pockets and purses for coppers and threepenny pieces, tidying children and reassuring themselves of the presence of their hats beneath the seats.

Murmurs caught Eli's uneasy ear: 'So John James didn' have his queer fruit ripe after all!' 'Thought better of givin' them to harvest-home, p'raps.' 'If y'ask me, I don' believe the things ever grew at all, at all!'

He caught a glimpse of Quilleash sitting puzzled, as his neighbours questioned in whispers.

An ill-mannered brat in the front row stared unwinkingly at Eli while he passed the plate along, until her mother corrected her. He saw the child whisper as he moved back, and people turned to glance at him quickly.

Eli felt uncomfortable, hardly noticing even that someone had placed a sovereign upon the blue velvet.

Heads turned, faces stared, as the hands to which they belonged offered pence or silver. 'Hush, child! Mr. Cain is a good man,' a woman behind him rebuked.

Old Watterson, the thatcher, let his last teeth show in a crooked grin, until, embarrassed by Eli's look, he began to search on the floor for the hymn book already clutched in his hand.

A young girl, who should have known better, gave a squeaky titter and hiccuped loudly.

Eli's ears burned. He stared across to the window, ignoring the worshippers, until the plate returned along the rows to his hand.

But instead of the backs of heads, faces were turned to him from the front pews he had passed. He was stung by the contemptuous stare of Mrs. Kermode under her shiny-black hat.

And at the end of the next row sat John James Quilleash.

Steadily Eli turned to his pew and submitted the partly filled plate.

Steadily Quilleash eyed him, his hands at his sides. There was a bitter-fat smile under his sandy moustache.

Everyone in the Chapel watched without a breath.

In an instant Quilleash's look changed. His eyes closed up and the grin of malice grew on his face. He spoke in a loud whisper that must have been heard by the very mice in the skirting.

'I hope you enjoyed my tomatoes, Mr. Cain,' he said. 'But, of course, you must have, since you ate the lot. Or p'raps you give one or two to Mr. Skillicorn?'

Eli was speechless. His face wobbled in bewilderment.

Quilleash prodded a fat finger forward, and flicked a tiny, shining thing from Eli's waistcoat.

Eli pressed his fingers to the place, and there, hidden by a fold, was a wet smear of pink juice and seeds. Caught by a horn button hung a long strip of red tomato skin.

Quilleash leaned forward confidentially. 'Thou'rt a sloppy eater, Mr. Cain.'

And the whole Chapel roared with laughter. Even the preacher.

Faces twisted and rolled before Eli as he stood blushing and sweating, like a man clutching a red wound. He gasped, 'I never done that! I never! Just you listen –'

But no one heard his words, and his tongue stopped working. Desperately he turned to the pulpit, and saw the bland faces of the three turnips, and the preacher wiping his eyes. The plate wobbled in his hand. A sixpence tinkled on the floor.

The grinning Mylroie took over, and Eli, recovered a little, dabbed wildly at his stomach as he fled to the back of the Chapel.

A streak of red juice sank into the leather of the new hymn book that he hid himself in, searching the pages frantically for nothing, to cover his confusion.

Still the Chapel vibrated with laughter, people standing up to stare at the pulpit and then back at the wretched Cain, until at last the preacher held up his hand, still smirking a little himself.

As the silence poured into Eli's soul like healing fluid, he realised that he was gasping and shivering. Willie Myhoie was beside him.

'Eli,' he said, his voice low and curious, 'what do they taste like?' But the look of hate that he received made him turn away. Perhaps they were poisonous after all, thought Mylroie.

No one noticed the remainder of the service, except that Eli Cain sat as if in a fever, quickly turning the pages of his hymn book one by one, and staring straight in front of him.

Occasionally there was a chuckle or a snigger or a nudging of elbows.

When it ended at last there was a rush for the door. But Eli Cain was before the first of his tormentors, hat in one hand, and book in the other, out in the road as they pressed through.

'Mr. Cain, I'm surprised at you!' he heard, and 'Better than turnips, eh, Eli?' 'Festival for somebody, anyway!'

He shambled up the road, mouth half-open, feeling as if the skin had been peeled off him. His brain had abandoned useless argument.

'Tomato Cain!' piped a voice, loud and shrill.

There was a great roar of laughter. That would be Joseph Kelly's cheeky Benjamin.

'Tomato Cain,' shouted others, and again. 'Tomato Cain!' Their noise filled the whole valley.

He quickened his steps, heart galloping, stopping only to snatch up the hymn book when it flew from his swinging hand into the mud.

The laughter continued louder as he glanced back, hunted.

'Tomato Cain!'

'Tomato! Tomato Cain!'

He knew, with a sudden twitch of agony, that Eli Cain Esquire had ceased to exist at a touch of Quilleash's podgy finger.

Panting, followed by a fading surge of chuckles, Tomato Cain fled up the hillside.

Enderby and the
Sleeping Beauty

A DOUBLE-SIZE CHIN. With a wide, pleasant mouth to say the thoughts from the long, tipped-back cranium above. These thoughts were just so many, docile and wholesome, like a well-ordered flock. Most concerned the laws and functions of machines, for Fred Enderby had been a mechanic since he began to screw strips of painted tin together in his mother's backyard in Warrington.

L.A.C. Enderby, Frederick, is the only man, I believe, to know the factual core of a legend that every child can tell when it has reached half a dozen years. How a princess pricked her finger on a magic needle and slept for a hundred years, with the whole palace, courtiers, scullions, dogs, in a trance where they fell. Round the palace grew a hedge of thorns so that no one could get in, or, once in, out. Until at the end of the appointed time, a handsome prince broke through and kissed the princess back to life, while every creature in the court stirred and moved again. That is the legend. Here are the facts:

In 1942, Enderby was in North Africa on maintenance duty with an R.A.F. survey truck. They were far to the south of the battle area when the great retreat to El Alamein reached its height. Helpless in the radio silence, knowing only from the rumbling, and the glow by night, that the enemy was closing on Egypt.

Several times the party spotted planes, slow, sightless specks. To avoid the chance of capture they turned to the south-east, deeper into the desert. Flat barrenness gave place gradually to the wallowing Sahara.

They were deep in that wilderness when the khamsin storm came upon them.

The wind was of unnatural violence, Enderby says. Sand shifted in whole dunes. The party were totally unprepared. To go on was impossible. To leave the truck seemed suicidal. The sides of the thing trembled and drummed. Cans of petrol and a spare wheel tumbled away into the whirling dust.

The truck itself became unstable. Twice they felt the three offside wheels lift and settle again. Then, even while they shifted gear to balance it, the vehicle went over.

The officer in charge had his head crushed by falling equipment. Another man was trapped. A third smelt petrol, forced his way out, and was choked to death a few yards from the truck he could no longer see.

Enderby was in the cab, unconscious.

He woke at last from his own coughing. There was sand in his mouth. He lay upside down across the body of the driver.

Enderby levered himself up and examined his mate. The man was dead, his face buried in a soft, suffocating layer that covered the inside of the splintered window.

Enderby forced up the other door. Sand poured from it. The simoon had become a gritty breeze across the reshaped land. He slid out, coughing.

The truck was half-buried. The rear door, once opened, had been held wide by the blast that poured inside. Nothing lived in there now. The man from Warrington rested a while, still half-stunned, among the smothered shapes.

When Enderby set off alone the sun was still fierce. He had water in a full bottle: some fresh, some from the truck's tank: and sufficient emergency rations to reach safety, if he could trust the sun and himself. He felt weakly bitter that the radio had smashed itself.

At the top of each rise he stopped and turned about, shading his eyes: blinked and went on. He walked slowly, to conserve his strength. The glare beat up against his body.

It was perhaps an hour after starting, Enderby says, that he first saw the thing.

As he came to the sliding, coarse top of a shallow dune, its brighter colour struck his eye. A few hundred yards away. There was something man-made about that pale stone that he could just barely see.

Enderby shouted once and began to run, slithering among the brown ripples.

It was a building. Sand was heaped about it on every side. Only a part jutted from the desert, like a half-buried box. The roof and corners were formless, the pale walls deeply corroded.

Enderby's heart sank. He walked haltingly along the bare side of the place, turned a corner into the black, cool shadow. Just where the desert rose up under his feet and hid the building, he found a door.

It was recessed between two of the flat, shallow buttresses that ran up the walls at intervals. Surprisingly, the lock was on the outside of the thin stone. (As Enderby said later, 'An ordinary lock mechanism with no cover. It was all made of stone bars and big – it must 'ave spread over 'alf the door.')

He was able to open it. His dread of the desert forced and fought the lock until it submitted. The door ground and scraped until there was a gap wide enough for a man to enter. On the other side was complete blackness. 'Allo, in there!' Enderby shouted. 'Ey!'

The answer was a long, clapping echo.

He found matches, stepped into the cool darkness and struck one. He was in a small, bricked antechamber. As the second match flared up he saw a heap of faggots. ('Sort of compressed fibre, they were made of,' Enderby said. 'They lit easily. Queer. Made you feel you were kind of expected.')

With the slow-burning, smoky torch held high, and two cold spares stuffed inside his shirt, he entered a passage. The air was dry and dead and sweet.

Then he dived to the wall, crouching, quivering.

Nothing stirred.

'Who's that?' said Enderby. 'If it's anybody, come 'ere!' Then, remembering, he threw the torch.

('I saw a statue,' he said afterwards. 'I felt – well, a sort of daft relief. Like a false alarm in a U certificate thriller.')

The figure stood man-high against the wall. Stone drapes exposed one polished shoulder and its arms were crossed. Round the head was a wide beaded band of blue stones. And the face –

('That's what'd given me the start,' said Enderby. 'The eyes, long, bulging black ovals – no pupils – they were the worst. And the mouth and that – as if 'e'd sucked every dirty thing in the world into 'is mind, and was damn 'appy about it.')

When he picked up the torch he began to see others. They stood in two facing rows, lining the walls of the high tunnel.

He walked in the middle. The black eyes flickered in the light. His feet were like a cat's in the deep, black dust.

The figures were of both men and women. Some were painted, in dull colours: blue and green stones sparkled in their dress: more than once Enderby saw gold in the carved folds of a woman's hair. And every face repelled him.

They were amazingly expressive, he said. Each seemed to have a double meaning. A twisting of the brows and a wrinkling round the empty eyes, and madness showed through the face's laugh. Where they were heavy and stupid, there was vicious cunning also. In eagerness was slavering depravity: in innocence treachery. Gentleness meant cruelty. ('It was like people in a bad dream. They wanted to make y' see through them. Indecent.') He was puzzled by small holes drilled in the centre of each forehead and throat, and in the robes below.

On the walls between them, depressed in the brick, were tablets of writing. Symbols were nicked out like tiny toothprints, row upon row. ('Like something a tike's chewed.')

The tunnel curved gradually. Enderby reckoned himself fifty yards along when he could no longer see the entrance. He began to whistle without a tune because hope had dropped to vague curiosity. The walls echoed against him. He walked in silence.

Then he saw that the figures ended just ahead. He passed the last leering face into an open darkness that must have been far under the desert. The air was thick.

Enderby crept like a glow-worm in his circle of light. His eyes went left and right.

He watched the guiding walls so intently that his knee struck what he did not see. It was a high-mounted slab. The top was carved to such a likeness of soft cushioning. ('Like petrified silk. It'd 'ave made y' sleepy to look at it. Like the mattress adverts.')

Enderby strongly disclaims any knowledge of art. Sculpture bores him and his only visit to a gallery was to the engineering section.

But what he saw on the stone couch, he says, was not sculpture.

He forgot the darkness, the unnatural figures, the choking air. He forgot the truck disaster and that he was lost in the desert.

('She wasn't just wonderful in the ordinary way. I can't tell you 'ow. Look 'ere, if y' take the most smashing film stars – Betty 'Utton, Garson – as many as y' like – and all they've got

between 'em, and multiply it by ten, and then... oh, I dunno!
She was different to them anyway – Eastern, of course – but
so different in other ways. What I said, I just can't begin to
describe her...')

But she was made of stone.

Enderby stood worshipping until the torch had sank and
the figure was shadowed.

He went to the magnificent head. The stone, he says, was
tinted to life, but no paint showed itself.

Light from one raised hand smoked down across the
Lancashire man's wide eyes and long chin and tunic: and over
the pale-sallow nestling stone creature with the sleeping eyes.
At last Enderby leaned forward.

Very gently he kissed the sculpture on the mouth.

('She was – I've told you. Oh, I suppose it was, well –
perverted. A statue, I mean. Her lips were cold.')

Then fear replaced all he felt.

For the figure moved.

Enderby started back. The delicate face had turned away.
Now it came back again, very slowly. Coy. Away, back. Away,
back. Rhythmically, swivelling on the carved throat, the
beautiful lady shook her head.

''Inge,' said Enderby's whisper, because he was very much
afraid. ''Inge, that.'

The movement grew stronger, pendulum-regular. And
now the eyes opened, black, horribly void. His throat seemed
to wither.

Points of light moved. In the tunnel. From side to side they
went, slowly. Jet eyes in metronome faces. ('Like the Chinese
ornaments that keep rocking their 'eads when y've started them.
Only slowly. Terribly slowly. And these shook them.')

Enderby sweated. He pulled the other faggots from his
shirt. A moment later the whole chamber flared into light.

From it led not one passage, he saw, but five. And in each

were figures that leered in perfect time. Somewhere there was a heavy murmuring rumble.

Enderby collected himself. He touched the icy stone body of the beauty. From a pocket of his shirt he fumbled a stump of blue copying pencil.

Across the perfect waist he printed, thick and almost steadily: 'F. ENDERBY, WARRINGTON, R.A.F. 1942.'

He stuffed the defiling pencil away. 'And now,' he said, much too loudly, 'I will go and get started again.'

It was when he turned towards the tunnels that he saw the spikes.

They were coming out very slowly. About the pace of a common slug in a Warrington allotment, and with no more noise.

One from the forehead, one from the throat and one from the folded hands; others from the studded robes. From each figure, and above to the ceiling, the points shone and grew, sprouting across the passages. Closing them.

'Christ!' Enderby said.

He sprang into the centre tunnel, opposite the slab, ran with the waving treble torch. It cast stubby points in a forest of pikes upon the ceiling. Nightmarishly, the dust muffled his boots.

Twice he kicked up yellow-white human fragments. He tripped on a carpeted cage of ribs and slashed his hand on a lengthening spike.

He saw no daylight.

Instead, a wall of arrow-lettered brick faced him at the end. He tore and kicked, trying to open it, before he realised he could be in the wrong passage.

Then he was flying back between the sprouting pikes. They covered half the space with a mass of jagged bars. Even the spaces between them would be death cages. Back across the bones.

The chamber itself, when he reached it, sprouted iron

from each wall. A deep throb shook everything. The whole building was thrusting at him.

Enderby panted by the slab without a glance. Down the left-hand tunnel.

At each nod from the jet–eyed lines, the points sprang a little farther across.

If he had not seen the light of the entrance, Enderby swears he would have been insane before the points took him.

As it was, he dragged himself through the last twenty feet when they were little more than a foot apart. Another second and the spike which ripped open his water bottle would have held him by the rib bones.

But he was outside. He stood in the shadowed sand with blood and water trickling together down his body ('In the nick of time. Like a film 'ero'). One of the last things he remembers is heaving the door shut and stumbling away from the ponderous booming that hung in the still heat.

Four days later Enderby was spotted by a reconnaissance car. He was walking in small circles.

When they brought him in, three of the deep lacerations in his side and arms were infected. He was totally collapsed. During his travels he had written two half-legible letters in his pay-book. One to his fiancée, a feverishly confused apology for something unspecified. The second was addressed to the Warrington Town Council, complaining of floods. He had almost died of thirst.

As he recovered, Enderby was eager at first to tell his story. Coupled with his letters, it made them prescribe further sleep.

'Do y' think it could 'ave been only that?' he asked me later. 'Sometimes it makes y' wonder.' Then he indicated the parallel scars. 'Truck accident, I don't think!'

16

He told me the story while he carved a piece of perspex into a Spitfire badge to send his fiancée. 'Y'know,' said Enderby, as I had not laughed, 'if I 'ad a lot more leave and that, I wouldn't mind 'aving a look back there some time. Bet it's covered up again, though.

'Y'see, I 'ardly touched 'er face more than a feather, like. And it started all that. Stone weights and pendulums, I suppose.

'Now, listen! Where did the acceleration come from? Tell me that!' He put down the transparent Spitfire and prodded me and paused to impress.

'There's a machine in that place, boy! Damn near perpetual motion, that's what. They'd be worth something, I tell y', them plans —'

First and last a mechanic, Enderby.

But also a prince. Who left his claim in writing.

Minuke

THE ESTATE AGENT KEPT an uncomfortable silence until we reached his car. 'Frankly, I wish you hadn't got wind of that,' he said. 'Don't know how you did: I thought I had the whole thing carefully disposed of. Oh, please get in.'

He pulled his door shut and frowned. 'It puts me in a rather awkward spot. I suppose I'd better tell you all I know about that case, or you'd be suspecting me of heaven-knows-what kinds of chicanery in your own.'

As we set off to see the property I was interested in, he shifted the cigarette to the side of his mouth.

'It's quite a distance, so I can tell you on the way there,' he said. 'We'll pass the very spot, as a matter of fact, and you can see it for yourself. Such as there is to see.'

It was away back before the war (said the estate agent). At the height of the building boom. You remember how it was: ribbon development in full blast everywhere; speculative builders sticking things up almost overnight. Though at least you could get a house when you wanted it in those days.

I've always been careful in what I handle – I want you to understand that. Then one day I was handed a packet of coast-road bungalows, for letting. Put up by one of these gone

19

tomorrow firms, and bought by a local man. I can't say I exactly jumped for joy, but for once the things looked all right, and – business is inclined to be business.

The desirable residence you heard about stood at the end of the row. Actually, it seemed to have the best site. On a sort of natural platform, as it were, raised above road level and looking straight out over the sea. Like all the rest, it had a simple two-bedroom, lounge, living room, kitchen, bathroom layout. Red-tiled roof, roughcast walls. Ornamental portico, garden strip all round. Sufficiently far from town, but with all conveniences.

It was taken by a man named Pritchard. Cinema projectionist, I think he was. Wife, a boy of ten or so, and a rather younger daughter. Oh – and dog, one of those black, lop-eared animals. They christened the place 'Minuke,' M-I-N-U-K-E. My Nook. Yes, that's what I said too. And not even the miserable excuse of its being phonetically correct. Still, hardly worse than most.

Well, at the start, everything seemed quite jolly. The Pritchards settled in and busied themselves with rearing a privet hedge and shoving flowers in. They'd paid the first quarter in advance, and as far as I was concerned, were out of the picture for a bit.

Then, about a fortnight after they'd moved in, I had a telephone call from Mrs. P. to say there was something odd about the kitchen tap. Apparently the thing had happened twice. The first time was when her sister was visiting them, and tried to fill the kettle: no water would come through for a long time, then suddenly squirted violently and almost soaked the woman. I gather the Pritchards hadn't really believed this – thought she was trying to find fault with their little nest – it had never happened before, and she couldn't make it happen again. Then, about a week later, it did: with Mrs. Pritchard this time. After her husband had examined the tap and could find nothing wrong with it, he decided the water supply must be faulty. So they got on to me.

I went round personally, as it was the first complaint from any of these bungalows. The tap seemed normal, and I remember asking if the schoolboy son could have been experimenting with their main stop, when Mrs. Pritchard, who had been fiddling with the tap, suddenly said, 'Quick, look at this! It's off now!' They were quite cocky about its happening when I was there.

It really was odd. I turned the tap to the limit, but – not a drop! Not even the sort of gasping gurgle you hear when the supply is turned off at the mains. After a couple of minutes, though, it came on. Water shot out with, I should say, about ten times normal force, as if it had been held under pressure. Then gradually it died down and ran steadily.

Both children were in the room with us until we all dodged out of the door to escape a soaking – it had splashed all over the ceiling – so they couldn't have been up to any tricks. I promised the Pritchards to have the pipes checked. Before returning to town, I called at the next two bungalows in the row: neither of the tenants had had any trouble at all with the water. I thought, well, that localised it at least.

When I reached my office there was a telephone message waiting, from Pritchard. I rang him back and he was obviously annoyed. 'Look here,' he said, 'not ten minutes after you left, we've had something else happen! The wall of the large bedroom's cracked from top to bottom. Big pieces of plaster fell, and the bed's in a terrible mess.' And then he said, 'You wouldn't have got me in a jerry-built place like this if I'd known!'

I had plasterers on the job next morning, and the whole water supply to 'Minuke' under examination. For about three days there was peace. The tap behaved itself, and absolutely nothing was found to be wrong. I was annoyed at what seemed to have been unnecessary expenditure. It looked as if the Pritchards were going to be difficult – and I've had my share of that type: fault-finding cranks occasionally carry eccentricity to the extent of a little private destruction, to prove their points. I was on the watch from now on.

Then it came again.

Pritchard rang me at my home, before nine in the morning. His voice sounded a bit off. Shaky.

'For God's sake can you come round here right away,' he said. 'Tell you about it when you get here.' And then he said, almost fiercely, but quietly and close to the mouthpiece, 'There's something damned queer about this place!' Dramatising is a typical feature of all cranks, I thought, but particularly the little mousy kind, like Pritchard.

I went to 'Minuke' and found that Mrs. Pritchard was in bed, in a state of collapse. The doctor had given her a sleeping dose.

Pritchard told me a tale that was chiefly remarkable for the expression on his face as he told it.

I don't know if you're familiar with the layout of that type of bungalow? The living room is in the front of the house, with the kitchen behind it. To get from one to the other you have to use the little hallway, through two doors. But for convenience at mealtimes, there's a serving hatch in the wall between these rooms. A small wooden door slides up and down over the hatch opening.

'The wife was just passing a big plate of bacon and eggs through from the kitchen,' Pritchard told me, 'when the hatch door came down on her wrists. I saw it and I heard her yell. I thought the cord must've snapped, so I said, 'All right, all right!' and went to pull it up because it's only a light wooden frame.'

Pritchard was a funny colour, and as far as I could judge, it was genuine.

'Do you know, it wouldn't come! I got my fingers under

it and heaved, but it might have weighed two hundredweight. Once it gave an inch or so, and then pressed harder. That was it – it was *pressing* down! I heard the wife groan. I said, 'Hold on!' and nipped round through the hall. When I got into the kitchen she was on the floor, fainted. And the hatch door was hitched up as right as ninepence. That gave me a turn!' He sat down, quite deflated; it didn't appear to be put on. Still, ordinary neurotics can be almost as troublesome as out-and-out cranks.

I tested the hatch, gingerly; and, of course, the cords were sound and it ran easily.

'Possibly a bit stiff at times, being new,' I said. 'They're apt to jam if you're rough with them.' And then, 'By the way, just what were you hinting on the phone?'

He looked at me. It was warm sunlight outside, with a bus passing. Normal enough to take the mike out of Frankenstein's monster. 'Never mind,' he said, and gave a sheepish half-grin. 'Bit of – well, funny construction in this house, though, eh?'

I'm afraid I was rather outspoken with him.

Let alone any twaddle about a month-old bungalow being haunted, I was determined to clamp down on this 'jerry-building' talk. Perhaps I was beginning to have doubts myself.

I wrote straight off to the building company when I'd managed to trace them, busy developing an arterial road about three counties away. I dare say my letter was on the insinuating side: I think I asked if they had any record of difficulties in the construction of this bungalow. At any rate, I got a sniffy reply by return, stating that the matter was out of their hands: in addition, their records were not available for discussion. Blind alley.

In the meantime, things at 'Minuke' had worsened to a really frightening degree. I dreaded the phone ringing. One morning the two Pritchards senior awoke to find that nearly all the furniture in their bedroom had been moved about, including the bed they had been sleeping in: they had felt absolutely nothing. Food became suddenly and revoltingly decomposed. All the chimney pots had come down, not just into the garden, but to the far side of the high road, except one which appeared, pulverised, on the living room floor. The obvious attempts of the Pritchards to keep a rational outlook had put paid to most of my suspicions by this time.

I managed to locate a local man who had been employed during the erection of the bungalows, as an extra hand. He had worked only on the foundations of 'Minuke', but what he had to say was interesting.

They had found the going slow because of striking a layer of enormous flat stones, apparently trimmed slate, but as the site was otherwise excellent, they pressed on, using the stone as foundation where it fitted in with the plan, and laying down rubble where it didn't. The concrete skin over the rubble – my ears burned when I heard about that, I can tell you – this wretched so-called concrete had cracked, or shattered, several times. Which wasn't entirely surprising, if it had been laid as he described. The flat stones, he said, had not been seriously disturbed. A workmate had referred to them as 'a giant's grave,' so it was possibly an old burial mound. Norse, perhaps – those are fairly common along this coast – or even very much older.

Apart from this – I'm no diehard sceptic, I may as well confess – I was beginning to admit modest theories about a poltergeist, in spite of a lack of corroborative knockings and ornament-throwing. There were two young children in the house, and the lore has it that kids are often unconsciously connected with phenomena of that sort, though usually adolescents. Still, in the real-estate profession you have to be careful, and if I could see the Pritchards safely off the premises without airing these possibilities, it might be kindest to the bungalow's future.

I went to 'Minuke' the same afternoon.

It was certainly turning out an odd nook. I found a departing policeman on the doorstep. That morning the back door had been burst in by a hundredweight or so of soil, and Mrs. Pritchard was trying to convince herself that a practical joker had it in for them. The policeman had taken some notes, and was giving vague advice about 'civil action' which showed that he was out of his depth.

Pritchard looked very tired, almost ill. 'I've got leave from my job, to look after them,' he said, when we were alone. I thought he was wise. He had given his wife's illness as the reason, and I was glad of that.

'I don't believe in – unnatural happenings,' he said.

I agreed with him, noncommittally.

'But I'm afraid of what ideas the kids might get. They're both at impressionable ages, y'know.'

I recognised the symptoms without disappointment. 'You mean, you'd rather move elsewhere,' I said.

He nodded. 'I like the district, mind you. But what I –'

There was a report like a gun in the very room.

I found myself with both arms up to cover my face. There were tiny splinters everywhere, and a dust of fibre in the air. The door had exploded. Literally.

To hark back to constructional details, it was one of those light, hollow frame-and-plywood jobs. As you'll know, it takes considerable force to splinter plywood: well, this was in tiny fragments. And the oddest thing was that we had felt no blast effect.

In the next room I heard their dog howling. Pritchard was as stiff as a poker.

'I felt it!' he said. 'I felt this lot coming. I've got to knowing when something's likely to happen. It's all round!' Of course I began to imagine I'd sensed something too, but I doubt if I had really; my shock came with the crash. Mrs. Pritchard was in the doorway by this time with the kids behind her. He motioned them out and grabbed my arm.

'The thing is,' he whispered, 'that I can still feel it! Stronger than ever, by God! Look, will you stay at home tonight, in case I need – well, in case things get worse? I can phone you.'

On my way back I called at the town library and managed to get hold of a volume on supernatural possession and whatnot. Yes, I was committed now. But the library didn't specialise in that line, and when I opened the book at home, I found it was very little help. 'Vampires of south-eastern Europe' type of stuff. I came across references to something the jargon called an 'elemental' which I took to be a good deal more vicious and destructive than any poltergeist. A thoroughly nasty form of manifestation, if it existed. Those Norse gravestones were fitting into the picture uncomfortably well; it was fashionable in those days to be buried with all the trimmings, human sacrifice and even more unmentionable attractions.

But I read on. After half a chapter on zombies and Romanian werewolves, the whole thing began to seem so fantastic that I turned seriously to working out methods of exploding somebody's door as a practical joke. Even a totally certifiable joker would be likelier than vampires. In no time I'd settled down with a whisky, doodling wiring diagrams, and only occasionally – like twinges of conscience – speculating on contacting the psychic investigation people.

When the phone rang I was hardly prepared for it.

It was a confused, distant voice, gabbling desperately, but I recognised it as Pritchard. 'For God's sake, don't lose a second! Get here – it's all hell on earth! Can't you hear it? My God, I'm going crazy!' And in the background I thought I was able to hear something. A sort of bubbling, shushing 'wah-wah' noise. Indescribable. But you hear some odd sounds on telephones at any time.

'Yes,' I said, 'I'll come immediately. Why don't you all

leave –' But the line had gone dead.

Probably I've never moved faster. I scrambled out to the car with untied shoes flopping, though I remembered to grab a heavy stick in the hall – whatever use it was to be. I drove like fury, heart belting, straight to 'Minuke', expecting to see heaven-knows-what.

But everything looked still and normal there. The moon was up and I could see the whole place clearly. Curtained lights in the windows. Not a sound.

I rang. After a moment Pritchard opened the door. He was quiet and seemed almost surprised to see me.

I pushed inside. 'Well?' I said. 'What's happened?'

'Not a thing, so far,' he said. 'That's why I didn't expect –'

I felt suddenly angry. 'Look here,' I said, 'what are you playing at? Seems to me that any hoaxing round here begins a lot nearer home than you'd have me believe!' Then the penny dropped. I saw by the fright in his face that he knew something had gone wrong. That was the most horrible, sickening moment of the whole affair for me.

'Didn't you ring?' I said.

And he shook his head.

I've been in some tight spots. But there was always some concrete, actual business in hand to screw the mind safely down to. I suppose panic is when the subconscious breaks loose and everything in your head dashes screaming out. It was only just in time that I found a touch of the concrete and actual. A kiddie's paintbox on the floor, very watery.

'The children,' I said. 'Where are they?'

'Wife's just putting the little 'un to bed. She's been restless tonight: just wouldn't go, crying and difficult. Arthur's in the bathroom. Look here, what's happened?'

I told him, making it as short and matter of fact as I could. He turned ghastly.

'Better get them dressed and out of here rights away,' I said.

'Make some excuse, not to alarm them.'

He'd gone before I finished speaking.

I smoked hard, trying to build up the idea of 'Hoax! Hoax!' in my mind. After all, it could have been. But I knew it wasn't.

Everything looked cosy and normal. Clock ticking. Fire red and mellow. Half-empty cocoa mug on the table. The sound of the sea from beyond the road. I went through to the kitchen. The dog was there, looking up from its sleeping-basket under the sink. 'Good dog,' I said, and it wriggled its tail.

Pritchard came in from the hall. He jumped when he saw me.

'Getting nervy!' he said. 'They won't be long. I don't know where we can go if we – well, if we have to – to leave tonight –'

'My car's outside,' I told him. 'I'll fix you up. Look here, did you ever "hear things"? Odd noises?' I hadn't told him that part of the telephone call.

He looked at me so oddly I thought he was going to collapse.

'I don't know,' he said. 'Can you?'

'At this moment?'

I listened.

'No,' I said. 'The clock on the shelf. The sea. Nothing else. No.'

'The sea,' he said, barely whispering. 'But you can't hear the sea in this kitchen!'

He was close to me in an instant. Absolutely terrified. 'Yes, I have heard this before! I think we all have. I said it was the sea: so as not to frighten them. But it isn't! And I recognised it when I came in here just now. That's what made me start. It's getting louder: it does that.'

He was right. Like slow breathing. It seemed to emanate from inside the walls, not at a particular spot, but everywhere. We went into the hall, then the living room: it was the same there. Mixed with it now was a sort of thin crying.

'That's Nellie,' Pritchard said. 'The dog: she always whimpers when it's on – too scared to howl. My God, I've never heard it as loud as this before!'

'Hurry them up, will you!' I almost shouted. He went.

The 'breathing' was ghastly. Slobbering. Stertorous, I think the term is. And faster. Oh, yes, I recognised it. The background music to the phone message. My skin was pure ice.

'Come along!' I yelled. I switched on the little radio to drown the noise. The old National Programme, as it was in those days, for late dance music. Believe it or not, what came through that loudspeaker was the same vile sighing noise, at double the volume. And when I tried to switch it off, it stayed the same.

The whole bungalow was trembling. The Pritchards came running in, she carrying the little girl. 'Get them into the car,' I shouted. We heard glass smashing somewhere.

Above our heads there was an almighty thump. Plaster showered down.

Halfway out of the door the little girl screamed, 'Nellie! Where's Nellie? Nellie, Nellie!'

'The dog,' Pritchard moaned. 'Oh, curse it!' He dragged them outside. I dived for the kitchen, where I'd seen the animal, feeling a lunatic for doing it. Plaster was springing out of the walls in painful showers.

In the kitchen I found water everywhere. One tap was squirting like a firehose. The other was missing, water belching across the window from a torn end of pipe.

'Nellie!' I called.

Then I saw the dog. It was lying near the oven, quite stiff. Round its neck was twisted a piece of painted piping with the other tap on the end.

Sheer funk got me then. The ground was moving under me. I bolted down the hall, nearly bumped into Pritchard.

I yelled and shoved. I could actually feel the house at my back.

We got outside. The noise was like a dreadful snoring, with rumbles and crashes thrown in. One of the lights went out. 'Nellie's run away,' I said, and we all got into the car, the kids bawling. I started up. People were coming out of the other bungalows – they're pretty far apart and the din was just beginning to make itself felt. Pritchard mumbled, 'We can stop now. Think it'd be safe to go back and grab some of the furniture?' As if he was at a fire: but I don't think he knew what he was doing.

'Daddy – look!' screeched the boy.

We saw it. The chimney of 'Minuke' was going up in a horrible way. In the moonlight it seemed to grow, quite slowly, to about sixty feet, like a giant crooked finger. And then – burst. I heard bricks thumping down. Somewhere somebody screamed.

There was a glare like an ungodly great lightning flash. It lasted for a second or so.

Of course we were dazzled, but I thought I saw the whole of 'Minuke' fall suddenly and instantaneously flat, like a swatted fly. I probably did, because that's what happened, anyway.

There isn't much more to tell.

Nobody was really hurt, and we were able to put down the whole thing to a serious electrical fault. Main fuses had blown throughout the whole district, which helped this theory out. Perhaps it was unfortunate in another respect, because a lot of people changed over to gas.

There wasn't much recognisably left of 'Minuke.' But some of the bits were rather unusual. Knots in pipes, for instance – I buried what was left of the dog myself. Wood and brick cleanly sliced. Small quantities of completely powdered metal. The bath had been squashed flat, like tinfoil. In fact, Pritchard was lucky to land the insurance money for his furniture.

My professional problem, of course, remained. The plot

where the wretched place had stood. I managed to persuade the owner it wasn't ideal for building on. Incidentally, lifting those stones might reveal something to somebody someday – but not to me, thank you!

I think my eventual solution showed a touch of wit: I let it very cheaply as a scrap-metal dump.

Well? I know I've never been able to make any sense out of it. I hate telling you all this stuff, because it must make me seem either a simpleton or a charlatan. In so far as there's any circumstantial evidence in looking at the place, you can see it in a moment or two. Here's the coast road...

The car pulled up at a bare spot beyond a sparse line of bungalows. The space was marked by a straggling, tufty square of privet bushes. Inside I could see a tangle of rusting iron: springs, a car chassis, oil drums.

'The hedge keeps it from being too unsightly,' said the estate agent, as we crossed to it. 'See – the remains of the gate.'

A few half-rotten slats dangled from an upright. One still bore part of a chrome-plated name. 'MI' and, a little farther on, 'K'.

'Nothing worth seeing now,' he said. I peered inside. 'Not that there ever was much – Look out!' I felt a violent push. In the same instant something zipped past my head and crashed against the car behind. 'My God! Went right at you!' gasped the agent.

It had shattered a window of the car and gone through the open door opposite. We found it in the road beyond, sizzling on the tarmac. A heavy steel nut, white-hot.

'I don't know about you,' the estate agent said, 'but I'm rather in favour of getting out of here.'

And we did. Quickly.

Clog-Dance for a Dead Farce

IF I EVER COME across a copy of *0, Frabjous Night* still flaunting itself as a Comedy in Three Acts, it will be flushed away immediately. Once, in desperate moments, I used to dream of scattering it upon stormy seas, or burning it, page by page, but both these methods smack of drama, with which it had nothing to do.

It was one of those shapeless attempts that are not comedy or farce because the author understands neither. Things without a naturally funny line, that make their actor-victims work like fiends to warm the corpse, and their audience-victims hate the seats they sit on. How this particular inanity achieved a West End showing will remain a secret: the hands that pulled the strings are probably stilled for ever, and the author's suffering name has changed obloquy for oblivion.

Possibly the thing is still performed occasionally by a broken and despairing repertory company, but this is how it died in the outer world.

'I've lost Kangaroo!' old Arnie said when I got into the dressing room at seven o'clock. 'He's gone! I can't find him.'

Kangaroo was the name he gave his mascot: it was made of coloured pipe cleaners and wool, and it had always looked to me like some sort of dry fly.

I helped him to search the waste basket and things, but it was no good. 'Fell off his hook and the cleaners got him, probably,' I said. 'They wouldn't know what he was.'

Arnold was cut up. 'Doesn't matter how it seemed to happen, boy,' he said. 'There's more in it. He's gone, and it's an opening night. First time since I've had him.'

The opening night of our last week, he meant. We were the tour version, doing the provinces with the usual weaker and cheaper cast: the London show had folded up some weeks before.

'Never listen to people who say mascots don't mean anything.' Arnold had given up the search and was rubbing greasepaint on his bald head. 'Keep your fingers crossed tonight, boy. Bang it out at them and take no chances.'

'Okay,' I said. I'd never gone in for mascots, but I believe in ghosts.

'Ah! I'll plug the broken doorbell business at the start. Aah!' he said, colouring his neck. He always smothered himself in greasepaint: it was a point of pride. None of that mask-and-white-neck stuff for him.

Most theatre people are failures. I don't mean they starve: they get along, just as clerks and taxidermists and boilermakers do: but they aim higher and drop shorter. There are lots of sorts of failures; even successful ones, financially. But chiefly they make two classes: the self-deluders and the realists. The first kind never know they're bad: they inhabit part of the same cuckoo world as the geniuses, only it's the slum area. The realists, though, know the worst. They know they won't enter the promised land, but they go right on, full of technique and guts and sometimes liquor. In spite of the mascot stuff, old Arnie was a realist.

He had a key part in this opera. Heavy Low Comedian. It wasn't a lead, but he was essential to such plot as there was, and had some of the best 'business' – after he had invented it himself. I was a juvenile; which shows how long ago it was.

Kangaroo's warning was soon borne out. When I got down to the stage for 'beginners,' I heard excited voices and a sort of moaning.

It was the stage manager. Our own S.M., who toured with us, a thin, jumpy type; he was all wrong for the job. Just now he was sitting on a prop bed in a terrible state.

'She's a devil,' he said to me. 'Oh, my God! She's the one that ought to be put away. My God! Having to hide like a rat in a trap!'

I knew he was divorced. Now it turned out there was a man outside with a judgement summons for unpaid alimony. The stage doorkeeper had been primed to tell the tale about the show being on, but the man said he would wait. The doorkeeper had to give him a chair.

'And she's earning money!' the S.M. whined. 'Nearly as much as I am! This'll finish me. I can't let them take me!'

We tried to persuade him to go and accept the writ, but he wasn't having any. He was so sure he was being arrested, he just sat and pitied himself.

It was bad. The two assistant stage managers would be upset too. A young girl fresh from drama school – I looked round, but I couldn't see her anywhere – and an unsavoury long-haired lad who never seemed to do anything.

Old Arnie appeared, looking a bit off form. 'Let's get started,' he said. 'Where's Miss Lane?'

The stage manager came partially to life. 'She's off,' he said.

'What!'

'Sprained ankle on the stairs as she came in, Dolly's going on for her.'

Dolly was the missing assistant S.M. She understudied as well. Arnie caught my eye.

'Poor kid!' said somebody. We all pitied an understudy in

that play. The thing had become so loaded with gags and comic business, it was like having to stand in for a member of a family acrobat team.

'Thank heaven it's a straightish part,' Arnie said, as she appeared. 'Good luck, Dolly! We're all behind you, remember. We'll see you through.' The usual remarks on these occasions.

Everyone wished her luck and said things about it being her big chance. She didn't seem to mind. She was either without nerves or half-paralysed with fright.

'Now for heaven's sake let's go!' said Arnie.

I came on quite near the beginning. After a few lines, I lay back in a chair and pretended to go to sleep, which is an excellent position for studying the audience if you're so inclined. Surprisingly, there were few empty seats. But something was odd.

You hear a lot about how audiences vary. They do. The weather; or the news; or the proportion of kids; or local conditions; or the varying quality of the show itself; all these affect them. This lot seemed to be mostly women: old women. They sat in rigid silence.

When I came off, I whispered to Arnie, 'Sticky house.'

'Suffragettes!' he said. The vote business had been settled a long time before this, of course; he used the word for description. 'I'll do my damnedest with the doorbell.'

It would be hard to describe Arnie's business with the broken doorbell. He had invented and perfected it during the run, at a place where the script became sheer calamity. It was a little masterpiece of timing and agile mime. He made me laugh whenever I saw it from the side, and I'd seen it a good many times. The audiences loved it. Most of them broke into a spontaneous round.

But not tonight.

Once I thought I heard somebody titter, but it may have been boots squeaking. Otherwise, dead silence.

I went on immediately after this. Arnie was insulted and furious at his stuff falling flat for the first time: it showed in the undercurrent in his voice, and the joyless way he was banging the stuff over. That's fatal. I tried to help him back into a good humour by being relaxed myself. He just made drooling–idiot faces each time his back was turned to them. It got worse and worse: not a flicker of response from that audience. We weren't as unfunny as all that, in spite of the play.

Little Dolly came on.

She was a pretty girl, excellent figure; but I saw the look her eyes held. It was fear all right.

She got started. Several lines were fine. Then her voice went faint. She didn't know it, of course; she was seeing only the lines.

On and on she went. Weaker and weaker. I could hardly hear her from the other side of the stage.

I put in a move, and whispered to her as I went across to make it a bit louder.

She tried, kept it up for a few lines; then it died again. Somebody out front started to cough. I was wondering wildly about jumping in ahead of cue, as a last resort, when Arnie spoke. He barked out, in character, 'Speak up, my girl! Speak up!'

And then he turned a look of loathing on the audience and said distinctly, and quite slowly, in his own voice: 'Not that it'll make a bloody bit of difference!'

There was a gasp of horrified amazement: their first reaction of the evening.

Arnie had turned his back on them.

It was useless after that. We and the house were sworn enemies.

At the interval I found poor Dolly in hysterics. She had thought Arnie meant her acting was so bad that it would make no difference if she spoke loudly, and that he had told the audience so. She deserved rows of medals for carrying on with the scene, thinking that. Arnie apologised and kissed her, and said she was wonderful, and explained how his hate of the audience had made him lose control, and how much he respected her self-possession. They steadied her with brandy.

One of the girls was looking through a split in the curtain. 'They're coming back for more,' she reported. 'Must be curiosity.'

'Been getting broken bottles in the bar, more likely!' someone else said.

Act Two was quite short: too short to build any suspense, as normal second acts do. Our author had known every point to miss.

The audience sat like jugs. It was uncanny, creepy, to act before them. As if they weren't there at all. Even the coughs and little rustlings and the murmur that fills every theatre had gone now. They were hating us.

Little Dolly had improved. She was audible and forging along, not letting herself dry. Once she cut a page or two of script, but nobody was sorry to see it go.

'Let's get it over!' Arnie said at the second interval. 'My God, they scare me now. Must be something in the water.'

This interval was a busy one for the stage crew, unfamiliar as they were with our scenery. A new set had to be rigged, a double one. It consisted of a small scene, 'Francesca's bedroom,' which was hauled up into the flies during a short scene-drop, to reveal a larger exterior scene, 'Outside the Château.' To complete this, a huge built-up centrepiece had to be wheeled into place at the back, representing the entrance to the Château. A stone doorway, with windows above.

We reached this scene change, and Francesca's bedroom sailed aloft.

Our nerves were wearing. It was like one of those dreams where you're trying to make a frantic escape in something about as fast as a steamroller, or where your fingers stick to things you've thrown away.

The curtain rose. 'Outside the Château.' This was the big action scene. After a few fatuous misunderstandings, the characters crept about, spying on each other. Gendarmes were called in, and nearly everybody managed to get arrested. An alleged denouement followed in a short separate scene: 'The same. Next morning.'

Just before I went on, the stage manager said to me, 'I can't stand this! It'll kill my mother!' The man was a wreck. I wondered what his mother had to do with it, and he said, 'He's still out there! Waiting!' I'd forgotten the process server.

On stage, Arnie sidled up. He murmured, 'Like a morgue. Somebody dropped a pin at the back of the gallery five minutes ago, and the echoes haven't died yet!'

The cast were hustling to get it over. The gendarmes – three burly supers – hurried in from the side, and up the two steps in the Château entrance at the back.

'No! No! Here I am! Help!' Dolly, as Francesca, was dragged out of a side door by Arnie and one of the girls. This was the cue for the gendarmes to come rushing back from the Château. They always came in a lump, sticking in the doorway because it was supposed to be funny.

Out they came, jammed according to plan, disentangled, ran down the two steps. Then I noticed the last of them hesitate and half turn back. I saw what he saw.

The Château was moving!

Very slowly, like a drunken duchess, the whole thing was tilting, tipping majestically over on to its face.

The last gendarme spluttered and grabbed at his colleagues.

Then we were all running to grab it. The thing was a light structure of canvas and wood, and not really dangerous.

We got the cracking monstrosity as it neared the ground, straining to support it. Myself and two of the gendarmes, that is. The third had his head stuck in a split in the canvas where it had hit him. The laths bent. The Château flopped most of its length on the stage.

In the gap it left, surprised and stricken like insects under a lifted stone, stood the stage manager and three scene-shifters. I saw old Arnie too, bending as if he was holding something down. Behind them were ropes, ladders, prop plants. And the back wall.

There was a strange noise.

A swelling, terrible roar that drowned the anguished mutterings of the gendarmes and the whispers in the wings.

The audience was laughing.

A harsh, derisive bellow that they had been saving up all the evening. They might have known this would happen.

I couldn't turn round. The laugh went on without slackening while we heaved at the bulging framework. The third gendarme had untangled himself and was pushing too. As it rose, stagehands pulled from behind.

The Château was in place again, a bit crooked, and with part of the stone fabric flapping where the gendarme's head had burst it. Why the curtain hadn't been dropped as soon as the accident happened, I couldn't think. But it hadn't, and we could only struggle on.

'I'll stay and watch it,' whispered one of the gendarmes. He stood by the doorway, trying to look busy, while the rest of us moved downstage.

Of course he was spotted. The audience's howl gained fresh strength. I tried to beckon him unobtrusively and he came forward. They yelled even louder. Suddenly, whatever we did, they laughed: but at us, not at the characters we were playing.

Other members of the cast were on stage now, bawling out their lines. Cues were lost in that appalling row out front.

I slid out.

'Take it down!' I said. Nobody seemed to be in charge.

'It's no use – we can't hold them now!'

The S.M. was on the point of collapse. Of course it was his fault the Château hadn't been properly braced. His brains were outside with the process server.

'The old chap's hurt!' he said. 'His back. I've sent for a doctor. What d'you think –?'

'Get the curtain down!' I said.

He did. The safety.

I could still hear that blanketed, half-hysterical laughter as I went to find Arnie. They had laid him on the prop bed. Apparently one of the loose steel braces had sprung round and hit him between the shoulders as he tried to grab the falling Château.

He was deathly white and evidently thought he was done for.

'They packed us up,' he said. 'They got us in the end. Tell somebody to play the King, very loudly.'

The S.M. managed to put the record on and it shook the nonsense out of them. There was peace after that.

'Is the doctor on his way?' I asked.

Arnie opened his eyes. 'I am dead, Horatio,' he said, and lifted one hand an inch or two. 'Report me... and my cause aright to the unsatisfied.' I wouldn't have thought Hamlet had been one of his parts, but you never know.

The girls were sniffing, what with the fiasco on stage, and now this. The S.M. was chewing his fingers, blaming himself desperately.

Arnie lay still. The greasepaint had been wiped off his face, but it still made his neck look ghoulishly healthy. The cast were all round him, hardly moving.

'It's as he would wish,' a voice near me breathed.

Old Arnie was making a beautiful finish. He was just going into Hamlet's dying words about the rest being silence, when the doctor came. We almost resented the intrusion.

He got his coat off and spoiled the whole thing. In two

minutes he had poor Arnold sitting up and telling where it hurt most. The old lad had chipped a bit off his spine, it turned out, but he was as fit as a flea by the pantomime season, and went on for years after that.

People trailed upstairs to remove make-up.

Later we found the S.M. had stolen the doctor's hat and coat and, with a prop bag to complete the disguise, had walked past the writ-server. So far as I know, he got clean away.

Occasionally I still get a reminder. I run into one of the cast now and then, though we don't talk about it. But where other people have nightmares about falling from heights, I get a vast craggy wall dropping on me, millions of tons of it, all crawling with gendarmes.

And I hear that audience laugh.

Essence of Strawberry

Poor May...

Every single evening, as soon as business slackened in the milk bar, I'd pick out a nice, unchipped glass for her and polish it clean – my assistant Valerie wasn't too particular about noticing lipstick stains – and I'd take it along the counter to the essence bottles. Into it I'd pour a double measure of strawberry – the thick, dark red syrup you colour milkshakes and sundaes with. This was a special standing order: for May. Just plain strawberry essence with a dash of warm water to soften the taste – that's how she'd always liked it. My wife had an uncommonly sweet tooth.

I'd say to Valerie: 'Keep an eye on things for a minute, duck.' And she'd let her sideways smile slip out at me holding the glass, and lift one neat, shaped eyebrow, like a big girl suffering to be in a kids' game, yet reminding them she's a big girl. 'O.K.,' she'd say. I'd go out the back door and upstairs.

And there would be poor, pale May, just her eyes moving.

All those hours helpless on her back, and she'd never stopped trying to keep bright – a thin, unreal brightness that belonged to her bedroom world. She'd say: 'Fred, do look at that face, like, there in the wallpaper. Isn't it funny? I *have* been laughing at it!' Or even: 'Now, Freddie, let me sit up and

43

surprise you!' She couldn't move.

I'd hold the glass of syrup to her lips, and she'd smile and drink. Sickly stuff, but she was crazy about it. Back in the days before she grew ill, when we used to run the milk bar together, she loved to sample all the sweet drinks; but strawberry was her favourite then, too.

Now she'd lie still, drain the glass and smile up at me again; I'd dab off a drop that had run down her lip. Sometimes those grateful smiles were more than I could stand: I knew she felt she owed them because she was a burden. Perhaps in a way I loved her all the time.

Downstairs, though, was Valerie.

One night – I'll not forget it: a rainy night, and no customers in. I was in the milk bar, filling May's glass from the essence bottle, and at the other end of the counter, rinsing cups and watching me out of the corner of her eye, was Valerie. Suddenly she burst out.

'My God!' she said. 'If you could only see your face! You look so sentimental and daft whenever you pour that stuff for her –'

'Ssh! Take it easy, kid!' I said.

'How May can drink that slop raw, I don't know! Small wonder she's an invalid!'

I didn't like this. 'All right, all right,' I said, and nodded at the stairway door. 'Sound carries, you know.'

Valerie threw the cloth down – I noticed how graceful she was, even doing that – and came over to me. She was flushed, and lovelier with it.

'No, no,' she said, 'hands off! I want to be serious, Fred, about us. We can't just go on like this, keeping it from her, whispering, putting on an act to the customers! Why don't you tell her?'

I'd been afraid of this.

'And then... if she doesn't want to stay, well, there are places for incurables, Fred. They look after them well.'

'No – I couldn't do that to her!'

'Look in my face. We've got our own lives, to *live!* Make a clean break – sell up this business and let's go away somewhere!'

I had to tell her then. 'This place and everything in it belongs to May.'

Valerie's breath caught.

'Anyway,' I said, 'I couldn't just walk out on her... after so long. It wouldn't be right, it wouldn't be... human. You do see what I mean, Val?'

'I see.'

'Oh God, it isn't that I don't want –'

She was watching me with that sharp expression of hers: I called it her X-ray look. 'I see. And she's been bedridden – how long altogether?'

'Seven years.'

'And in another seven years – you'll be quite an old man, Freddie. Won't you?'

Her eyes went up as if she was studying the greyness of my hair, and it was more than I could bear. 'No!' I said. 'She can't last that long! A year – maybe only a few months. The doctor says so, Val... the doctor, he says so...'

But looking into those cold eyes I didn't believe my own words. Valerie lowered her lids, a little smile of contempt for the glass of red syrup. And then the smile went, very slowly, and she was standing rigid.

'Fred... there's lots of doctors who believe in euthanasia.'

I stared at her.

Her breath sharpened, and her eyes came back on me, bright and fierce. 'It wouldn't be wrong, Fred! Can't you see? I'm sure May would even be glad. But she needn't know anything about it, Fred! That stuff she drinks – it's so sweet you could put something in it and she wouldn't know!' For a moment I didn't really take it in. This wasn't Valerie and

45

me: it was something out of a book. She whispered:

'Well, Fred?'

I got control of myself, I grabbed her by the shoulders.

'This – this didn't happen!' I said. 'Forget about it – every word you've just said – or it's all finished between us. For God's sake be real again, Val!'

The tension went out of her suddenly, left her limp. She gave a sob that might have been relief, or disappointment, or just misery. 'O.K.,' she said.

From that moment there was strain in the air. Her manner with customers was colder, and they didn't like it. At times I'd find her watching me furtively, guiltily. Even in repeating orders along the counter, she took to muttering under her breath. 'Come on, kid, give yourself a break!' I'd say, and for a time she'd relax. Gradually I began to hope we'd got over that particular crisis.

Then, between five and six weeks later, it happened.

About quarter to eight one night, I took May her usual glass of strawberry. I noticed at once how pale and stiff her face was, and I asked her how she felt.

She smiled. The nicest smile I'd seen on her for a long time, but so strange. 'I'm all right, love,' she said. 'I've been looking forward to my drink.'

I held the glass to her lips, but she could take only a little.

'No… I can't. It was just a fancy,' she said. There were tears in her eyes now. 'Fred, thank you for being good to me. You have been kind.'

'May, what is it?'

She looked like a mother telling a dull child what it should have known. 'I'm dying, love,' she whispered. 'I've been dying this hour or so, I think, and it won't take much longer. Just sit and hold my hand, and I'll be all right.'

I mumbled something.

'No, Fred… it's been coming for ages. Now just stay close!'

I sat with her there – I don't know how long. And things went on in my head that I didn't know could. Until, quite suddenly, she died. And then, when it couldn't hurt her to be moved, I took her in my arms, and really kissed her.

Afterwards, I found my way downstairs.

There was Valerie, both hands full, in a temper. 'Where have you been?' she said. 'Leaving me on my own all this time, with all the rush from the flicks, too!" She looked hard at me. 'Fred, what's the matter?'

I pulled myself together.

'She's gone,' I said. Valerie put down her tray and came over to me. Then she went white. 'In your hand!' she whispered. I looked down: it was the glass, still two-thirds full of red liquid. I must have picked it up as usual when I left May.

Without a word, Valerie took it from me. She hustled me into the back room – the kitchen – and closed the door. 'You fool! Oh, you utter fool!' she said, 'to come walking down with it in your hand. They might have seen it out there!'

I tried to understand.

'She couldn't drink it,' I found myself saying. 'She could take only part.'

Valerie was busy at the tap, rinsing the glass over and over again. 'My God,' she said, 'it's a good job I saw you! Didn't you realise – it'd have been evidence!' She took a cloth and began to dry the glass thoroughly.

'Valerie,' I said, 'what do you think has been happening?'

She had a look of dreadful satisfaction. 'I'll see you through, Freddie! I won't let anything happen to you – there's not the slightest reason why they should suspect now – if only you didn't leave anything else around. The doctor can give a certificate –'

'Stop it!' I said. 'You think I killed her?'

'Fred, there's no need to pretend with me. We've got to trust each other. We're free now, Fred – just keep that in your mind – we're free!'

I believe that was the only time I came near the thought of murder – when I saw *her* in front of me, alive with this ghastly excitement. I wanted to crush her like a wriggling insect – to stop her exulting in what had happened upstairs. Or what she thought had.

'Get out of here!' I shouted. 'Quick – get out of my sight!'

I pulled the door open and swung her through; she was screaming about me being crazy. I pushed her into the milk bar, flung her along behind the counter, with all the wondering eyes of the customers on us. 'Get out!' I was yelling. 'Get out before I finish you – get out!'

There was uproar everywhere. People scrambling about. Some youths got hold of me, to protect Valerie, I suppose. A woman began to scream for the police, and somewhere I could hear the smashing of sundae glasses – I remember that distinctly: some part of my brain was reckoning their cost.

Soon afterwards, the police arrived. They cleared the place and talked to Valerie in the kitchen, and then two of them went upstairs. A doctor came, and then a photographer. I sat watching the police examine things. One of them came from the kitchen carrying the glass Valerie had washed: it was dry and polished, but he took it away.

The following days have never become very clear.

I was charged with my wife's murder. At the inquest Valerie played the woman scorned: she told everything about us, ripped her own reputation to rags, blackened herself as an accessory to the crime – the way we'd planned it together, how she'd washed the poison glass. The jury had me damned in every glance. And then three doctors came, one after the other – a Home Office pathologist among them – and swore no poison had been found at the post-mortem. The contents of the stomach, they said, revealed only strawberry essence; and they read out its harmless formula. May had died from natural causes: the jury had to find so.

When it was all over, and the official apologies made, I went back to the milk bar, and opened it up.

But the damage was done. Nobody came near.

Even the little spiv kids with padded shoulders stayed away, skulking under the railway bridge. Occasionally a lorry driver would drop in who didn't know the town, and he would wonder, over his tea and sandwich, when he saw people across the street stare and nudge each other. I cancelled most of the milk – nobody was going to ask for a shake – and stopped placing orders with the wholesalers. It was getting time to pack up.

One rainy night I was sitting over a coffee, reading by the light of a single bulb. It was late, but I'd got out of the habit of noticing that.

I heard the rustle of a plastic mac, and looked up.

It was Valerie.

We watched each other like two cats for a long time, not speaking. At last she sat on one of the swivel-topped stools by the counter. 'So,' she said, 'after all, you didn't have the guts to do it!'

I kept quiet.

She rubbed her finger along the chromium edge of the counter. 'Wants a polish,' she said. 'The whole place is a mess. Fred, don't keep looking at me like that, please!'

I just sat.

'Fred, I'm not to blame. The way you suddenly went for me that night, it made me go crazy. Now, I'm sorry.' Her lips trembled 'Fred – look, we could still make a go of it together.'

'Could we?' I said. 'I don't know. It doesn't matter now.'

I was going to ask her if she wanted a coffee when I noticed her eyes. They were going over my face with that X-ray look, harder than ever I'd seen it. She hadn't made up her mind about me, even yet.

And I had a notion.

I said: 'Yes, we might make a go of it after all.'

Steadily, as if I'd been prepared for it, I got the milkshake beaker and squirted jets of essence into it, a strong measure; added milk and hooked it on the electric mixer. I sat and watched Valerie again.

She was nervous, fiddling with her gloves. 'That's been mixing long enough – it'll foam out,' she said soon.

I smiled. In my own time I switched off and filled two glasses from the beaker. Close up against the counter where she couldn't see, I stirred them with a spoon.

'What are you doing there?' she said, peering. 'What's going on – putting gin in it, Fred?' I wasn't doing anything, only stirring.

'Strawberry,' I said, 'for old times' sake. Just the two of us.' I smiled again and put the glasses up on the counter; pink foamy bubbles split on the surface and they looked tempting.

After a moment her eyes came up to mine, slowly, jumpily, as if she had to force them.

'Come on, Val,' I said, 'drink up!'

But instead, she slid from the stool and backed away. Her eyes were wide and frightened.

'*Did* you…?' she said. '*How*… did you…?'

One of her hands picked its way across the front of her mac. A strange, painful sob came from her, a kind of whimper of bewilderment. Then she swung round and ran out of the doorway.

I listened to her high heels click jerkily away down the street.

For some time, I sat gazing out into the darkness. There was no sign of anyone else coming, so I drank the two milkshakes myself – not to waste good food – locked up, and went to bed.

Lotus for Jamie

JAMIE WIPED THE HOMEMADE hair cream from his fingers on to his soft brown beard, while sister Emily neatly arranged his parting.

'Emily,' said Jamie.

'Yes, dear,' said Emily.

'I couldn't sleep last night, Emily. I just lay quiet and there were little pains in my head, Emily. Why couldn't I sleep?'

'Your brain was upset, dear,' said Emily. 'I think there are still one or two aspirins left and I would have given them to you if you had called me.'

'Yes,' said Jamie, 'I like to have an aspirin when I can't sleep. Because, after a while, I have lovely dreams, Emily.'

'Do you, dear?' said Emily.

She smiled with the little wise look in her eyes that came there when Jamie told about himself.

'I see all sorts of exciting things, Emily. Like it says about in books. I do exciting things too, Emily. I do brave things. There's people. There's a man – a sort of little man. He's got a beard like me. And he's awful kind as well, Emily. But I'm stronger than he is.'

'It's all dreams, Jamie,' said Emily.

'Sometimes we go hunting in the woods, Emily, and there's big animals and things there, and then I'm frightened – a bit. But we always win, Emily.'

'Yes, dear,' said Emily.

When the postman came with a letter, Emily read it with tiny lines between her eyes and said, 'I've got to go away for the day, Jamie. Uncle Jacob is very ill.'

'Poor Uncle Jacob,' said Jamie.

'I'll lay the table for your meals,' said Emily. 'You must be quiet: and if I don't come back early, go to bed at eight o'clock.'

When she had gone, Jamie sat in the garden and looked at the pictures in his comics. He read one or two of the stories, but they were not so interesting as the pictures and took too long to make out.

In the afternoon, when he had drunk his milk and eaten his salad, he sat in the sunny garden again and tried hard to think of the bearded dream-man. But he would not come into Jamie's head, nor the wood with the strange animals.

There was just the yellow hot field beyond the garden.

Suddenly he had an idea.

It was a clever idea, and Jamie smiled and pulled at his brown beard in pleasure. He found his black tin money-box with the slot to put pennies in. Once he had had one shaped like a dog, but Emily said that it was too silly for a man of forty.

Jamie opened it with a heavy stone and took the money in his big white hands. There were a number of pennies, and two bright shillings, and five half-crowns. He put the coppers in one pocket and the silver in another, and with his best hat in his hand, set off down the lane.

He waited a long time at the place where the brown bus stopped. At last it came. It made a great noise, and for a moment Jamie was frightened.

The conductor had a loud voice. 'Don't you want to get in?'

Jamie took a seat at the front, and his wide eyes watched trees and poles and houses fly past.

Presently the conductor came and Jamie gave him one of the pennies. The conductor winked at a man behind and said something Jamie did not understand, about 'tip.'

'It's to pay for the bus,' said Jamie. 'I'm going to town.'

The conductor made a hissing laugh and began to explain in a slow, loud voice.

At last Jamie gave him one of the shillings.

All the people in the bus were laughing. A young woman with two ducks on her knee looked at him and said 'Ought not to be allowed on buses!' Jamie wondered if she meant the ducks.

He put the pretty blue ticket carefully inside his hat-band, as Emily had once shown him.

When they reached the town, he looked round anxiously, but he remembered to stay in his place until all the other people had left. Then he went too. Near the marketplace he bought a cake; a pretty cake made of red and green stuff with cream on it. He ate it slowly and rapturously as he went towards the chemist's.

At this shop, he wiped his hands on his coat before remembering he was not to do so. He took all the money in his sticky fingers, and tried to talk in the way Emily said was proper, because he was doing an important task.

'I want aspirins,' he told the chemist, and added, 'sir.'

The man produced a very small bottle with a printed label. 'I want a lot,' said Jamie. 'Emily and me, we live a long way from places. I want them to last a long long time – sir.'

The man brought two more bottles.

'Another one as well,' said Jamie.

That made four.

'They're bottles of fifty,' said the chemist.

Jamie laid the half-crowns out on the counter and looked at the chemist. The man's eyes closed a little, and his mouth quivered as if a smile was trying to come. He handed three of the coins back to Jamie, and also a shilling from a machine that rang.

Jamie put the bottles in his pocket and left the shop, the coins clutched in his hand.

His ears burned.

He had forgotten to say 'Thank you.'

There were many people in the streets as he went to finish his shopping, and a great noise of talk and walking and cars and lorries. Jamie's head jerked from side to side as he watched. He knew his mouth was open, and he shut it hard, as he had been told.

A little girl who went by said, 'That man's got cream on his beard,' and Jamie wondered whom she meant.

He could see no one with a beard.

At the newspaper shop he spent a long time looking at the comics, until the shopkeeper asked him what he wanted. Then he took three of a kind of comic that had no stories and many pictures, and counted pennies into the man's hand until he was satisfied.

It was not until Jamie was in the brown bus again that he found the comics were all exactly the same.

At first he felt angry with the shopkeeper: then he tore two of them up and threw them under the seat.

The conductor said, 'You back again, chum?' and made him buy another ticket before the bus started. 'You wanted a return,' he said, and winked at the driver, who peered back from his seat like the funny horse in the comic, looking though a gate.

Jamie did not understand, but he felt the pockets where the shining bottles were, to make sure they were safe, and looked at the pictures in his comic while the bus took him slowly home.

When he looked up, still smiling at the funniness of the jokes, he did not know where they were, and a strange cold feeling came in his head, and his legs trembled.

He sat stiffly, with the comic in one hand and the hot half-crowns and the ticket in the other; he knew his mouth was open, and he looked out of the window, then across through the one opposite.

At last the conductor came and patted his shoulder.

'This is where you want to get off, chum,' he said, and giggled at the driver as the bus slowed down.

Jamie climbed out of the bus and crossed the road.

It was the right place.

'Hi, you've forgotten something,' shouted the conductor.

When Jamie went back, he handed him the torn-up comics. Jamie took them politely, and the half-crowns clattered on the ground from his open hand. The blue ticket floated into a pool of oil.

The conductor was winking at an old man on the back seat as the bus rumbled on up the hill.

Jamie found the money, and hurriedly hid the wasteful, torn papers in a deep briar bush.

The precious aspirin bottles were safe.

It was a long walk home past Clew's old empty farm and the waterfall and the three broken cottages. As Jamie went by the waterfall and smelled the warm wetness of the hedges that the high trees shaded, he saw something move in the long grass at the side of the road.

A dark-coloured furry creature crept out and raised a pointed nose, sniffing blindly.

Jamie stuffed the last comic into his pocket with the aspirins, and picked the mole up. It did not struggle, and Jamie stroked its loose coat gently as he held it against his chest.

Animals never ran away from him as they did from other

people. 'It must be because you're sort of – special, Jamie, dear,' Emily had told him.

When he reached home, it was growing late and cool, for the bus ride had been a long one. He set the aspirins in a neat row on the table.

'You're my friend now,' he said to the mole.

Its tiny black eyes winked, not like the bus conductor's, but honestly.

'You're Mister Mole,' said Jamie.

After supper, he gathered the sleepy animal into his big hands and put it down on the foot of his bed. He brought a heavy blue-patterned jug of water to drink, and began to prepare for bed, for it was eight o'clock.

Mister Mole yawned; his wet pink mouth shone in the darkness of his fur as Jamie patted him.

Emily came back some time later.

'Are you all right, dear?' she called softly, and when a sleepy voice answered, she opened the door of Jamie's room. Seeing her, the mole scrambled clumsily down from the foot of the bed and crept into a corner.

'Whatever's that!' she said.

Small empty bottles chinked on the bed as Jamie swallowed the last few of the two hundred aspirins, and lowered the jug.

He looked up drowsily with eyes that were black slits.

'Em'ly,' he said, 'they'll last a nice long time. I do like dreams, Em'ly.'

Oh, Mirror, Mirror

'The Old Queen possessed a wonderful mirror and when she stepped before it and said:
"Oh, mirror, mirror on the wall,
Who is the fairest one of all?"
it replied:
"Thou art the fairest, Lady Queen."
Then she was pleased.'

'Snow White and the Seven Dwarfs'
Grimm's Fairy Tales

THERE'S NO CALL TO start so, Judith. It's only your auntie.

Lie back in the bed now. Let me pull the covers round you against the draught. And a sip of water: your forehead's hot.

No, you're wrong, dearest. It's hot, not normal. So often that way; I don't like it – Oh! You mustn't listen when I say such things, talking to myself. I'm such a silly: I meant nothing. Really – nothing. Yes, I know it feels cool to you, but then – never mind! Poor little Judy!

I'm going to sit with you for a while. There! What jolly cane chairs you have in your room, haven't you? I think they are two of the cosiest in the whole house. Age doesn't matter with really good articles, you know that. Don't you? And fumbling repairs sometimes spoil things we've grown used to, and fond of.

Now I want you to lie quite still and restful. I'm going to talk to you, dear.

Yes, it's about what happened yesterday afternoon.

Won't you tell me why you did it, Judith? You may as well. Because I know anyway; more than you do.

No? No?

Don't hide your face like that! Oh, it hurts your auntie more than you can tell when the little girl won't speak to her.

Yesterday I was arranging her tea, and wondering what would please her most. I had found a bright, clean napkin for her tray and I was cutting bread thin as thin, and cornerwise, because that is how she likes it. And then I looked out of the window.

What I saw upset me very much. It was my little girl running, wasn't it? Running far down the garden to where the wall joins the big door. And peeping behind her to see if I watched. But I was behind the curtains.

Then I felt something inside me. Here. A tight, cold feeling all round my heart.

Because of two things. One was that she should go so terribly against my wishes. So many times I have said, since she was quite tiny, 'You mustn't go outside the garden, Judith,' and 'You ought never to run.' But there she was, in spite of all I had said and done for her. It made your auntie extremely unhappy, Judith.

But the second reason was sadder still. As I ran out on to the lawn, I was saying to myself, 'Now she will have to be told everything, and it may break her heart. Something wicked has made her do this, and she must know, so that she can resist it.' That's what I said to myself as I was running down the path. 'She will have to be told,' I said.

You weren't able to go very fast, were you, dear? You are so young, and I am your old aunt, and yet I caught up with you among the pear trees. Was it really that you slipped upon the path? Or was it perhaps, something else?

Now I want you to take another sip of water – there! – are you quite comfortable? You must be very brave. Give me your hand, dear. Such a frail little hand, tight in mine.

Very brave indeed, Judith. I'll have to tell you something that will be a very great shock. I'm going to be as gentle as I can, but it will still be a shock.

Let me see. You remember that fairy tale from when you were very small – 'The Ugly Duckling'? It looked so odd and different that the other ducks and everybody drove it away. And then it changed and grew into a beautiful swan. Do you know what 'beautiful' *is,* Judy? You liked that story very much, though.

Now just think, dear. Supposing – just supposing that the duckling hadn't changed at all. Supposing it became a still uglier one? That wouldn't have made a happy ending, would it?

Hold your auntie's hand very tightly, my love, and try to be ever such a brave girl. You see, Judith, I'm afraid you're that kind of duckling.

There, there!

Ever since you came here as a tiny tot with no mother and daddy, I've known someday I'd have to tell you that you were – different from other people.

Now you're understanding. Why nobody comes here. Why I have to have a high, safe wall round the garden, that you never go outside. And why your auntie takes such care of you, every minute of the day.

I suppose you've often wondered why it was like that. Haven't you? But you've always been so good, and done as auntie bid, and auntie loves you so very much.

It would have been the same if your – parents had lived. Your lovely mamma would have done what I did: we understood each other so well, as sisters do. I knew everything she should have, every single thing that was best for her. And then she married your father – she had no right –

We – we'll not talk about that. It's only what I said before. He wasn't really for her. Not for her. That's it, he wasn't – good enough.

And so, they've both gone a long time; and poor old auntie's minding this little girl instead.

And the little girl wants to know why she cannot go out and see the world at last. Because she's grown to fifteen years old.

Well now, just wait a minute.

Here's the mirror, down from its hook. I can rest it against the foot of the bed. Carefully does it when the frame is loose.

Can you see into it, Judith? Raise yourself a little, dear. There. See the precious duckling clearly?

This is the part that is going to hurt, even with her auntie's arm tight round her.

I want you to look at that shape in the mirror, Judy. Such a slender, curvy body, isn't it? So soft and pale. Those swollen little breasts.

Did you think that was right? Did you?

Now look at me, dear. I'm not like that at all. See how strong and solid I am, straight everywhere, in every line? That's the way people are, Judith. People outside.

That little face of yours, Judy. Pale, nearly like the bed sheets, except for two pinky cheeks and red lips. Eyes as blue as – copper rot. Mine are dark brown, and my skin is dark and tough. And hair – look in the mirror, dear; see that thin, soft, shiny yellow, like fading grass? Not thick and black, like other people's.

My little Judy – crying! Oh, what sobs!

You just didn't know how – different you were. I've always kept it from you. That is why there are no pictures of people in the rooms. I didn't want you to be hurt.

Brown-skinned and hard, they are, with strong black hair. I'm one of them.

So I can go out and talk among them. And they don't know about you, these dark people. Only I think of my little girl at home that's – different.

Now, Judy, do you know what would have happened if your old auntie hadn't cared for you yesterday, and run to stop you and guide you back to this house? Do you know what would have happened if you had gone past the pear trees and the green water tank, and up to the big door? And if it hadn't been locked – but it always is – and you had opened it and walked outside?

Something very horrible, Judith.

You would have seen people like me – all like me, Judy, only not smiling, I'm afraid.

You would have seen them halt in the distance, and point, and murmur to each other in their dry, grey roads; and move softly in the shadows. And presently as you walked, you would hear tiny shufflings and mutterings. And you would glimpse a head of a person on the other side of a wall, keeping pace with you; or grey hand signalling in a doorway. And then things would come quietly through the hot dust. They would be people. And they would be following you. Because you were different.

Remember how all the animals were unkind to the Ugly Duckling? People can be far crueller.

You might speak to one of them; but your voice would be tiny with fright. His head would turn away, with eyes remaining on you, and he would talk loudly and hard. Not to you: to the others. You would feel the whisper run through, sealing them against you, and teeth and eyes would shine out from the whole band of them. Then they would be thrusting, jostling, screaming; and all the roads clattering with laughter. 'Look at the eyes!' they would shout. 'See it! How it cries! There, it is running!' And the shouts would become the echo of your own feet beating along the middle of the lanes, and the stones ringing under them. Running until you couldn't go any longer! And behind, they would be coming, closing on you!

Like one of those dreams auntie calls nightmares; but this time it would be true, Judy. Perhaps, in your dreams, you know.

It's terrible to be different.

But your auntie's here. She understands. And there's a high wall, and nothing to be afraid of, if they don't see inside.

And when you make that singing, or sit watching the clouds and wondering, or tremble at the thunder, there's only auntie to know that you're doing what no one else does, isn't there? And auntie's your friend who understands.

My Judith is brave, and she won't cry any more now, will she? Just one last look in the mirror at that strange little face, so that she'll know finally what her auntie meant.

Oh, my poor girl! Can't she bear to look? Can't she, then.

Don't hide in the bedclothes, dear. You're never strange to me, you know.

Take the mirror away? Wait, Judith.

I've something for you. I knew what a horrible shock it would be, and I got what may help my little girl to bear it.

There. Right in her little hand. Do you know what it is, dear? A bottle of stain – quite harmless brown stain. It smells rather sweet.

If she wants, she can add a little to her washing water. To darken those hands and those pink and white cheeks. And when she looks in the mirror, she won't seem so different after all. She can pretend to be like me. Can't she?

And after that we must simply be patient, and auntie loving, because we haven't so very long in the world, have we? And if we're not ordinary –

Now if the little girl stops crying, and lies quietly and still, she shall have a plate of bread and butter cut just as she likes it. And some little secret treat. Her auntie will sit with her in this beautiful cosy room, and we shall have a game of ludo.

For I understand. And she's my very own. For always.

Poor little Judy.

God and Daphne

DAPHNE WAS FOUR AND had a white frock. Aunt Susan and Aunt Janet were very old indeed, and dressed in black.

Aunt Susan had eyes that let tiny tears run down from the corners all day.

Aunt Janet had one brown tooth, and white ones that wobbled when she chewed.

When Daphne was four years and six hours old – so Aunt Susan said – it was breakfast time and there were birthday presents on the table: a little green purse to keep pennies in, from Aunt Janet; a new blue jumper that Aunt Susan had made; and some money from Uncle James, who lived a long way off. Aunt Janet put the money away so that it should not be wasted.

Daphne kissed Aunt Susan on the cheek, and there was a salty taste from the little tear that shone there.

She kissed Aunt Janet also, but not on the cheek, for that had a mole with black hairs hanging from it.

She wrote a letter to Uncle James to thank him. Daphne held the pen with the long sharp nib while Aunt Susan made it form the marks. 'We should write our thanks before we have time to forget,' said Aunt Janet.

When Daphne had eaten the porridge that was for breakfast, Aunt Susan gave her a dish with stewed apple rings in it. 'Eat them up, dear,' she said. 'They are good for you.'

Daphne ate one slowly, pulling it into stretchy pieces. Apple rings were tough and old-smelling, like the dusty things in the lumber-room.

When Aunt Susan and Aunt Janet went out of the room with the used dishes, Daphne took the apple rings that were left, some in each hand, and dropped them out of the window. They fell on to the path outside with a tiny noise. She saw a striped cat smell them and walk on.

She wiped her hands on the underside of the table. Aunt Susan came back and said, 'That's a good girl, but do I see something left?' Daphne drank the juice, while Aunt Susan waited for the dish.

When the aunts had washed all the plates, they came back into the room, where Daphne was playing with the green purse.

'Don't spoil it,' said Aunt Janet, and they sat in their chairs by the fire.

'Just think,' said Aunt Susan, 'Daphne's four whole years old!' She smiled and a small tear ran down her face.

Aunt Janet went out of the room and came back with the big shiny book that the aunts sometimes looked at late on Sundays. 'Daphne is old enough to know about the Bible, Susan,' she said.

She opened the book on her knee. It had no pictures, and the pages were covered with tiny words. 'This is the Bible, Daphne,' said Aunt Janet. 'It tells all about God and is the most important book in the world.'

'Did God write it all?' asked Daphne.

'Not exactly, dear,' said Aunt Susan, 'but it tells what He did.'

'He made the earth, and the sun, and the moon, and the stars,' said Aunt Janet.

'He must be very big,' said Daphne.

'Very big,' said Aunt Janet.

'God is very good and kind,' said Aunt Susan. 'When people die —'

'Like Mrs. Stebbings' puppy?' asked Daphne.

Aunt Janet nodded. 'Like the puppy. But people go to Heaven, and puppies don't.'

'Where is Heaven?' asked Daphne.

'No one exactly knows, dear,' Aunt Susan said. 'But God is there, and it is very beautiful.'

'Though God does not like bad people who do wicked deeds. They do not go to Heaven,' said Aunt Janet.

'Wicked deeds?' said Daphne.

'Like making dirt, and worrying people, and wasting good things,' Aunt Janet told her.

Daphne remembered the apple rings lying outside on the path.

'How does God talk to people, Aunt Janet?'

'Sometimes He sends an angel with wings to talk to them. And sometimes He makes a sign.'

'Like a bush going on fire without any matches, dear,' said Aunt Susan.

Aunt Janet read a little from the Bible, which had a word called 'begat' in it. Then she closed it.

Daphne went into the garden and looked at the apple rings. They had soil on them and could not be eaten. She dug a small hole with her fingers and gently buried them.

It was very wicked. She walked away down the path. Tears ran out of her eyes; Aunt Susan and Aunt Janet were going to Heaven and she was not.

She knelt by a flowerbed and when she had moved a stone from under her knee, she put her hands together like saying prayers and said, 'I am sorry about the apple rings, God.'

Nothing happened, and Daphne cried again.

'Please say I'm not wicked,' said Daphne. 'Please, God, make a sign.'

There was the noise of a big drop of water on the path beside her, and a tiny bead splashed her leg.

Daphne looked up into the sky that the drop of rain had fallen from. It was bright blue, and hot, and nowhere was there the smallest scrap of cloud. Her aunts had told her that rain came from clouds, but except for one of God's birds flying ever so high above, the sky was quite empty and clear.

It was a sign.

Only a little sign, but there had been only a few apple rings.

'Thank you, God,' said Daphne, politely and full of gladness. She watched God's bird fly slowly with white wings that shone in the sunlight.

Jeremy in the Wind

YES, IT WAS WINDY when I first met him, Mister.

He was standing in the middle of a field, waving his arms at the big black birds who steal the little seeds men put in the ground. My word, he could swing his arms about!

So I climbed over the wall and went up – keeping low, because you're not supposed to go into men's fields, are you?

When I reached him, I saw how thin he was. You could almost see the wind blowing through him – you could, really! He had a long black coat down to the ground, and a brown hat and black gloves with little holes in at the ends.

But I liked his face. I said, 'I do like your face, Jeremy.' You see I knew his name was Jeremy. It was a sort of special face, pretty big, and greeny-coloured, with black eyes you could see right inside. And a big smiling mouth; but I think his lips were sore: they were split and flaky-looking.

I had to shout because it was so windy. 'Will you come for a walk with me, Jeremy?' I shouted it right up close to him and then – you'll never guess what happened. Three little yellow mice came out of Jeremy's mouth and ran down his coat to the ground. I like those sort of mice.

When they had run right away, I took Jeremy's arm. Poor

old Jeremy! He could hardly move because his feet – his foot, it was really, because he only had one – it was buried deep in the earth. So I got it out for him and then he was taller than I am – I had to look right up at him, like you look up at your daddy when you're a little boy. As the wind blew, Jeremy waved his arms about and shook his head. I don't think he wanted the wind to blow that way.

Then I heard him talk for the first time. He's got a sort of dry rattly voice, and you have to listen very hard to tell what he's saying.

Jeremy said, 'Let's go now. Go.' So I put my arm round him and we went along down the field, with his foot dragging in the soil because it was so stiff.

I don't think it's very exciting to just stand in a field like he was, do you?

We travelled on the road together for a while: Jeremy was leaning on me and it was pretty steep, so at last we stopped. Jeremy rested against the hedge while I had a drink out of a stream: the water was cold because it was so windy.

A man came along on a horse-cart full of cabbages, and presently he stopped and looked at us.

'What have you got there?' said the man. 'Jolly old pals, eh?' And he started to laugh till his eyes shut.

Then there was another huge gust of wind, and Jeremy's coat billowed out and he wagged his hand towards the man on the cart, and made a noise in his throat.

'He's bad,' said Jeremy, and his head nodded at me. I knew the man had upset him.

So I left Jeremy against the hedge and ran at the man. He stopped laughing then and swished at me with his whip – there's the mark just by where my hair begins, see? – but I pulled him down into the road and knocked him, over and over again, until he stopped moving.

The horse was frightened, I think, because he ran away,

and cabbages were falling out of the cart all over the road. Birds flew from the bushes and little things ran about in the hedges. And when I walked away with Jeremy, I saw something dark sort of spreading round the man.

But Jeremy – he just chuckled.

As we went along, he talked to me – funny sort of voice he's got – until a pebble fell out of his mouth.

Then he stopped, and didn't say anything at all. So I thought perhaps the pebble helped him, and when I saw a nice shiny yellow one by the roadside, I popped it into his mouth like a sweet. At the top of the next hill he started to talk again, and when gusts of wind came, he swung his arms.

I think we must have walked a long way after that, and my feet were sore. It was about sunset too, when we came to a village; not very far from here, I think.

There was a kind of shop where they sold tea, and we went in.

'We'll have food now,' I said to Jeremy. But he said nothing and he didn't move, because everything was still in the shop. Funny, isn't it? He's so quiet when the wind doesn't blow.

In a bit a woman came out. When she saw Jeremy she said, 'Take that thing out of here!' But he didn't do anything.

She looked at me again and then back at Jeremy and gave a little scream. 'Oh!' she said – her voice came out squeaky – 'it's you! That poor carter! – you – you –' She ran out into the room behind the shop and there was a noise of bells ringing.

I said, 'We'll get some tea all right, Jeremy,' and patted him on the back: little pieces of straw fell out of his hand. I was hungry and cold and I said loudly, 'We want some tea!' But nobody answered.

After a minute – yes, it was only a minute – I heard more feet coming outside, and the door opened.

I don't like policemen, do you? Well, it was one of them,

and he looked at me and Jeremy, and licked his lips quickly and said, 'You'd better come with me, I think.'

You can't guess what happened then.

Jeremy fell on the policeman!

They tumbled to the ground and I saw Jeremy's hat and the policeman's helmet roll under a table. The policeman grabbed at Jeremy's greeny-yellow head, but I knocked him and pulled Jeremy away.

I think I knocked that policeman pretty hard too.

I got my arm round Jeremy and we ran out of the shop as fast as anything. I could hear the old policeman groaning behind, and the woman shouting.

So now I'm here, Mister.

I like your house. It's nice to sit by a warm fire and see good things about you. I'd like to stay here always.

Why don't you look at that window over there? That's right.

Oh, you don't need to jump like that: it's only Jeremy. He's standing just where I left him. Don't you think he's got a pretty nice face?

He must be cold out there, and he hasn't got any hat either, poor old Jeremy.

Now I'm going to give you a surprise.

Jeremy and me are going to live here: in this house: always.

No, don't jump about and try to pick that thing up. I know what it is. A telephone.

And you mustn't run away! I'll just have to knock you. Hard.

And then I – me and Jeremy'll be in this house always. And sometimes we'll sit in the garden and he can talk to me.

On windy days.

The Excursion

MR. CLUCAS KEPT A defiant eye on the greyness above as he rubbed the mildew off the leather seats in the pony trap, hoping rain would not send him to chapel after all. He worked with the polishing cloth until the faded leather had lost its dullness. The morning air was cold, and exercise warmed him.

From his kitchen he brought scones and egg sandwiches, and locked all the doors. Overhead it was beginning to turn blue: the cloudiness must be sea mist that the sun was drying.

He harnessed Robert and made the old pony comfortable between the shafts. The whip went smartly into its socket. 'Hup!' said Mr. Clucas. He shooed his two cats from the side of the track as he was carried past.

The air was still. Through the earthy thumping of Robert's hoofs, he could hear a lark somewhere above the mist. 'Fine day, Rob!' he said. It felt almost an adventure to go to town after so long. Talk on the way should be pleasant too; he tried to think up subjects: the prospects for the hay crop, the coming diamond jubilee – there would be plenty to say.

Near the bend where Callister the smith's cottage was, he smoothed his whiskers and pulled the pony's head up smartly.

Young Callister was waiting in his Sunday suit by the little painted gate, face shining. 'Hallo, Mr. Clucas,' he said. 'Oh, don't get down at all – Nellie won't be a minute. She's gettin' a shawl. It's chillier than we thought.'

Mr. Clucas dropped his voice, looking at the door. 'She – she'll be all right, ye're sure? The bumpin' won't – trouble her?'

Young Canister smiled at the pony's nose.

'There's months to go yet, Mr. Clucas. And she's eager for this trip: it'll do her good. Nellie!' he called. 'Mr. Clucas is here. Quick – we're off!'

Clucas's sixty-two years always hung more lightly when he saw Nellie. She came now in a bright new bonnet with silk inside it, and over her dress a heavy embroidered shawl she had made. She was younger than her husband, but altogether bigger-framed.

Her soft face was flushed. 'All right?' Canister said.

Darker still went her cheeks, with Mr. Clucas watching. 'Get out with ye! Of course I am.' She grasped the side of the trap. 'Here – give us a hand up!' The trap's owner stretched out his arm. 'Oh! Mr. Clucas, I didn't mean you!' she giggled. 'It's this Jemmy – he drives a person to rudeness with his fussin'. How are ye, Mr. Clucas?'

Her husband grinned, pleased. 'She needs fussin'. She'd be snorin' yet!' And, as she exclaimed a pretence of anger to Mr. Clucas, 'Look at this: she's forgot the cakes like I told her she would!' He ran into the house.

Nellie laughed up to Clucas. 'He's at me all the time, teasin'. I haven't had a minute's peace with him. Aw, Mr. Clucas, what can I do?'

He felt quite fatherly as he started Robert with the young couple behind him.

'I was thinkin',' he said. 'It'll be quite an adventure for me. D'ye know, I haven't been into Peel since I don't know when. Not since Christmas.'

'Us too,' said Callister, an arm round his wife. 'I believe the last time we were down was for this one to stock her bottom drawer.'

She half-whispered, 'No, it wasn't!'

He thought. 'No – there was one day on the honeymoon we went there. Oh, she shocked the natives that time! Wait while I tell Mr. Clucas – hi! hey!'

He was pretending to bite the hand she held over his mouth when they came on Mrs. Kaighin, with her children, Grace and Edward John.

'Hallo there, Mrs. Kaighin!'

The big-bosomed woman was excited under her shiny hat.

'Hallo! Hallo, Nellie. Oh, Mr. Clucas – Mr. Clucas, I hope it's not goin' to be a terrible bother to ye – oh, dear!' Something was on the widow's mind.

'Not a bit, now!' Clucas waved down at the children. 'We didn't expect to meet you an' the little fellas here on the road. I'd have come by your place. Here, let me help!'

Mrs. Kaighin had not finished. 'Grace, put your foot up on the step. No, Mr. Clucas – it's th' ould Miss Barlows. Th' English ones. Could ye push thim in somewheres, d'ye think?' At their surprise, she finished desperately, 'I was talkin' to thim last night, poor craythurs, they can't think where to put thimselves. An' when I said we was goin' to Peel, they ast if they could come too, an' I went an' said it would be all right. Oh, did I do wrong, Mr. Clucas?'

She cuffed Edward John's hand from his nose as she took her seat.

Mr. Clucas looked at Robert's grey ears.

'Ye're givin' him a proper load, Mrs. Kaighin,' said Callister.

Words sprang out of the widow. 'If it's too much for the beast, me an' the childher can stay behind, Mr. Clucas! Can't we, Grace?' Full of self-sacrifice now, she shook the child's hand.

Grace sniffed. 'That's what we'll do, Mr. Clucas! An' then th' ould ladies can go. They're terrible wantin' to look at the shops.'

'But it's Sunday,' said Nellie.

The widow was firm. 'They can peep in the ones that hasn't got blinds. Yes. Well then, come on, Grace! Edward John! Mr. Callister, will ye help get thim out?'

The eight-year-old gave a whine of objection as his mother prised him from his seat. 'Hush! The buggane'll get ye!' said Mrs. Kaighin.

'Aw, let the kids go,' said Callister. 'Nellie an' me can get there some other –'

'No!' said Mr. Clucas. He strode round the trap with the solid step of a man who has decided to hide his doubts. 'We can all get in. If ye don't mind squeezin' a bit.' He took his place.

Behind his back, they agreed about knees for the children to sit on.

'And maybe walk up the hills.' His eyes were on the jogging Robert.

'What age is he now?' asked Callister.

'Ah – he's gettin' on.' Mr. Clucas felt that his age should be Robert's secret. To give it, amid head shakes, would be like shortening the animal's life. He asked, 'Are th' ould women at home?'

Mrs. Kaighin turned from wiping Grace's nose. 'They said they'd wait at the four roads. Aren't we nearly there? Yes, see yonder – that's thim!'

The two old ladies squeezed aboard, softly finical about their clothes and the iron steps. Mrs. Kaighin introduced everybody.

'It is most kind of you to take us along, Mr. Clucas,' said the taller, and seemingly older, in her English voice.

He felt uncomfortable. 'No, no. We were goin' anyway. I – I'm glad ye could come.'

'We are deeply obliged,' said the younger Miss Barlow.

The beat of Robert's hoofs became slower on a gentle gradient.

'We have not been to the town for a considerable time,' the elder added. On her mother's knee, Grace was beginning to fidget.

Nellie Callister said, 'It's quite an adventure, isn't it? Mr. Clucas was sayin' before we started.' It sounded false and silly, and she blushed.

'Yes,' said the younger Miss Barlow.

Mrs. Kaighin began to quieten her daughter with sharp, soft smacks. 'Didn't I tell ye! Be still, or th' black man'll get ye!' The child buried her head and whimpered. The widow's face was sullen with anger at herself.

The young Callisters were whispering. Edward John lay asleep against the young man's chest. As if their lives depended on it, the two English ladies studied the fields and sky.

Sunlight was rolling the mist up towards the mountains. Bright gorse spattered the hedges with yellow.

But behind Mr. Clucas was silence: embarrassment, regret and dislike. Only essential words were heard when they dismounted at a steep hill and climbed in again at the top; or when food was eaten, near noon. Once they heard church bells and a little whisper of guilt ran round, but that was all.

At last Mr. Clucas tapped Callister and pointed.

'I always think it looks nice from here.'

The little sandstone town was coming into view. Chimneys first: then the broad empty bay, and the crumbling red castle on its islet.

'Very charming,' said the younger Miss Barlow.

They agreed to split up and find their separate pleasures, afterwards meeting in time for tea. Mr. Clucas suggested it, seeing the situation, and they fell in with the plan so quickly that they felt uncomfortable.

Downhill through the narrow empty streets to the market square, and there four of the party alighted. 'We can find the shops nicely from here,' said the elder spinster. The young Callisters were going to the castle. 'I haven't ever been inside it,' Nellie said. 'Just fancy! I've been in Peel many a time, but I never went there.'

The trap creaked on down the narrow whitewashed lanes.

The smell of Sunday dinners still mingled with the kippery air from the curing-sheds. In the doorways, newly-fed cats washed themselves.

At the stables, Mr. Clucas found an acquaintance who would see to Robert's needs. He lingered a few minutes to help with the harness. The children watched, while their mother strayed, fretting, down the road outside.

'What did that man mean?' said Edward John, and Mr. Clucas hurried them on to catch up the widow. 'He said Robert was going down a hill. What hill?'

'Nothin'!' Mr. Clucas felt angry with the boy for saying it. 'He just likes to talk.'

They went with Mrs. Kaighin to the shore, with its dry, white sand piled steeply above the high-water mark.

'Terrible stuff. It's never out of your clothes for a week.' Mrs. Kaighin took the children's shoes and stockings, and sent them to play, calling a stream of warnings after them. 'Don't go in deep, now, d'ye hear! Or the tarroo-ushtey'll get ye, and pull y' under! And watch for broken glass! Edward John, take her hand, now!'

She sighed. 'Childher's a dreadful worry, aren't they, Mr. Clucas?'

'Well, yes,' said Mr. Clucas. His wife had died without having any.

She looked along the almost empty seafront, with its black windows, and back at the two small figures nearing the water's edge. 'I think I'll lay down here a bit: keep an eye on thim.

There's a newspaper in me bag. Would ye like a sheet to sit on?'

He sat and smoked at her side. He could see the woman was still blaming herself for breaking up the party, though she was less wild now. Good-hearted but desperate in her ways. He looked at her over his pipe. Her eyes were wet.

'Never mind me, Mr. Clucas,' she said, dabbing. 'Silly!'

'I'll go,' he said. She might be going to ask him to forgive her.

'No! Don't move. It'll do ye good here in the sunshine. I was just thinkin'. Look at thim playin' down yonder. Babies. An' there's me havin' to shout at thim, an' friken thim, with all sorts of silly bogies. Like an ould screetchin' witch-woman.' She lay on her back and her big bosom shook.

'Aw, now.' He gently patted her hand. 'Don't say such a thing that isn't true.'

'Yes, it is, I can't manage thim, that's what it is!'

Missing a father, thought Clucas. He said, 'They're right enough.'

She sniffed and sat up. 'Where's me hankie?' Her nose blew. As if she had known his thought, she said, 'Nearly three years now he went. He was a good husband. I'm at me wits' end to feed thim sometimes. If it wasn't for gettin' knittin' to do, like this —!' From the bag she brought a man's jersey, half-finished. Her hands dropped into her lap as she watched the water line.

She stiffened. 'Edward John!' she shouted; then her voice softened self-consciously. 'Watch your sister there, will ye! There's a boy.'

When she looked round, Mr. Clucas had gone.

The streets seemed smaller than when he had lived in the town years ago. And tidier. Clean, but mean, he thought.

He felt ashamed, now, of running away from Mrs. Kaighin. A decent woman. But her talk had alarmed him, and he had found a protective feeling growing in him. It was best to leave her. He was happy with the remains of his old life.

He wandered about the tiny, sloping streets, with their bright paint. There were new business names about, and shops selling different goods. His rare visits had lost track of the changes.

People were few. It was too early for visitors. A pair of young men in bowler hats went past on an afternoon stroll; he did not know them. A woman sitting half-asleep in a sunny doorway said, 'Good day to you,' but it was only for civility.

At last he reached the shadowed street where he had lived with his wife, and looked down it with a casual, stranger's eye. Three chattering children ran from it on their way to Sunday School. He felt nothing. It was just like any other street.

Then he saw the stone. One of the worn sandstone blocks that made the street corner, shoulder-high.

He stood staring. Those same cracks and marks of wear had met him before. Two or three times a day; every day. Remembering, it held him minute after minute.

Finally he turned away, half dizzy, one hand feeling the wall to steady himself. Everything had rushed upon him, unaltered. He could not enter that street again.

He would go to the harbour and look at the herring boats.

As he went, breathing hard, it seemed that all over the bright streets danced little ghosts of familiar stones.

'I know perfectly well which I mean! And it distinctly says three-and-eleven per yard,' said the elder Miss Barlow. She crouched in a shop doorway, peering behind the lowered blinds.

'Five-and-eleven,' said her sister, beside her. 'It's a five that looks like a three. Look again and see whether I'm not right.'

The elder turned. Pale, her hairy upper lip trembling, she had straightened. 'Anne, you must be ailing! Ever since we arrived, you have been determined to spoil my afternoon with all manner of petty contradictions.'

'Nonsense, Ethel –'

'It is not! You began with the street names. Then you took me to task over my own mother's birthday!'

'Our mother.'

'And ever since, I haven't been able to make a single observation that has gone uncorrected by you!' She seized her sister's arm tightly, and her voice dropped to a whisper. 'What are you trying to do? Persuade me I'm senile?'

The younger was horrified. 'Ethel! Remember where we are!' She tried to twist free and see if they were still alone. 'Let me go, if you please!' She was released. Her sister began to cry softly, leaning against the shop window.

'Ethel. Have you a handkerchief? Come away; people will look at you!'

The elder lady was past control. 'It was your fault that we ever left England! Why did we come to this horrible place?'

'Ethel – please!'

'I'll tell you! Because you insisted on it, and badgered me until – oh, get out of my sight!'

Miss Anne patted miserably at her sister's shoulders, peeping about for watching windows. Luckily, most of the street seemed to consist of a long, blank wall.

'They don't want us here! Tell them we've no money, and see if they do! Tell them we come to the shops on Sunday because we've nothing to spend! They hate us!'

'Nonsense! Everyone has tried to be most kind.'

Miss Ethel made a sound between a cry and a cough.

'Nonsense again? That's the last time you'll say it! I'm going to leave you! I'm going to, I swear it! By God and by heaven I swear −' Her voice became shriller as she was seized by the shoulders and shaken.

Only a window-ledge cat seemed to see the old ladies struggle, black dresses rustling in the sun.

'Ethel − look!' The commotion suddenly stopped. 'Mr. Clucas!'

The sight of him completed the shocking of the elder out of her hysteria. She turned away and took out a handkerchief.

'Oh, Mr. Clucas!' said Anne, as he came up. She tried to control her breathing. 'Isn't − isn't it warm?'

He seemed not to notice her, and she was relieved. 'My sister felt unwell. Might we walk with you a little way?'

'Yes. Of course,' he said.

As they started, a window squeaked open somewhere behind them, but none of them turned. Not looking at each other, they went slowly towards the harbour, the older lady growing steadier on her feet and sniffing less.

A high, wide causeway ran to the islet, and the gateway of the red, broken castle that covered it. Inside the walls, thick springy grass had cushioned the old parade ground, and filled the roofless chapel and armouries, making them comfortable for picnickers. The empty embrasures gave the peeping visitor picture-postcard views of the bay, and the softly smoking town, and the shallow harbour where the herring fleet tied up. Only one or two of the positions still held an ancient, black cannon.

'Aw, Nell! It's harmless.' He caught his wife up. 'The thing's dreadful ould, all bunged up with rust an' tar. It'll never go off.' He looked sideways into her face. 'What's up, Nell?'

'Nothin'.' She looked past him, among the ruins. 'Let's find a place to sit.' So quietly, for her, that he was uneasy.

On the warm turf by the round tower, he took her hand.

'Nell, love – Oh, my lord, look at this!' he said. 'Sunday School outing!' Children of all ages, with adults in the rear, were spreading noisily along the battlements. 'I bet it's kids that tears the place down, not ould age.' He tried to catch her eye. 'Aw, they needn't bother us, eh?'

An old man sat down nearby and began to open a paper bag with shaking fingers.

'Jem,' she whispered. 'Love you.' Half-forgiving, half-apologetic.

Relief warmed little Callister till he felt the expression on his face change, and make the old man look at him.

'I get pains if I go long without a bite,' said the old man. An egg lay on the grass beside him, and his stiff fingers were clumsily shelling another.

'Ye'll be right enough with those inside ye,' said Callister. But he was not really noticing the old man. Nellie had slipped off her bonnet and rested her head on his shoulder.

'Jemmy,' she said.

He pressed his cheek to her hair.

'For once ye didn't fuss me.' He smiled. The old man stared out across the bay, munching.

'I loved it all, Jemmy,' she said. 'It was awful nice.' She giggled. 'That fat fella that nearly stuck in the staircase! But then – we went to that damp hole of a place. Would they really shut up people there? All their lives?'

'Aw – I don't know. I don't suppose anybody knows, nowadays.'

She nodded. 'An' then I seen th' ould gun. Pointin' down on the people in the harbour. It would be a terrible killin' thing once.'

The old man's eggshells crackled. A gust of children's squeals echoed in the skeleton of the armoury.

Callister felt her laugh then, and he was relieved.

'I might be puttin' a mark on the child, thinkin' these things,' she whispered.

'A neat little cannon on his chest,' he said in her ear, 'might be quite decorative if it was well carried out.'

She smiled. 'Or a dungeon.'

'Woman,' he said. 'If you can produce a birthmark to look like a dungeon, we'll exhibit it an' charge admission!' She kicked at his ankle.

The old man had finished his eggs. He brushed crumbs from his beard as he rose.

'Good day,' he said.

Canister turned to nod to him, then felt himself held. His wife suddenly twisted in his arms and gripped him tightly. 'Jemmy!' She was staring into his face; as if she saw a mile behind his eyes. 'Jemmy!'

He whispered: 'Love?'

The frightening look went from her, and she pushed her face into his shoulder.

'Oh, Jemmy. I just felt suddenly – I don't know. Sort of glad that we don't live a long time ago.'

He did not smile. She went on:

'It'd be no sort of a world for a child. When they killed each other, and shut each other in dark places till the end of their days.'

She looked up. Like a creature startled at its own voice.

'Say I'm a fool and make me laugh, Jemmy, will ye?'

'Ah, here's two of them now,' said Mr. Clucas. 'Come from seeing the sights.'

The odd silence of the English ladies had puzzled him, and he was glad when the young Callisters appeared. The five of them wound among the afternoon strollers on the seafront.

'Somewhere here I left her – there's the childher anyhow.'

They reached the place; and the children had heaped sand on their mother; and there was polite laughing, and supernatural threats by the widow, swearing her knitting was ruined; and it was time for tea.

'I've arranged it to be all ready for us,' said Mr. Clucas.

They feasted on kippers fresh from the curing-shed, cooked so that the smoky juice would run, and whet the appetite for more. And as the big brown teapot was emptied and watered and emptied again, they began to talk to each other.

The civilities of passing food grew into chatter about the town. They talked about the things they had seen and forgot about the things they had felt. By the time they left the house where teas were made, Callister had a child holding each hand and his wife was in deep gossip with the English ladies.

'I'll maybe be puttin' a sight on ye one day soon.' Mr. Clucas was last, with the widow. 'To see the childher's behavin'. If ye'd like.'

She nodded. 'Oh, I'd be glad if ye would. Come down tomorrow; an' we'll have a bite of tea. Little devils – I'm smothered in sand still!'

Mr. Clucas stepped off to find Robert, and trotted him up to the market square just in time to meet the passengers.

They drew up the hill out of the town, walking the steep part, and halted to look at the castle, black on the track of the sun as it dropped towards Ireland.

Small talk soon tired itself, and when they passed a roofless, overgrown cottage, Mr. Clucas left Robert to manage himself while he told of the man who had lived in it. A desperate believer in fairies, till one mid-summer night they found him floating face down on a pond, dressed only in a robe of cat-skins, with a bunch of herbs in his hand. It had been a struggle to get him a Christian burial.

There were many murmurs in the trap.

'Ah, some queer ones there were round here,' said Callister. 'My da used to tell of a fella that spent himself cloth' th' ould Manx Bible into English for the benefit of the heathen across the water!'

The old ladies laughed as delightedly as if it were a personal compliment.

'Indeed, perhaps he was not so far wrong after all,' said Miss Anne. 'Our minister at home in Wiltshire often remarked –'

'Stop the trap!'

The widow had slipped Grace from her knee and was bending across Nellie Callister.

'What's up?' The young husband's voice shot high.

'She's sick.'

There was a frightened stillness in the trap.

'Jemmy, get down and help me get her out.' The widow was in charge. 'Edward John, get you a cup from me basket and run to find a well. Easy now with her!'

They supported the collapsing girl to the roadside. 'In through the trees there,' said Mrs. Kaighin. 'There's a patch where she can lay flat.' Among the early foxgloves she turned. 'Now get along back with ye, Jemmy. Leave me. I'll do better alone.'

Callister's face was like a wet day. He came and grasped the wheel of the trap and trembled.

'Easy, lad,' said Mr. Clucas.

The smith looked up past the old ladies, who sat like button-eyed stuffed birds. 'If she loses it, I – I don't know –'

Something like a groan came from the roadside.

'No! Wait, boy,' said Mr. Clucas. 'Ah – here's the water.' Some was spilt, though Edward John had ran carefully. 'Give it here, sonny,' said Clucas. 'I'll take it to your mother. Promise to wait, Jemmy.'

He stepped across the road. On the verge he almost collided with Mrs. Kaighin.

The widow was laughing. With relief.

'It must have been the kippers! She'll be all right in just a minute, the darlin'! Oh, good – I'll give her this to drink.'

The wild change in Jemmy, and having his wife back in the trap, shadowy but able to smile, and all their assistance, made the old pony square his feet against the shaking of the shafts. Mr. Clucas even took out the whip and cracked it, when Mrs. Kaighin said they could go on.

Gaiety grew all the way.

The younger Miss Barlow started it, with the softest singing of a hymn, as a form of lullaby. Her sister took it up, still almost as clear as in a Wiltshire choir-stall. And soon the singing of all of them, scandalous and happy, was bringing people to their cottage doors to wave goodnight.

Flo

A MAN CAME OUT of the pawnbroker's, blinking in the sunlight. From a little below the eyes, whitening stubble crept down his face: his eyes were fiery red. He was very low and thick-bodied, as if the earth had drawn him to it and shortened him. It was Mr. Percy Hurd.

He pushed the perforated slip into his jacket pocket. In the other hand he held three cold half-crowns.

He looked back into the dark shop, where his overcoat was being hung away with a white duplicate ticket pinned to the collar. He called, 'Flo! Come on, Flo!' and squeaked persuasively with his lips.

An old half-bred collie padded stiffly out into the light, eyelids quivering. Her muzzle was white, and the brindled body heavy and sagging. She grunted with the jolt the step gave her.

She stood quietly while Mr. Hurd passed a length of string through her collar and rubbed her head. 'Good dog. Now where are we going, eh?' The old creature's claws clacked loudly on the pavement as they walked. From time to time she raised her head, peering, and sniffed in the nature of shops and walls and people she could hardly see.

A man stood on a corner, sorting his stock of early newspapers. Mr. Hurd pulled back on the string and stopped to speak to him.

'Another day off, Perce?' said the man.

Mr. Hurd smiled. 'Just like you was saying – it's bright today. Know what's special about it?'

The other man shouted a headline and said, 'Eh?'

'Ten years ago today my old woman went.' Mr. Hurd watched his friend make a sale, and repeated, 'Poor old girl died ten years ago this very afternoon. Day to celebrate, eh?' He grinned a jagged outline of teeth, and winked at the paper-seller as he moved off.

He liked to look in the window of the next shop he visited. Before going inside, he stood admiring the huge bottles of coloured liquid that stood high up in the window, above the dummy packets of laxative and sleeping tablets. They looked good.

'Give us a pint of meths,' he said to the chemist.

The man came back licking the label. He looked up through his eyebrows at Mr. Hurd's face, and said, 'For fuel?'

Mr. Hurd pocketed the heavy bottle coldly and said, 'Going to clean an overcoat. How much?' He waited in the shop, insultingly, while he counted the change aloud.

'Come on, Flo,' he said, and patted the dog as they reached the pavement.

They turned down a side street, past a disused church with auction labels stuck on it, and between two untidy stables. Stems of chaff blew beneath their feet. The dog sniffed at the horse smell. Her master did the same. 'Good hearty stink, eh, girl?'

Beyond the stables, they came into a bleak field where shiny patches of bald earth shone through the grass. The animal panted shallowly after her walk.

'Lie down, Flo,' said Mr. Hurd. 'Good dog, lie down!'

The creature's white eyebrows flickered as she watched him. Slowly she sat, then paddled her forepaws along until she was stretched out: she rolled her stout body sideways for greater comfort.

'Good dog,' said Mr. Hurd. He wound her ear between his short fingers. 'Good dog, does what her master says.' The long ragged tail swept the ground, wagging.

Mr. Hurd took the bottle of spirits from his pocket, removed the cork and sniffed the contents. He placed the bottle's mouth to his own and tipped his head back. There was a quick bubbling in the thin blue liquid. It sparkled in the light.

He swallowed, twisting his face and screwing up his eyes into a tangle of lines. He lowered the bottle and sighed several times with his mouth wide open. He patted his chest heavily, and then his stomach, through the tight buttons of his jacket.

'Fire,' said Mr. Hurd.

He drank again. Presently he blew a gust of breath at the old beast's head. 'Lady!' he murmured. 'Turns her head away, yah!'

The tail wagged at his voice.

'One day, a long time ago,' he said, 'I hadn' no dog. Then I got a pup. Fat ugly pup with a long tail.' His toe gently stirred the fur of her side.

'Know who it was? It was you.' Mr. Hurd lay back and regarded her for a time: when he spoke again his voice became foolish. 'I said: "I'm goin' to call her Flo." And I did.' He took another mouthful. 'My old woman didn' like dogs. No, she didn', no. Funny about that: why shouldn' she like —? But she died and it didn't matter. And what did we used to do? We used to rat-hunt. Me and Flo used to rat-hunt.' He chuckled. 'I bet old Mounsey she could catch I don' know how many rats in one day, and she caught even more. Old Mounsey never paid up, either —'

He took the morning's money from his pocket, counted and replaced it.

'Could run like the wind and fetch stones.' His hand searched about until he found a half-buried flint and worried it out of the ground. He held the clayey thing up for the bitch to see, and said, 'Good girl! Fetch it, Flo!' He threw it and it bounced a few yards away. She pulled herself to her feet, trotted slowly over to the flint and picked it up carefully to drop it near him.

He grunted and tossed the stone high again. The animal's watery, blinking eyes followed it and lost it.

'Well, where is it?' said Mr. Hurd. He wiped his lips. 'Got that stone?'

She looked to each side and walked a few aimless steps. Her tail wagged, drooping.

Her master watched. 'Fetch it!' he said. 'Fetch it!' She blinked at him along her white muzzle. 'Fetch it!' Mr. Hurd shouted. His face showed a darkening red network.

The dog stood with her feet wide apart. Her pale tongue trembled for an instant between her lips.

Mr. Hurd pulled the neck of his shirt open. 'Too old to know what to do with yourself! Where did I – where did I say I was going to send you?' He held the bottle close to his eyes and pressed the cork hard into it, then lowered it into his pocket. 'Don't know why I didn't.'

He stretched out a hand. 'Come here!' The animal stood still, wagging her tail slavishly. Mr. Hurd rose on his knees. 'Come here – coward!'

One foot at a time, she crept towards him, the tongue slipping in and out of her lips.

'Got to do what – you're told until – I say leave – off!' pronounced the man loudly. He tugged her by the collar. Beneath the old, fine fur he felt her trembling. 'Good dog,' he said. He frowned fiercely in bringing his eyes to bear: his breath caught. 'What are you scared of? Silly old bitch! Don't be – so – bloody – frightened!' he shouted. At each word he rolled her from side to side by a handful of the loose skin above her shoulders.

He felt the vibration of the thin sound in her throat.

He stopped shaking her and shouted into her face, 'What did you do? You growl at me?' He threw her with a thud on to her side. She snarled with fear and he felt teeth glance across his hand: old, blunt teeth. He drew back.

At last he said, 'So – turn on me, would you! Use teeth on me, eh? We'll see about that!'

He braced himself and stood up: then he was as steady as always. She lay looking at him through half-closed eyes, trembling from head to foot. The lips were still drawn back from her teeth.

'You done for yourself now, my lady! Get up!' His furious voice shot across the field and cracked up an echo from the railway embankment.

He pulled the string from his pocket, frowning. With one foot he held her jaws down against the earth, growling and twisting. He stooped, tightened her collar and fumblingly worked the string through it. He had to drag her to her feet. Then he ran, jerking her along behind him.

They went back through the stables. 'Come along!' he shouted.

He found his way somehow, after some mistaken turnings. When he stopped, it was by a shop with a blue-painted window. He knocked loudly.

The bitch struggled to slip her collar. He seized a handful of her coat and dragged her back to the door. He hammered again. From inside came a hurt animal cry. Then footsteps, and the door opened. A man appeared; he had sleeves rolled up on his long arms, and a pale face, angry at being interrupted.

'Well, well, what is it?'

'You the vet?' said Mr. Hurd thickly. The man nodded wearily.

'Then take this brute and do her in! She turned on me, vicious! Turned on – me with her teeth!' Mr. Hurd tugged the string and put it into the vet's hand.

'She's old,' said the vet; he pulled her lip down to look at her teeth. 'Very well, that'll be three and six.'

Mr. Hurd stared. 'Wait a minute! I thought –' He snorted and jabbed a hand into his pocket. 'All right! Nobody say I – didn' have it done right!'

A woman's voice shouted inside, 'Be quick, it's trying to get loose!'

'All right, I'm coming!' the vet called. 'Injured cat,' he said. 'Hurry up!'

'Half a – crown. Shillin'. Three'n'six. There!' said Mr. Hurd. 'Good money all waste on – old cur!' He swung away.

'Do you want her afterwards?'

'Wha'?'

'D'you want the carcase, man? Oh, all right, I'm coming!' The vet hurried inside, pulling the bitch after him in spite of her resistance. She was still trying to wriggle out of the collar, but it was too tight.

Mr. Hurd felt confused. He growled, and shook his fist at the street: now that the excitement had gone, everything annoyed him. He found suddenly that he was very sleepy and his eyes ached.

It was difficult to wake up because of the pain in his head. When he forced himself to sit and look round at last, he was in one of the stables. A streak of evening sunlight was licking his trouser leg with a beautiful orange colour; across his hand ran a money spider. He seemed to be alone.

'Flo!' said Mr. Hurd.

He squeaked with his lips, and frowned to remember whether he had left her behind when he came out.

He stood and put his hands in his pockets. There was money there. Three and six, he thought, what was that about three and six? He drew in a great aching breath, remembering.

'No!' he said, and ran out of the stable. He began to trot, saying, 'No, no, no,' under his breath. He soon tired, and had to stop to lean on a wall; he rubbed his face in his hands and ran on.

When he came to the shop with the blue-painted window, he said, 'No!' again. But he rang the bell.

A tall, thin-faced man came. A familiar face, somehow. He knew Mr. Hurd and said, 'Well, what is it? I did what you wanted.'

'You – put –?'

'I tried to ask you if you wanted the carcase, but you simply disappeared,' said the vet.

Mr. Hurd grabbed him by the coat and yelled into his face, 'What have you done? What have you? When I came to you I was drunk! I –'

'Get your hands off!' snapped the thin man. 'I know you were, but that was your own business!' He seemed about to slam the door. Then he said, 'Look here, it couldn't have lived much longer anyway. Too old. I haven't had time to dispose of the carcase yet – if you want it.'

Mr. Hurd followed him through a passage into a small stone yard at the back. On a narrow ledge, next to a dead white cat with a gashed side, lay the familiar brindled body. She might have been asleep, except that her head hung limply over the ledge.

'I took the collar off,' said the vet. 'You can have it if you wish – may come in useful for another – Get a grip on yourself, man! It was only an old bitch, after all.'

Mr. Hurd was kneeling by the ledge. He took one of the

dead animal's forepaws in each hand, and stroked them with his thumbs. He ruffled her ear.

'Better take it away,' said the vet. Mr. Hurd put his arm clumsily round the corpse and lifted it.

'Bit stiff,' he said. He rubbed his chin against the fur. 'You don't want her?'

The vet breathed in sharply and shook his head. 'This way,' he said.

'Catch rats in hundreds,' Mr. Hurd said. Their steps echoed in the passage. 'When she was young. Fetch stones. Just like a human. Understood every word.' As he went out past the blue window, the vet called after him, 'Look here, the collar; d'you want it?'

Mr. Hurd did not hear.

He was looking down at the brindled fur. He saw a wet drop appear on it. He looked at the ground to see if it was raining, and felt a cold line down his face from his left eye. He put his head down to his hand, and wiped it as he made his way though some playing children.

One of them whispered, 'He's dead, that dog!'

Farther on, somebody must have recognised him. A voice shouted, 'What's up, Perce? Had an accident, lad?' He did not wish to look round.

A man was attending a drain, and water spread over the street from it, rippling round Mr. Hurd's boots as he walked. A bread van with a broken, flapping side halted noisily to let him pass in front of it. Once a hand pulled him on to the pavement. 'Plenty of better spots for suicide, chum!' It was growing dark. Soon it was hard for him to see what it was he carried. Passing cars shone lights that hurt his eyes.

He sat down at last on a seat where there were no people, and put the body gently across his knees.

He buried his face in the stale coat. Sparrows flew away, startled by his tearing sobs.

Long after midnight, the constable heard moaning, muffled by the heavy, continuous rain. He switched on his lamp, quickly alert. It picked out a tall, dripping statue, scroll in hand. Sitting at the base of it, a man had dropped his head almost between his knees. Rainwater trickled through his hair and dripped from his nose. On the ground beside him lay a brindled dog.

The policeman's light seemed to wake him. He sat up with a hand over his eyes. 'You can't stay here,' said the constable.

The man gave an exhausted sigh. His clothing was sodden. He stood, leaning on the policeman's arm. His feet crunched in broken glass as he did so. There was a reek of chemical spirits from him.

'Can't – stay here, no. Somethin' this afternoon, awful! Awful!' he repeated, as if trying to remember what it had been. 'It was – it was – this afternoon, my old woman, she died! I can't go on any longer.'

His eyes were bright with discovery. 'Know why she died, my poor old woman? She was bitten! She – bitten by this brute here!'

An empty cigarette carton floated between her paws. Her muzzle lay in a pool of black water that was kept bobbing by the heavy pattering drops from above.

He kicked savagely at the animal.

The Putting Away of
Uncle Quaggin

As ONE OF HIS descendants remarked, the twentieth of June, 1897, was marked by public rejoicings throughout the Empire: Ezra Quaggin had died in the night. It was also the day of Queen Victoria's diamond jubilee.

He had lived alone on his farm, working it with hired labour, sending out occasional blasts of hate at the male members of the family. Then one night when he was concealing money in the chimney he was choked by a mouthful of soot, fell, fractured his hip and began a lingering end.

He was visited in hospital by fat Tom-Billy Teare the joiner, who had married the old man's niece, and was troubled. But Ezra presently told him he had forgiven the females, who could not be expected to know better.

'I've seen to it that your Sallie's all right. Now listen: me will is in a proper black box on top o' the kitchen dresser. They all know I've made one; leave her there till you read her to them. Do the – th' arrangements, y'self, Tom-Billy. Keep it in the family, like. An' then maybe the cost...?' His niece's husband was an undertaker on occasion.

Teare went away happy, full of his executorship. He told

his wife Sallie, and she was content, and stayed in town on market day to buy a black dress.

Five days passed. Then the sad news came from the hospital and she was able to put it on.

After Teare had informed the relatives, carefully pencilling down the expenses, he and his wife shut up their home in the village and moved quickly into the Quaggin farmhouse to look after it.

They found the flimsy black deed box in its place on the dresser. Having no lock, it invited a look inside.

Under a layer of old receipts, a backless prayer book, and letters dealing with an unsatisfactory grubber, was the will. A long sky-blue paper. It was in the old man's handwriting, with strange words in places, but clear in their meaning.

Teare hugged his wife delightedly. She had been left the farm itself! A few small bequests disposed of the Quaggins.

'We're made, woman!' he said.

But later he fell into some small dispute with the heiress when she wished to cut down expenses now that there was nobody worth pleasing. He considered a heavy meal would be necessary to keep the family quiet during the will-reading. Particularly this will.

On the day of his funeral, the old man lay clean and tidy in the coffin Teare had made for him, ready for those who came to make sure he was gone.

They arrived earlier and in greater numbers than expected, caused the waiting meat plates to be recast in more and smaller portions.

Teare received the mourners at the door. Quaggins, most of them, the men short and sandy, sharp-nosed; the women pale-faced and shiftily prim. Black clothes, hastily dyed, showed smothered patterns. And expectation showed through the reverence.

The weather was fine, lighting up the dead man's fields for valuation. People went to the windows under pretence of admiring his industry, and gazed hungrily out.

The mourners' conduct was sober while in the house; sober, too, in the black varnished carriages as they crept in line behind the hearse; sober and musical in the draughty little church, as they listened to a long-winded service. At the graveside they began to cheer up; for the unpleasant part of the day was over.

On the return journey talk in the carriages grew bright. Quaggin the Cruelty, the animals inspector, thrust his red whiskers out of a window to hail a friend. From another vehicle Teare thought he heard something suspiciously like song. He frowned at his wife.

The little procession trotted briskly along the road that ran behind the village, and turned up towards the farm.

A tense proprietary excitement filled each jogging group. Eyes were fixed with modest greed on every field they passed. The dutch barn, the old pigsty, the cows. They rounded the orchard.

Teare's carriage was the first. As it drew in towards the house, he saw a figure moving near the rose-covered porch. As if coming from the side where the dairy was, and the back entrance. Teare had visions of unlocked doors. He scrambled out of the carriage.

'Well, who —?'

'Hallo, there' called the man. 'I missed the poor ould fella, eh?'

Short and sandy, with a sharp nose. A Quaggin, undoubtedly.

'Don't ye remember me, Tom-Billy?'

'Uh — yes. Of course.' Teare shook hands dubiously. Now he knew; it was some sort of cousin, a man they called Lawyer Quaggin because he had once worked as an advocate's clerk. Then a sign-writer or something, and for a time, they said, he had tried to live by raising ferrets. A spry man.

'Hallo, all!' called Lawyer Quaggin. People were

descending from the carriages. 'I was just sayin' to Tom-Billy here, business missed a train for me, an' I came too late for to see him under!' The relatives hailed him, crowding round.

Teare hurried in after his wife. He motioned her into the kitchen.

'Sallie, just a minute —'

Outside in the hall they could hear old Mrs. Kneen weeping over 'the beautiful internment' and the bass voices of her three sons.

'Well?' said Sallie.

Teare jerked his head and whispered, 'Did y' see that Lawyer character? Skulkin' round the house just as we come up. Keep an eye on him — he's fit for anythin', that fella!'

The parlour was already seething.

Teare dodged about, fitting people into places for the meal. The three huge Kneen boys were prowling gloweringly about, comparing the size of the platefuls. A child cried to be taken home. Then somehow a chicken had got into the room, fluttering among the black legs. Women pulled their skirts out of the way. Men jostled, shooing and hooting.

In desperation Teare grabbed a thin arm that led to a long face. 'Mr. Cain, for pity's sake start a hymn or somethin'!'

The thin man struck a fork on a plate and began to sing 'Abide with Me' in a grating voice that struck piercingly through the uproar. Gradually silence came.

The Quaggins sat, unwillingly, one by one.

'So beautiful,' said old Mrs. Kneen in the hush that followed the solo. She added, to the thin man's confusion and anger, 'I mean the way the table is laid. Look at it, boys.'

Soon Sallie had the tea urn working and there were polite murmurs of appreciation. Everyone held back patiently while cups joggled perilously round.

Then the food went down with a rush.

Quaggin the Cruelty called for a second cup through

steaming whiskers. The Kneen boys tore seriously at their cold beef. Pickle glasses emptied. Faces bulged.

Tom-Billy glanced round. Lawyer Quaggin was at the second table and it was difficult to see him. He seemed very quiet. Teare shifted back uneasily. The meat was tasteless in his mouth.

'My boys say they're enjoying it ever so much, my dear,' called Mrs. Kneen. Her sons chewed on, unnoticing.

Teare whispered to his wife, 'Is anybody out watchin' the kitchen?' She shook her head. His face sagged. 'Come, come, Mr. Teare! Eat up!' said a neighbour. 'Don't let the sad business distress ye too much!'

Plates were collected and fresh courses sent round. Creamy cakes and scones oozing with butter. As appetites grew less, droning reminiscences began. Teare heard everywhere the working-out of remote family connections.

He suddenly stiffened. His wife had nudged him. She whispered, 'Look – Lawyer!'

He screwed round, trying to make his face seem lightly interested in the company. Lawyer Quaggin's place was empty. He was not in the room.

Tom-Billy half rose. He sat again, heart tapping, and whispered, 'Did ye see him go?'

'No, I just turned round, and – oh, look, look! Here he is again.'

The short sandy man was sliding into his seat, a strange look upon his face, it seemed to Tom-Billy. A mixture that might have been self-conscious innocence and satisfaction; uneasy satisfaction. He caught Teare's eye and grinned. A nervous smile that suddenly became too hearty.

Tom-Billy felt his face tighten. He stood up. One or two people looked at him, and his wife's hand touched him warningly.

'Uh – get more bread,' he mumbled, and pushed his way

between the chair backs. Once the door was safely shut behind him, he ran the few steps to the kitchen. He pulled a stool up beside the dresser, climbed on to it, and clutched the tin deed box down from its place. A bead of sweat fogged his eye as he opened the lid.

The heart folded up inside him, and he grasped a shelf for support.

Ezra's will had gone!

He stumbled down, and scattered across the table all the contents of the box. The loose papers, the prayer book, the letters. He swayed as the empty black bottom of the tin stared back at him. A moment later an old chair's wicker seat split under his sudden weight.

Like scalding steam, a stream of explosive hissing curses reddened his face. Then the remembered need for silence bottled up his fury, and drove it into his head and muddled his thoughts. They took several minutes to clear.

It was Lawyer all right! He must have found out the will's hiding-place by spying through the kitchen window during the funeral. And now he had stolen it; the guilt was there on his face when he sneaked back into the parlour just now.

Tom-Billy sat trying to control himself and picture the next move.

The other room was full of Quaggins waiting to hear the thing read. If he showed the empty box, they would rend him, the keeper of it. Useless to protest that Sallie had been left everything; each man jack of them would fancy himself cheated out of a huge legacy.

Go in there and denounce the thief? No, that was as bad. Lawyer would be ready, knowing the Quaggins distrusted him nearly as much as they did Tom-Billy. He would have the will hidden somewhere, and brazenly deny everything. And later, in his own crafty time, he would tell the Quaggins in secret what it said.

Either way, the will would never be seen again. The farm would be divided amongst the whole brood.

Tom-Billy groaned with anguish.

Something must be done immediately; he had no idea what. Often he had wondered what a fattened beast felt when it sniffed the smell of slaughter. Now he knew; it prayed for the neighbourhood to be struck with catastrophe, to give it a chance of escape.

An earthquake. At least a whirlwind.

Words were dancing in front of his eyes. 'All your problems solved,' they read. He tried to blink them away like liver spots, but they persisted. They seemed to be printed on a packet lying by the wall. A little more cold sweat formed on his face.

He rose. He approached the improbable packet.

'Vesuvius Brand Lighters. All your firefighting problems solved!' he read. So he still had his senses. His pulse slackened. He had been tricked by the crumpled label.

A bag of patent things that Sallie must have bought; old Quaggin would have died of cold before spending money on them. 'Vesuvius Brand.' There was a clumsy little picture of people in long nightshirts running about clutching bundles and boxes, and a flaming mountain in the background. He slowly picked up the smelly packet.

A desperate idea was coming. The most desperate he had ever had.

He pulled the split wicker chair into the middle of the room and stacked the firelighters carefully upon it. Five of them the packet held. Quickly he added crushed newspapers, some greasy cleaning rags he found in a cupboard, and two meal sacks. The old stool and table he arranged close to the chair, in natural positions. A jarful of rendered fat completed the preparations.

He replaced the scattered papers in their tin box, and put it exactly where it belonged, up on top of the dresser.

In fearful haste now, dreading that somebody would come to look for him, Tom-Billy struck a match and put it to the tarry shavings. The flame crept over the problem-solving lighters.

As he closed the kitchen door behind him, he began to count slowly.

One, two, three –

He wiped the sweat from his face. At about a hundred it should be safe to raise the alarm.

Conversation was lively when he re-entered the parlour.

Only the Kneen boys were still eating, urged on by their mother's busy hands. The animals inspector was performing a balancing trick with lumps of sugar. Crammed, a child had fallen asleep.

Foxy Lawyer was sitting without any expression, as if biding his time.

Tom-Billy sank into his place beside his wife. He answered nothing to her questioning eyes.

Twenty-one, twenty-two, twenty-three.

He accepted another cake and ate it slowly, as calmly as he could.

Fifty-seven. Fifty-eight.

He was praying that no one would leave the room yet. Once, to his horror, Quaggin the Cruelty rose and squeezed from his place, but it was only to borrow another basin of sugar. Tom-Billy watched him sit again and go on with his tricks.

Seventy-one. Seventy-two.

The family histories were still proceeding. Nearby, a monotonous voice worked out a line that was proving intricate; '– And this Quine I'm tellin' about was a cousin of Quine the draper, an' he married the widow of a fella that had a brother in the mines; now let me think what his first name would be –'

Eighty-three.

A sandy man leaned across the table and winked. 'What about the will-readin', Mr. Teare?' he said quietly.

Instantly, it seemed, they were all deathly still; full of fierce attention. 'Yis, the time is suitable enough now,' said a woman, with a kind of desperate reasonableness.

There were murmurs of, 'The will!'

'He's goin' to read it!'

'Oh, yes, the will. I'd clean forgot about that.'

'Is it you that has charge of it, Tom-Billy?'

Teare was frozen in his chair. Bright eyes were on him from every side. In his head he had counted ninety-one. He nerved himself to pretend that he suddenly heard crackling or smelt smoke.

He was forestalled.

'D'ye smell burnin'?' said a voice. There were sniffs.

'Somethin's on fire!'

There was a moment of silent alarm. Then Quaggin the Cruelty dropped his sugar and scrambled towards the door. He pulled at it. A cloud of thin, foul smoke was swept into the room.

There was uproar. People rushed to the narrow hallway, Tom-Billy Teare fighting to be at the head. Behind, there were frightened, coughing cries; a banging at the jammed window. Somebody was roaring, 'Save the women!'

When they reached the kitchen the smoke became black and choking. Flames could be seen in it. Men hung back unhappily.

'Come on! Quick!' shouted Teare, and dived inside to kick apart the evidence of his fire-raising. His eyes streamed. 'Fling everythin' – out of the – the back door here!' He heaved it open as he shouted, and threw a smouldering cushion into the stone yard. Drew breath, then back into the room.

Men were blundering about the sides of the kitchen, eager

to save what might become their own property. Mrs. Kneen's voice was raised somewhere, commanding her sons to keep out of danger.

A chair was tossed outside, then a glowing table leg.

The women crowded in the yard, filling buckets at the pump and passing them from hand to hand.

Watching savagely, Teare was in agony. Through the smoke faces were hard to recognise. He felt a small draught of despair; if Lawyer had run away, the whole plan was wasted.

Suddenly he saw the little clerk on the other side of the kitchen, jostled in from the hall by a bulky helper; he looked nervous.

Teare sprang for the dresser and snatched down the black box. Almost in the same movement he had Lawyer held fast in the hug of a thick arm, and rushed him strongly through the burning room to the yard door. Into clear earshot of everybody; particularly the women. 'Here, take this! An' keep it safe!' he shouted. 'Uncle Ezra's will is inside it!'

For a moment their eyes locked. Seeing the fury in Lawyer's, Teare knew he had been right.

There was a tense pause in the clattering and fuss and sluicing of water. The word 'will' had struck home. Every jealous eye was on the little foxy man clutching the box.

'Watch it close and no monkey business!' Teare yelled after him, with a wink round at the rest. He felt that the wink was a good touch.

Now he had to make sure Lawyer was left alone with it.

'Come on, everybody – one last big slap at it!' With something like cheerfulness, he flung himself at the dying fire. The Quaggins followed suit.

Tom-Billy busied himself in the yard, finding work for every pair of hands. Except one. Lawyer sat alone in a strawy corner, the box on his knees. But there must be no witness to say he had not meddled with it; Teare kept everyone on the move, shouting at them, directing, comforting. His flannel shirt was soaked with sweat as well as water.

Once he caught sight of Mrs. Kneen approaching Lawyer as if to sit and share his guardianship. He ran and caught her arm. 'Oh, Mrs. Kneen; would ye look to the child yonder – I think she's taken with fright!' Lawyer glowered.

A minute or two later, when Teare turned from dousing the last smouldering remains of the table, the corner was empty. He thought he glimpsed Lawyer, slipping round a corner of the cowhouse.

The idea must be working!

'It's all out now!' called one of the Kneen boys from inside. Water dripped from everything in the kitchen and swilled across the stone floor. The ceiling was blackened. Otherwise damage was small, though wives' voices rose when they saw their men's singed suits, and the Cruelty was anxiously feeling the shape of his beard. Dye had run on splashed dresses.

Tom-Billy pulled a sack over his shoulders and looked round. There must be no waiting.

'Where's – who did I give it to? The will box?' He hoped his frown looked honestly puzzled.

They knew.

'Lawyer!' shouted voices. 'Where's Lawyer? I seen him a minute ago!' The unmistakable cry of hungry, suspicious animals. 'Where did he get to? Lawyer! Did you see him go?'

'Lawyer, the fire's out!' shouted Quaggin the Cruelty. 'Where the divil have ye put yeself?'

'Lawyer! Lawyer!'

There was a hush.

The little foxy man was coming from the direction of the cowhouse, the box in his hands. His hair seemed a brighter ginger, or his face was whiter. Suspicious eyes were all on the tin.

Without a word, expressionless, Lawyer handed it to Tom–

Billy. This time his eyes told nothing.

'Ah – thanks,' Teare said. 'We wouldn't have had this lost for the world, eh? Thanks for keepin' it safe, Lawyer.'

There was a chorus of excited approval.

'Good oul' Lawyer! Bad job if the will had gone on fire!' 'If they found even a singe –'

'Better make sure it's safe,' said the man who had suggested the reading.

Tom-Billy's hands trembled violently as he put the box down among the trickling water and singed cushion feathers that covered the yard. 'Heat injures the nerves,' murmured Mrs. Kneen, interestedly; nobody noticed her.

The black box squeaked open. Tom-Billy's hand went inside and fumbled quickly. A pause.

He drew out a long, sky-blue paper.

'This aforesaid document,' he read shakily, 'is the only will whatever of me, Ezra John Quaggin, pig, general, dairy and poultry farmer –'

His head sang with relief as he looked round the grimy, eager faces.

'Go on! Go on, Tom-Billy,' they cried.

He found the place, cleared his throat, and read again. Soon, he knew, the real fun would begin.

The Photograph

WHEN HE STUCK THEM sideways out of the bed, his legs felt as if they were doing a new thing, something they did not understand.

'Dress quickly, now,' said Mamma. 'It is easy to catch cold after being so long in bed. I shall call your sister to help you.'

It was hard to keep upright. His legs were still sore in the places where they bent; his arms, too, when he held them up to go through sleeves.

'Feel funny?' said his sister, Gladys. 'Hold on to the bedpost while I fasten these buttons. Why, Raymond, I do believe you've grown taller in bed, dear!'

He saw a face low down in the great wardrobe mirror.

For a moment everything in him stopped.

A terrible, thin face. With perfectly round shiny eyes; shadows you could almost see through, that belonged to a thing, not a person; dull, dull, tangled hair.

'Well, how do you look?' said Gladys.

She was putting a kind of jolliness into her voice. Her head came down beside his, to see. She was healthy, different only in the way all people looked in mirrors.

Mamma brought out his green suit with the white curly

111

collar, and laid it on the bed. He watched little creases being smoothed from its special cloth.

'Is it Sunday?' he said.

Lines folded deeper in Mamma's face; her bright eyes fixed on him so hard that he felt guilty, and blinked several times. 'No,' she said in a low voice, 'but you are to wear it today. I am taking you to have your photograph made.'

Gladys squeezed him. 'The doctor says you're a lot better now, Raymond. Won't it be nice?'

He clutched her warm arm. Sideways, through Gladys's hair, he could see Mamma standing still, watching.

'Silly! Little silly boy! He's frightened!' said Gladys. 'I had it done last year – you know that. And Mamma has. Everybody has. There, funny boy.'

She brushed his hair till it was smooth, and cut off some little pieces and put them in an envelope.

'Glad,' he said, 'what are you crying for?'

But instead of answering she began to dab his face gently with a puff of her own powder.

It was cold downstairs. Everything felt hard and big, and the linoleum looked like frozen water. 'Button his overcoat up,' said Mamma. 'Stay quietly in that chair, Raymond, until the cab comes. Close to the fire.'

The yellow-tiled grate turned on him an unfamiliar, quivering heat that made him blink often. Soon the little pains in his knees died out. He was damp and hot inside his clothes.

'You must behave well,' said Mamma. 'Do exactly as the gentleman directs. Keep very still for him – that is the most important thing. Are you warm?'

'The cab!' Gladys called. 'It's here!' She came into the room. 'Oh, how much better he looks! He'll be sorry to leave such a nice fire, won't you, Raymond?'

They got into the cab. There was a strange smell of its leatheriness, and some kind of scent, and pipe smoke were in the thick blue cloth of the seat, and the padded walls. He sat between Mamma and Gladys and watched the tall roofs stream past the window.

'Isn't it fun?' said Gladys. 'Listen to the horse's feet! Trotting as fast as he can go. All specially for this little boy!'

When they climbed down the cab's iron steps, it was in a street with shops and high buildings. Mamma stopped to talk to the driver. 'Come along,' said Gladys. 'Up we go. Let me help you, old mister shaky-legs!'

There were many stairs inside the building; whenever they stopped, they saw more leading upwards. 'Must be growing while we climb them!' Gladys panted. She had both arms tightly round him, almost carrying him. From below, Mamma was calling softly and crossly, 'Gladys! Wait a moment, if you please! We must all go in together!'

They came to the last of the stairs, and there was a door that was partly made of glass, with printed letters on it.

'Come,' said Mamma.

The man inside wore black clothes. There was no hair on his head, and he had yellow eyes that moved in a sort of liquid. He said, 'So this is the little man! A bright chap! In no time you'll be as fit as a fiddle, eh?' He held a hand down to Raymond. The fingers were dark brown, and some of the nails had split until you could see into the cracks.

'Shake hands with the gentleman, Raymond,' said Mamma.

He could do nothing.

'Not altogether surprising,' said the man, and made a noise like a laugh; but he was not pleased. 'Chemicals ruin the hands, madam. Sit down in this nice chair, little man.'

He began to talk to Mamma in a whisper, glancing sideways.

The room was very big, with wide windows in the ceiling, but they were painted streaky white and no sky showed through them. Tall shining things made of wood and glass and yellow metal stood everywhere.

'Now,' said the man. 'Let us begin. The little fellow's overcoat off, please, madam?'

Then Raymond was on a different chair. His legs hung down from the huge leather seat. The man picked up his hand and pressed it on to the chair's cold, knobbed arm as if it belonged there. A polished table stood close by; on it were a book made of leather and a shiny plant like Mamma's. 'Genuine antiques,' the man was saying to Mamma. 'The floral background is hand-painted in oils.'

'Tidy his hair, Gladys,' whispered Mamma.

A burning brightness came, high up. His eyes itched and watered. The man said, 'Don't look at the lights, little fellow,' and moved metal things that clicked, under a black cloth.

Raymond shivered. He seemed to be in another place, feeling nothing; like being asleep and not dreaming. He could hear Gladys blowing her nose somewhere behind the brightness.

'Ah, yes,' said the man, busy jerking things in the dark, 'doesn't he look a picture?' He cleared his throat. 'Steady, now! Still as a mouse. See what I've got in my hand?' And, as if he was singing a little tune, 'Keep-quite-quite-quite-still –'

Clack, went his machine. 'Now, again –'

When the lights went out at last, everything broke into spots of purple darkness.

'This very evening, madam,' the man was saying; on one hand he had put a glove with a head like a monkey. 'Without fail. In the circumstances.' His voice had a secret in it. 'I'm so very sorry –'

On the way downstairs, Raymond sneezed.

He lay quietly in the bed. When he moved, all the old pains jumped in his arms and legs, worse than weeks ago. His nose was running.

For a time, the sun made slow reddish squares on the wallpaper. Then it disappeared.

His heart began to hurry, bumping until it hurt. The bed seemed to shake. A tiny ticking noise began, somewhere down among the springs; keeping time with his heart.

The door opened; it was Gladys again.

'How now, dear?' she said, and put her cheek against his forehead. 'The shivering's stopped, and now he's too hot. Poor little sick Raymond!' She sat on the bed. 'I've got a surprise for you,' she said. 'Lie very still, and I'll show you. It's just this moment arrived.'

'Look!' She held something up, high above his chest. A reddish-brown picture. He knew the table in it, the huge chair, the book, the shiny plant, from some time in the past.

There, too, was that terrible face.

After a moment he turned to her. She smiled and nodded. 'It's the photograph, darling. Isn't it nice?'

He twisted his head away, and his neck ached. Tears came out of his eyes. He felt angry and frightened; as if he had lost part of himself.

Gladys was tightening the bedclothes round him. 'Poor dear! Does it hurt to look up? I'll put the photo here on the mantelpiece, and light the candle so that you can see it all the time. We're going to have another big one, in a frame, to hang downstairs. Mamma is so pleased and – and –' Her voice turned down and trembled.

Suddenly he felt himself held tightly. 'Raymond!' Gladys was crying again, and a tear ran down inside his collar. 'Oh, my little –'

She squeezed him until he gasped. Then she ran out of the room and the door thudded.

He felt cold and small.

Then, in the same instant, he was enormous. His head stretched from the pillow until it touched the walls. His huge hands were pressing down through the bed to the floor. From far below came the ringing click of the bedspring, like distant hoofbeats.

On the mantelpiece was the little brown picture-child. His face was white and horrible and still. He clung to his chair and stared at Raymond.

The candle was too bright to look at. And when it flickered, the whole room bobbed. Waves of fright rushed over him, up through the bed. His ears were bursting with the noise.

'Keep still,' said something inside him. Keep-quite-quite-quite-still!'

His head was changing its shape because it was so heavy, and the beating, bubbling heart climbed up to meet it.

'Keep-quite-quite-quite-still,' said a voice.

It sounded like his own, but this time it was not inside his head. It was outside, close to his ear. He twisted himself through the hot clothes, crying because it hurt; and looked.

He nearly screamed with terror.

By the bed stood the picture-child. Alive. In the green suit, but now it was reddish-brown. His face was the narrow photograph-face. Like a hollow, china thing.

'Still!' said the boy. 'Keep-quite-quite-quite-still, little man.'

He put out a hand and laid it on the rumpled sheet. Brown fingers, and the nails were split wide open. 'Your heart's going to burst,' he said.

The whole of the bedroom roared and crackled; yet at the same time it was utterly quiet. The boy smiled. Little bony teeth.

'I'm going to have your toys,' he said. 'The new ones too.'

The bedspring kept time like a great bell.

'And in this bed will be me. Just-keep-quite-quite-quite-still. You won't be anything at all.

'Feel it bursting?'

Downstairs, they were arguing.

'Crass folly –!'

She twisted a handkerchief in her fingers, and tried to hold her lips firm; but they trembled.

'Kindly remember, Doctor, that I am the child's mother! I wanted this memory of him, to keep. More than anything you could ever understand!'

'Nonsense, madam!' said the doctor. 'Think I wouldn't have told you if he was dying? But now – I can't answer for what you may have done today. Let me see him at once.'

Halfway up the first flight of stairs, they heard the cries in his bedroom, and ran the rest of the way. The doctor threw the white door open.

'Raymond!' his mother exclaimed.

He was crouching near the window in his nightshirt, but over it he had pulled the jacket of his best green suit. The trousers were clasped to his chest. His eyes were bright with delirium, staring towards the bed.

'I won't! I won't be still!' The screaming went on, hoarse and terrified.

He did not seem to see them. From the window-ledge he snatched a picture book and held it tightly.

'I won't! No! No! I won't go on the mantelpiece!'

Chains

CHAINS, MASTER?

You've found the right man if it's them you're wanting. I lay you'd travel from here to Old Scratch's bosom, and never light on another stock like mine. You're in a sweat, master; due out on the next tide and short of tackle, I wager? Pretty fix, that. But you came to me, and I never let a sailor-man down yet.

Here – I'll just set a spark to me lantern; it's a filthy bastard of a night round the harbour for an old man. Crabber, you brute – hup! Old dog, too, sir; we're both stiff in every joint. Now we'll be off!

Only a few steps away, my shed is. My palace. Thirty feet to the ceiling, if it's a pygmy's inch. And all heaped with the treasures of the deep blue sea.

Of course you understand my stores aren't new, exactly. Honourable labour, you might say, has been their lot. So often a big-bellied shipowner, or it might be a wharf-lubber, or just a poxy carter, they'll say, 'These here chains is wore out,' and they'll throw them away. But do you – heel, Crabber! – do you just chip off the pitch and rust, and run 'em through a tub of rock-oil, why, many a one'll see good

119

service again. Test 'em and take out the weak links, that's all.

Of course, they comes cheaper than the new, master; but you'll find 'em well cared for, and I sell only the best. Big demand for 'em sometimes, so I like the sight of moneys in hand, of course – Oh, yes, sir; yes, I see. Naturally I knew I could trust you. Nice to deal with a gentleman, sir.

It's remarkable, you know, what kinds and degrees there is in chains. Rare masterpieces, sometimes. Craft and wisdom I've found in some of mine, that no ordinary ironman would ever know of, even in this year of grace 1731. The way they'll take any sort of strain, yet when they're slack they'll lie neat as a lady's hand. Queer-shaped foreign links you see, you'd think they had human sinews the way they act. 'Course they're not all like that; some are clumsy, sheer weight, and treacherous in a ship.

And here we are, master. Big place, eh? Would you hold the lantern just a moment; salt gets into the lock and it sticks. That's it – thank you kindly. Just follow me.

Now watch when I hold up the lamp. There! Chains enough for you, eh? See how they go right up to the very roof? Looped and coiled over the cross-beams, most of 'em. Mark where you walk, there's that many on the floor; it's slippery, too, from the oil that drips down.

Quite an inheritance, eh, master?

That's what it was, you know. My grandfather had it first, and then my father. When I came back from the sea – oh, yes, I sailed in southern waters for many a year – my father said, 'You've had a hard life, Samuel,' he said. 'With my blessing, do you take this store which has been built up to a paying business by me and my father.' Meaning grandfather, you see. I told him he was a liar. He was right, though. Remarkable what money there is in them, too; gentry wanting a rare piece of chain for some fancy purpose, and whatnot.

Here's me chattering, and you got to sail on the next tide!

Now, master, just what's your requirements? Spare anchor chain? Some fine lengths here, full weight. See that in the corner? Washed up out of a Dutchman in van Tromp's time; too old to use now, though.

Something lighter? – right! This way, sir.

Mark that dog – after a rat, just as if he isn't past catching them! Fetch, Crabber! His wits are gone; what would rats live on in a place like –?

Hsst! Listen to that, master? Hear it? A tiny slithering, metally sound, and then a soft plop. That'd be what the dog heard, and it isn't a rat. Guess what it is?

Well, it's chain, master. A little chain. Sliding and slithering through the heavier lengths and down to the floor. They'll hang here quiet, month after month, and then – it's the way heat and cold work on them, or a gust of wind through a crack – they'll shift just enough, and come wriggling down like iron snakes. Queer, eh? Opening the door must have set that joey off.

Mind that patch of grease, master! With the light so dim, you need to watch where you put your feet.

Yes, sometimes I'll be in my cottage yonder, and in the middle of the night there'll be hell's own crashing and whipping from this shed. And next morning I'll find chains lying tangled all about, like those huge dead devil-snakes that floats and stinks on the Sargasso; I lay you seen them. So I have to set to, and drag 'em out in order again.

Now, master, would these be more to your liking? Not too heavy, but there's a deal of life in 'em yet. Stand on a length and pull hard as you like – you'll find no weak links.

Would that be your ship lying across the bay now, master – the *Lampedusa?* Sailing for the Ivory coast, they say; would that be right? Pick up cargo there for the Americas?

So the chains you'd be wanting wouldn't be ordinary ones. Eh?

But about three feet long, with a stout ring at one end, and shackles at the other; such that'll hold a blackey secure. Well, master. I reckon I can help you there. Just a bit farther along, if you please. Not that I've had many asking for them – bastards want new ones because they're scared of the blackbirds breaking loose!

Now watch your step! If you slip and clutch at 'em, there's no telling what they'll do. Crush a man's head like a barnacle if they come down sudden.

Look, over in that corner yonder – them's the ones you want. I had 'em strung up along that wall out of the way. Most of 'em seen service in slavers before, and half a hundred from – guess where – old Newgate Gaol. You might find some of the gyves rusted on the inside by sweat and that; but on the whole, they're in fair condition.

Queer, come to think of it; how much power there is in this place. Just waiting. All these chains here are made for holding and binding ships, and men. Eh, master? So the bastards'll do what they're told, and work hard till they're done with. That's right, ain't it? Eh? Eh? Oh, you're one as appreciates a cunning bit of chain. 'A real sailor-man,' says I when I seen you first. And there's good money going for blackbirds now in Virginia.

Now, how's them, master? Strong, ain't they? Take more than a black savage to work his way out of them fetters; just feel 'em! Funny how they eat into the skin, and when the raw salt of a ship gets at the sores –

Forgive me chattering.

You'll take 'em all? All them with fetters and anklets. I'll have 'em down directly then, and maybe some of your crew would be along in a few minutes to collect 'em. I'll just light you back to the door, sir.

No, no, this is the way we came. Watch your head. Just place your feet where I do, master, and you'll dodge the slippery patches. Glad I've been able to help you out; I often –

Oh! That's a fine thing – telling you to be careful, and – tumbling myself like that. Don't move, sir. Just stand dead still a moment while I – relight the lantern. Don't move an inch now.

Hallo!

Something's slipping up aloft! Listen! They're on the move, all of them! Don't budge, whatever you do!

Oh –! Master –!

Lord, that was a smash! Curse this damp tinder – can't see a thing!

There! A bit of light at last! All right, Crabber? Good dog! Now where is he? Somewhere back here. Fetch him out, Crabber! Oh, what a monstrous mess of chain!

Heel, you brute!

Yes. That's his hand, with the dirty lace at the cuff. Might be – might be twenty fathoms of anchor chain there, lying on him; must have grabbed at a piece because he felt himself slipping in the dark. Poor, simple, honest blackbirder, he just didn't know his way about here. Was that it, dog? Maybe if you could see in the darkness like a cat, you'd think different.

Look, here's his fancy purse. His fancy gentleman's purse. Take a good sniff at that, dog. Don't mean a thing to you, eh?

Poor bastard, how he screamed! A sound I never did like to hear from a man.

Eh, well, master. So you've died. And spoiled my chance to tell you about my merry life; you'd have listened kindly to it, being as you're a sailor-man. How I sweated in the shipyards before I ran off to sea. And the women I've known; now, they would have made a story for you, some of them. And how the yellow jack took me, and I came through it. And how – and how, for instance, I was seven years aboard the Spaniard galley. In chains.

Crabber! Come away, you filthy brute!

The Tarroo-Ushtey

IN FAR-OFF DAYS BEFORE the preachers and the schoolmasters came, the island held a great many creatures besides people and beasts. The place swarmed with monsters.

A man would think twice before answering his cottage door on a windy night, in dread of a visit from his own ghost. The high mountain roads rang in the darkness with the thunderous tiffs of the bugganes, which had unspeakable shapes and heads bigger than houses; while a walk along the seashore after the sun had set was to invite the misty appearance of a tarroo-ushtey, in the likeness of a monstrous bull, ready to rush the beholder into the sea and devour him. At harvest-time the hairy troll-man, the phynodderee, might come springing out of his elder tree to assist in the reaping, to the farmer's dismay; for the best-intentioned of the beings were no more helpful than interfering neighbours, and likely to finish the day pulling the thatch off the house or trying to teach the hens to swim. What with the little people, the fairies themselves, so numerous that they were under everybody's feet, turning milk sour and jamming locks and putting the fire out; and with witches waiting at every other bend in the road with their evil eye ready to paralyse the horses, ordinary people led a difficult life. It was necessary to carry charm-herbs, or beads, and to remember warding-off rhymes that had been taught in early childhood.

As the generations went by and people took to speaking English on polite occasions, the old creatures grew scarcer. By the time that travellers from the packet boats had spread the story about a girl named Victoria being the new queen of the English, their influence was slipping; at night people put out milk for the fairies more from habit than fear, half-guessing it would be drunk by the cat; if they heard a midnight clamour from the henhouse, they reached for a musket, not a bunch of hawthorn. But back hair could still rise on a dark mountain road.

From the gradual loss of the old knowledge, came dependence on the wise men and women.

Charlsie Quilliam was one of these.

He was the fattest man on the island, said those who had travelled all over it and could speak with authority.

He carried his enormous body with special care, like a man with a brim-full jug; but he still stuck in doors and caused chairs to collapse; and people meeting him on a narrow path had to climb the hedge to let him pass. The right of way was always Charlsie's.

His fatness, coupled with a huge black beard, left little shape to his face, but his eyes were quick. Above them, like a heathery ledge, ran a single, unbroken line of eyebrow, which denoted second sight.

Whatever question was asked, he would be able to answer it. Even if he said nothing, the expression in his eyes showed that he knew, but considered the questioner would be better in ignorance. It was Charlsie who had had a vision of the potato blight crossing to Ireland in a black cloud, but he kept the frightening secret to himself until long afterwards, when the subsequent famine was common talk and nobody could be alarmed by what he had seen.

Old secret customs; birth-charms and death-charms, and rites for other dark days; Charlsie's big head held them all. Folk in trouble might set out for the minister's house, think better of it, and go to find Charlsie where he sat on a hump of earth outside his cottage, his thick fingers busy with scraps of coloured wool and feathers.

Ever since he became too fat for other work, his secret knowledge had supported him; and gifts of food from grateful clients kept his weight creeping up.

Many a winter night he would be at the centre of a fireside gathering. Charlsie's guttural, hoarse voice could hold a packed cottage in frightened suspense for hours as it laid horror upon horror. Personal experience of dealing with witches was his chief subject. Most of his stories had little point, which made them all the more uncanny and likely. People went home in groups after an evening with Charlsie.

Apart from the witches, he had only one open enemy.

This was a Scottish peddler named McRae. The man had lost a leg in the Crimea, and called himself a Calvinist. He sneered at the old beliefs and tried to tell his own war experiences instead; but people were chary of listening, in case Charlsie got to know. They bought Duncan McRae's buttons and shut the door quickly.

The little Scot hated it. At hardly a single house in the fat man's territory could he get himself invited inside for a free meal; even the news he brought from the towns was received with suspicion, when at all, as if he had made it up on the road. He would have cut the district out altogether, except that he sold more elastic there than anywhere else.

One hot afternoon in the late summer, the peddler sweated up the hill towards the village.

A dense sea fog had smothered the sun, the air was close,

and his pack wearied him. Time after time he had to rest his wooden leg.

Duncan McRae had news. A titbit he had picked up before he left town particularly pleased him, and had gone down well in two villages already. For once it was an item that people would be able to put to the proof themselves later on.

A new machine was to be tested on the English side of the channel, less than thirty miles away. It was said to be able to warn ships in fog.

McRae hastened. He had heard that when the new 'fog horn,' as they called it, was tested, people on the island might be able to hear it blowing faintly. Today's weather seemed very suitable for such an experiment, but even if nothing happened, surely this story at least had enough interest to call for hospitality.

At the top of the hill he leaned on a hedge to ease his leg. The air was heavy, and the quietness a relief after the clumping of his iron-tipped stump in the grit.

He held his breath, listening.

Far away there was a moan. He pulled himself up the hedge and faced towards the fog-blanketed sea.

The sound came again, faint and eerie; a growl so low-pitched that it could hardly be heard at all. It could only be one thing.

Excitedly, McRae slid down the hedge and straightened his pack. Within ten minutes, bursting with news, he had reached the first outlying cottage door. He rattled the latch and pushed it open.

'Hallo, there!' he called. 'D'ye hear the new invention yonder?'

There was silence; no one at home.

He hurried out, and on to the next fuchsia-hedged cabin. 'Hallo, missis! D'ye hear the wonders that's going on across the water —?'

No one to be seen.

McRae frowned. He was at the top end of the village now, looking down the winding street as it sloped towards the sea. There was nobody moving in it, and no sound. Even the blacksmith's forge was silent.

The peddler shouted, 'Where is everybody? Is there no' a single body up the day?'

His voice went quietly away into the mist.

Charlsie Quilliam had been in his cottage when they came for him. He was threading a dried caul on a neckband as a cure against shipwreck, working indoors because the damp grieved his chest.

People came clustering round his door, muttering.

'Come in or go out!' called Charlsie. He pricked his thumb. 'Devil take it! This caul is like the hide of a crocodile!'

They saw that he did not hear what they heard; he suffered at times from deafness. At last old Juan Corjeag persuaded him to come outside.

Charlsie was surprised to see nearly all the village assembled at his door.

'Just listen, Charlsie!' said old Juan.

The frightened faces seemed to be expecting something from him. 'Well, what is it at all?' he said after a moment.

'Oh – listen, do!'

Then Charlsie heard it. A sound that might have been made by a coughing cow far away on a calm night.

'Some beast that wants lookin' to,' he decided. 'Is that all? Whatever's got into everybody?'

Old Juan's face was too horrified to express anything. He pointed.

'Them sounds is from out at sea!' he said. There was a shocked murmur from the villagers at the speaking of the words.

Charlsie made no move. His little eyes sharpened.

'Tell us what it is, Charlsie! What've we got to do? Oh, an' it's far worse down by the water! The twist of the land smothers it here!'

Without a word Charlsie Quilliam turned back into his cottage; the crowd were alarmed by his stillness. When he reappeared, he had his big blackthorn walking-stick in one hand; in the other was a bunch of dried leaves.

'I'm goin' down there for a sight,' he said. 'Anybody that wants to, can come.'

He set ponderously off.

For a little space they hesitated, whispering among themselves. Old Juan licked his lips and went after Charlsie. When he looked round, a few dozen paces down the shore path, he saw the rest following behind him in a body on the sandy track.

Charlsie stopped for breath. Old Juan caught him up.

'Ye're right. It's clearer down here.'

Old Juan spoke slowly. 'Charlsie, I'm hopin' it won't put bad luck on me, but I was the first that heard it.' He swallowed, remembering. 'Down in the tide, diggin' for lug-worms.'

'Ah?' said Charlsie. He grunted. 'Let's get nearer.'

As they came over the low brow of the foreshore, where the yellow sandy grass ended and the pebbles began, the sound hit them. It travelled straight in along the surface of the water; still very far away, but plainer to the ear; so unnatural that it shocked everybody afresh. It ended with a throaty gulp.

Charlsie made his way slowly across the stones, picking his way with the stick among the puddles. They all followed in silence towards the water's edge.

There he stood, leaning and listening.

Again and again and again the distant cry came from the fog, and they shivered. Old Juan made to speak, but Charlsie silenced him.

'Yes,' said Charlsie, turning back casually, 'it's a tarroo-ushtey.'

A woman screamed and had a hand clapped across her mouth. People drew back hastily from the creamy water's edge.

'What'll happen?' whispered old Juan.

Charlsie's single brow bent in a frown. 'Queer thing for it to come out in the daylight,' he said. 'It goes to prove such creatures is no fancy.'

He turned to the crowd and addressed them.

'Now listen, all! It's a tarroo-ushtey out yonder. Hush, now, hush! It's in trouble over somethin' – maybe lost an' callin' out to another one.'

'Aye, its mate, likely!' said Juan.

Charlsie ignored him. 'For all that they're not of this world, they can get lost in thick fog like any other creature. It's a terrible long way off at present; so the best thing to do is be quiet and go home, and do nothin' to draw it this way.

'An' I'll tell ye what he's like. They look like a tremendous big black bull, but their feet is webbed. An' in th' ould days they've had many a person eaten. So nobody must come down here tonight, for fear of the fog clearin' and it seein' him. There's no tellin' what it might do if it got up in the village.'

He showed the bunch of herbs in his left hand. 'Now everybody go home quiet, an' I'll see about layin' a charm on the water. Keep all the childher indoors!'

He sat on a low rock near the tide as they went.

Peering back at him, they saw him wave the leaves back and forth in his hand. He seemed to be chanting something. In the sight of old Juan, the last to cross the sandy bluff, he finished by tossing the bunch into the sea and turning abruptly away.

Charlsie laboured up the track without a look behind. The lowing sounds still continued. He felt satisfied with what he had done, but was checking the rites over in his mind to make sure. Ahead, the last stragglers reached the safety of the village.

But when he came to the houses, Charlsie found people still talking in small groups.

'Look here, I told ye to get the childher out of sight!' he said. 'An' it'd be just as well if everybody kept themselves –'

A commotion was going on farther up the street.

'What the devil is it now?' Charlsie shouted; he felt privileged to make a noise.

Old Juan hobbled towards him. 'It's that Scotch peddler!' he said. 'He's got some nonsense tale! Oh, ye'd better give him a word, Charlsie – he'll be puttin' foolishness in their heads!'

Charlsie scowled.

He came ponderously to where Duncan McRae sat on a wooden bench outside a cottage. People parted before him, but he felt that there was a questioning quality in their respect.

'What's goin' on here?' he said.

The little Scot grinned up, hands tucked comfortably behind his head.

'Och, I've been sitting here wondering if ye'd all fled awa' into a far country. I was thinking ye had a nice day for it,' he said.

'What are ye bletherin' about?'

'Have ye got a straightjacket on yon sea monster?' The peddler chuckled. 'Look him in the eye, man. That's what they say; look him in the eye and put salt on his tail. I've a new brand of table salt in ma pack – would ye care to try some?' He began to laugh loudly.

Charlsie's face was purple. 'Is the feller crazy or what? Shut up, will ye!' He seized the little man by the hair and shook him violently. 'Stop laughin'! Haven't I ordered quiet!'

The peddler squealed as he tried to escape; his wooden leg skidded, and he thrashed about.

The staring villagers broke into explanation.

'He's got a tale that the noises is from a machine, Charlsie!'

'A warnin' of fog, for the ships!'

'That's what he said.'

There was dead silence, apart from the spluttering breath of the dazed peddler. Charlsie slowly released him.

They were all tense, watching Charlsie's face. It showed no expression; he might have been thinking, or working something out, or studying his victim, or listening. 'Juan,' he said at last, pointedly.

'Yes, Charlsie?'

'Can ye still hear it?'

They all waited, listening. The noise at sea had stopped.

'No, Charlsie. No! It's gone!'

It was Charlsie's moment. He glowered down at the wretched peddler, and took a chance.

'It's gone because I stopped it,' he said. 'I put a charm on the water to send it away. Now tell me somethin', me little Scotchman! Could I ha' done that if it was only some kind of a steam engine across the water?'

He felt the awe all round him.

'Ye poor ignorant cuss, ye're not worth mindin'! I pity ye,' said Charlsie kindly.

'Och, look here! You go down to the town, and they'll tell ye there –'

Charlsie gave a laugh. It began deep inside him, where there was plenty of room, and rose in a throaty bellow.

'In the town! Oh – oh, my!' Charlsie was overcome. 'Ye'd better stick to sellin' buttons, master! He heard it in the town! An' he believed it! In the town! – where they're washin' themselves from mornin' to night, an' where they have to give each other little bits of cardboard to know who they are, an' get special knives out for t'eat a fish! There was a feller in the town thought he was Napoleon of the French! Oh, yes, the town! That's where they know everythin'! I'm sure!'

There was a howl of laughter.

It was a complete victory. The peddler protested and raged against their laughter, but he could do nothing to stop it; only

Charlsie could do that, by a finger to his lips and a warning nod at the sea.

Charlsie watched McRae go stumping away in a fury without selling anything. His face was dark and thoughtful.

'Juan,' he said, loudly enough for others to hear, and with great conviction, 'this has given me an idea! Ye know, the sound of a tarroo–ushtey's voice would be a good thing t'imitate, as a warnin' to the ships; it needs a frightenin' sort of a noise. I've a mind to suggest that to th' English government! In fact, I will; I'll send the letter now. An' describe how it can be done.'

He went indoors, where he felt weak now that the crisis was over; praying for the silence to continue, but ready to make another journey to the beach with a bunch of herbs. His luck held.

The foghorn did not sound again that day, or again for more than a week.

When at last it did, Charlsie reassured the village and bade them observe the sound: they would find, he said, that it was copied from the cry of the tarroo–ushtey, according to a simple invention of his own. They listened, and it was so.

He was often to be seen after that, sitting outside his home on foggy days, listening to the far-off hooting with a critical expression. When he went indoors, they said it was to write to the English government again, advising them.

Charlsie's fame as an inventor spread. He was rumoured to be working on a device for closing gates automatically, and another to condense water from clouds. Even strangers came to the village to have their ailments or troubles charmed away, or to undergo his new massage treatment.

But Duncan McRae did not sell another inch of elastic in the whole district.

Mrs. Mancini

A RAY OF SUNLIGHT came through the curtains and deliberately struck Mrs. Mancini in the eye. Half-asleep, she muttered at it and rolled over, but her eye watered until she had to grope under the pillow for a handkerchief. Presently she sat up and lifted the pillow: there was no handkerchief. 'God damn it!' she moaned, and dried her eye on the sheet.

It was no good now: she was awake. She leaned back on her hands, yawning and blinking slowly at the spotty, sun-yellowed curtains. 'That's the way I am,' she said aloud to herself. 'When once I wake up I can never drop off again.' Her voice was thick and husky. She cleared her throat. 'Never,' she added.

When she felt able, she threw the bedclothes aside and slewed her legs to the floor. 'God, Rose, look at that fat!' she said, and smacked her knee; it shook. She ripped her nightdress open and let it fall round her feet while she lit a cigarette. She dressed slowly, humming through her nose and exhaling smoke at the same time, occasionally laying the cigarette down to pull a garment over her head. Pouchy eyes watched her from the mirror: thin grey hair; a long nose; cheeks hollowed because their fullness had slipped, through the years, down towards her neck. Holding her facecloth by one corner, she lowered it into the big jug for moisture and applied scented soap thoughtfully. 'A bright-eyed, beautiful old lady,' she said. 'You could see that she had once been strikingly handsome.' She regarded the mirror earnestly, holding the cloth poised. 'No, Rosie. Never mind, you had character, my dear.' The face's lower lip trembled.

With a long sniff, she pulled the clothes back over the bed, ready for night. This looked suspiciously like the start of a patch of misery.

Entering the other room, she knocked over an ashtray full of stubs, and was sure of it. She took the cover from the parrot's cage; as usual, it crouched with skinny claws clamped on the perch, grey eyes artfully closed; like a miser hatching a plan for theft. 'You old devil – stop pretending!' cried Mrs. Mancini, and shook the cage until the bird struggled for balance; it looked at her resentfully. She put her head close to the bars and mocked it by imitating its rattling laugh. She was forestalling it. Sooner or later in the day, it would start talking in her dead husband's voice.

There was no bread in the flat. She quivered with anger at the way there was no bread; nothing but an old, curling crust that she threw furiously out of the back window, hitting the stone yard below with a dry crack. In a basin she found margarine. 'Oh, thank you, thank you!' she said sarcastically, and began to smear it on biscuits from the red glass jar that stood on the sideboard, sticking them together in pairs. Biscuits for breakfast.

Tea made, she sat drinking slowly. Biscuit crumbs scattered into the upholstery of the big streamlined chair. 'Comfort, by God!' she said, and suddenly felt light-headed at the thought of the furnishers' demand-letters pinned behind the door. *Dear Madam*, they said, *Unless you make some attempts to discharge the arrears due,* they said. 'Dear Madam, dear darling lovely Madam,' she sniggered. 'Don't they know they hate me? Or are they trying to be sly? That's it – stupid fools!' A settee and two armchairs, all new; seventeen weeks old, to be exact; with chromium-plated bands round the arms. Well, they could have one of those chairs back; they didn't think anybody could sit in two chairs at once, did they, the fools!

Noises rose from the flat below. Miss Abbott was awake. By the amount of running about that she did when she got up, anybody would think she was training for something – to catch a husband, perhaps! Stupid old maid, no mind, chasing like a hen that follows its nose. Just listen to her down there – scurrying, hunting, rooting about among boxes and tins, looking for the bread or something.

'Rose,' said the parrot, 'you got my shoes?'

It was Mr. Mancini's voice: his deep, accented voice, hollowed by echoing in the bird's beak.

'Rose, you got my shoes?'

Her husband had been a waiter and she always polished his shoes; she insisted, because he did it badly. He used to lean over the bannisters and say that, and she would pass the shoes up to him. The linoleum of the hall chilled his stockinged feet.

'Rose,' the parrot repeated, and paused as Mr. Mancini had sometimes done. 'You got my shoes?'

'No, Louis,' she had the fancy to say, 'they're not ready. Sit on the stairs and wait.' She smiled. That would put him in his place.

Her family hadn't liked the marriage: Mr. Mancini was a foreigner. They thought it was beneath her to marry a foreigner, not understanding that she thought so too but had her reasons. She smiled cunningly at her husband's photograph on the mantelpiece; at the same time tears ran down her face, and one fell on the biscuit she was holding. Without really noticing, she wiped it dry on her skirt, and sniffed.

'We didn't have any babies, Louis!'

Mr. Mancini said nothing: the parrot was eating its coloured seed.

'It wasn't me, Louis. I know for certain it wasn't me!' she whimpered. 'Unless – perhaps I was too old then.' You couldn't tell Mr. Mancini you had had a secret baby before you met him. Poor, second-best Mr. Mancini!

'When they adopt somebody,' she said, looking straight through the short net curtains at the fish-and-chip shop across the street, 'I wonder if he ever finds out. Does he say to himself: "I'm not one of these people, I don't belong to them; I don't look like them and I don't even think like them, so I must have a real mother somewhere else." Does he ever say that?' Her voice had become shrill; now she stood quietly, tiny ripples running through her cheeks. At last she turned. 'It's interesting to speculate about things,' she said. 'I was well brought up, and often amuse myself in that way.' In case something should be heard: you never know.

'Rose,' said the parrot, 'Rose, Rose, Rose.' It imitated a dog growling, and cracked a red seed.

She lit another cigarette. She was going to be in a mood today, a hell of a mood, everything pointed to it. Now where was the string bag with her ration book in it? And she fancied her green shawl to pull round her; she had sewn a fur edge on it.

'Dear Rose,' sighed the parrot, 'this house will be yours.'

Mrs. Mancini felt her face go hot. The bloody creature kept repeating that as if it had heard nothing else, but Mr. Mancini had only used the expression about twice in his life.

'Don't! Stop saying that!' she shouted.

'Rose, Rose! Got a nut?' The parrot had caught her excitement and left its perch, clutching the side and roof wires. 'This house will be yours!'

'Shut up!' she screamed, nearly weeping. If only she hadn't had to sell it four months after he died; a perfect little cosy home. The blasted lodgers had run off with her money, she was sure of it, sure of it! If only she had that house now, instead of this stinking flat with the damned shared kitchen! 'Shut up, will you!'

'This house, house, house! Got a nut?'

In a fury, she struck at the cage, set it swinging wildly. The terrified bird screeched, and the room rang; all the air quivered.

Mrs. Mancini slammed the door and stumbled down the dark stairs, flushed and loathing the parrot that still cried piercingly behind her.

In the narrow hallway she found Miss Abbott standing and staring, with the newspapers in her hand; her own unreadable thing and Mrs. Mancini's *Daily Mirror*.

'What's the matter with the parrot?' she said.

Mrs. Mancini's eyes narrowed. 'He was cleaning his feathers, and he nipped himself accidentally!' she said, with ice in every word. 'I'll take my paper, thank you!' She put it in the string bag and left the house.

Bloody sauce! Snivelling, prying old maid, trying to read somebody else's *Mirror* on the cheap; getting nosy about the bird! Tell her a lie, tell her a good one. 'Always tell lies,' murmured Mrs. Mancini as she glanced into the shop windows, 'but believe every word yourself as soon as you tell them. That's the trick, Rosie, my dear; that's what puts it over. Poor blasted parrot, nipping himself!'

People were looking at her, and she liked it. They noticed that she talked to herself. Well, why shouldn't she, could anybody tell her that? 'Eccentric means behaving,' she remarked, 'as you like, instead of how you think people expect. Eccentric's natural.'

Mrs. Mancini ruffled her hair up, to emphasise her hatlessness, and hitched the shawl more tightly round her. A small boy whistled, and she smiled – cynically, she thought.

At the butcher's, where she knew they had come to dread her, she raged about her ration and accused them of cheating her. She shook the string bag at them, and, seeing the newspaper in it, remembered something she had read a day or two before. 'Look here, you! Rations drove a poor honest woman to put her head in the gas oven last week!' she shouted. 'It was you and your sort that hounded her to her grave!' That made the butcher lick his lips and glance nervously at his other customers. 'Hounded to her untimely grave!' she repeated. She was offered an extra chop, and took it.

Her ankles began to ache, so she turned aside for a coffee. The snack bar was almost empty. She made faces at herself in the mirror opposite, but nobody noticed except a cat that came up and tried to drink her coffee. Mrs. Mancini pushed it off the counter into a bowl of split peaches, and shouted righteous insults at the horrified assistant.

'Rosie, Rosie! The truth is that in your own little home you're possessed by a devil,' she decided in the next street, 'but outside, get after other people. And cats.' She muttered 'possessed by a devil' in several interesting ways, and frightened an old man.

She came to the furniture shop.

'Oh!' In the big window was a suite like her own; exactly like hers – no, it actually had more chromium fittings. But it was cheaper, the bloody thieves! Full of hate, she glared at the display. And they were going to come and take hers away, were they? Well, she would just lock the doors if they came! She would tell them lies, fool them into taking Miss Abbott's furniture – what was the good of that idiot having chairs anyway? She never sat down.

Mrs. Mancini had a mind to fling a stone through that big heartless window. She walked along, studying the gutters.

The search for a stone still occupied her when she came on a wedding: chattering women crowded round the church door as usual, waiting. Mrs. Mancini joined them, noticing with pleasure that she seemed to be recognised, and twitched her head. 'It's only a wedding, my dear,' she told herself aloud 'Will you care to stay, do you think, Rose?' She squinted a good crazy glance at her two nearest neighbours; both women moved away.

'Here they come!' ran the silly whispers. The organ whined inside the church, and a dolled-up photographer began to fidget with his ridiculous-looking machinery; faint squeals of admiration spread near the doorway; the bride and groom came creeping out. 'Ho, I wonder if she'll think this was worthwhile in a year's time!' Mrs. Mancini let one side of her face slip into what felt like a cynical smile. 'Stupid, creamy little cat, grinning and smirking there! The greatest hour of her life! But dressing up in white doesn't mean she's any better than she ought to be, not with those eyelashes!' The cheers drowned what she said. Only one woman seemed to hear, and turned a dirty look: Mrs. Mancini bettered it.

Yet, pottering through the confetti afterwards, she felt the long, deep strokes of regret coming over her. 'Pangs, my dear,' she whispered, and sat on a wall to feel sorry for herself.

The sun was warm. She was basking in it, whimpering from time to time and thinking about white wedding dresses, when a child approached her. Mrs. Mancini had watched his mother send him from the other side of the road with a pat on the head: a small pretty child in a blue coat.

He stopped in front of Mrs. Mancini and held out something that caught the sun. A shilling.

'For you,' he said, as if remembering what he had been told.

Mrs. Mancini sat astonished. Then she jumped up and knocked the coin tinkling from the boy's hand. 'I'm not a beggar!' she shouted. Without thinking, she pulled a face at him.

His mouth twisted and he seemed to grow smaller, to

shrink down on the pavement far beneath her. It was not until he had run, shrieking, back to his white-faced mother, and was being hurried comfortingly down the road, that Mrs. Mancini's brains began to work.

'Dangling little dirty shillings! Cheek! Don't you take it, Rose!' She strained to catch sight of the child's face again, but he was too far away. She remembered only how he had looked: mouth open, lips drawn right back, eyes popping. He had nearly fallen backwards into the gutter. She giggled, but the uneasy feeling would not go. 'Rosie, my dear –' she began, and found nothing she wanted to say. The road was empty; the child and his mother had turned a corner.

With dignity, Mrs. Mancini picked up the shilling and left it on the wall; took her string bag with the extra chop and the *Mirror*.

When she passed the furniture shop it was without seeing it.

At the next corner she had an unexpected impulse to speak to a policeman. 'Constable,' she said, her fingertips twisting together.

'What is it this time?' He recognised her.

'If – if you had a baby, and he was adopted, and thought about you, would it frighten him like that?'

The policeman watched her before speaking, 'Frighten who? Trying to make out somebody's lost, or is this supposed to be funny?'

Of course he wouldn't be a baby now; he would be a man.

'He's a man now,' Mrs. Mancini said. 'I haven't lost anybody, no...'

The policeman drew his breath in and told her to go home and rest; he was busy, he had to see to the traffic.

Mrs, Mancini walked with the string bag dangling at her side. Once or twice she turned to see whether the child and his mother might be following, but they never were. She kept close to the wall, pictures dancing through her head. It must feel dreadful to be suddenly frightened in that way, all over a shilling! Tears of misery began to stream down her face. People looked curiously at her, but she was used to that.

When she reached her own door she was shivering from head to foot. Suppose — suppose somebody was adopted and grew up. Suppose he met you then — say, in the street, a grown man, not knowing who you were, of course, and you not knowing him. And suppose he felt alarmed or annoyed or amused when he met you, just like anybody else; that would be terrible, because neither of you would ever know the truth. It might even have happened so, and neither of you had known!

'Got a nut? Got a nut?' said the parrot, when she went in.

She scattered a handful of seed into his cage, and the bird scrambled for it. Then she set about feeding him properly, because one's last acts should always be deliberate. She filled the feed and water containers, and slid them into position on the sides of the cage.

'Ha, aha, ha,' chuckled the parrot, 'Rose, you got my shoes?'

The thought from the back of her mind had taken full possession now. She sat down and brought out her writing-pad; for once she wrote on the lines, because of the occasion, 'To his honour the Coroner,' she put, in her irregular, jerky hand, 'I can go on no longer. What with rations and the insults of the butcher. The furniture men are hounding me to death. Chief of all, there is a secret in my past that I cannot reveal, but please let that alone, your honour. Please, sir, take care of the parrot. He is clean in his habits.' She signed it and sobbed, overcome by the solemnity of what she was doing. It was the very last time she would ever handle a pen.

She blotted the note and took it downstairs to the kitchen. Miss Abbott was always out in the middle of the day.

The note looked well, she thought, gently laid on a clean

part of the floury table: to think that those words might be appearing in the *Mirror* in a day or two! Remembering accounts of such things, she took out a box of cleaning rags and stuffed them round the window and door. She had discovered that Miss Abbott kept a few shillings handy in a cream-of-tartar tin; now she took one and put it in the gas meter.

Inside, the oven was foul: neither of its users had been prepared to clean it for the other's benefit. She slid the wire grills out of their grooves and placed them on the floor.

She considered. Should she turn on the tap before putting her head inside? In that case she might be momentarily overcome by the rush of gas, fall clear and recover. She decided to get inside first, and then turn the tap.

The coconut matting was harsh under her knees and made her grunt. From her crouched position, she looked sadly round the kitchen: her last view of the world. 'Poor old Rose!' she whispered, and put her head in the oven. There was nowhere to rest it. Only pools of burnt grease.

She sat up, shaking all over, and replaced the lowest grill, cursing when it jammed; then laid her head on it, surrounded by the smell of dinners she had cooked and eaten months before. With her free hand she felt about for the tap. Her neck was hurting; something had caught in her hair, and one ear was being nipped agonisingly against the grill. She found the tap at last, and turned it, clenching her teeth. Cold and putrid, the gas rushed over her face.

In the same instant, she dragged herself out with a cry of pain, and clutched her ear.

Gas was hissing slowly from the oven. She coughed, shivering, glaring at the black, open hole she had just been in. She had forgotten they always had a bloody pillow!

She listened stupidly, wheezing.

Her head was singing with blood and her heart thumped,

but it was as if she could hear bells also... A bell... the front doorbell. Somebody out there must be pulling at it repeatedly.

She moaned and lurched forward to turn the gas off.

'Oh dear, oh... dear!'

Perhaps it was that old jangling bell that had called to her inside the oven, and made her take her head out. 'Rose,' she whispered, 'yes, Rose, that's what it was! You weren't afraid, Rosie! Not you, never!' But her teeth chattered.

Oh, why did they have to keep on ringing like that!

Why did they –

'Oh – oh, my dear!' Tears began to trickle all over her face as she panted, swaying, back to her feet. 'Salvation! They've come to save you! Salvation, Rose, salvation in the very nick – God damn!' She wept with fury and thankfulness together, struggling to free the door from the rags she had packed round it. 'Come out of it!' she sobbed, nails stinging. 'What in the name –!'

The key turned, and she staggered through in a gust of gas.

'I'm coming!' she called, and leaned against the wall to cough. Her head swam in the sudden freshness of the air. The hall was like a long dark cave that echoed her breathing and was lit with strange flashes and spots of colour. She felt her way along by the wall, trembling with anxiety. 'I'm coming – don't go away!'

The front door had always been easy to open.

'There, you see – I'm alive! You got here in time...'

It was the postman.

She stared at him in stupefaction, too surprised to understand what he might want. His face showed no interest, only peevishness at being kept waiting. 'What? Here – you all right, ma?' He was holding something out: a registered letter. 'Look a bit queer, you know. Better go and sit down. Sign here, please.' She leaned against the doorpost and let him put his dirty little pencil in her hand. 'It's with hurrying,' she whispered, attacking him out of habit. 'Why d'you make people run like this!'

He left her holding the envelope. It had a typed address and everything.

'You were right after all, Rose – providence! Oh, my poor old dear, whatever can it be? P'raps it's from the pension people, I shouldn't wonder – even a bit extra that Louis left –' She ripped it open across the side, hungrily, and snatched the letter out.

It was from the furnishers. Final notice that they intended to recover their suite, failing full payment in three days.

Her face flushed slowly.

If only somebody would pass by – no matter who; she wanted to bash somebody. She beat her fists slowly and heavily on the door, the letter crushed in one of them, and the envelope in the other.

Suddenly her face creased and she giggled. Several rapid panting breaths, then all the air was thrown from her body in a great gust. Her eyes squeezed shut. Shrill, echoing squeals rang out, running down the scale before being restored by a convulsive whoop. Gasps and hiccups interrupted. Then she settled into long, rolling, joyful shrieks that purpled her face and brought the neighbours to watch.

Sitting on the front doorstep, Rose Mancini was enjoying one of the biggest laughs of her life.

Curphey's Follower

IT BEGAN ONE NIGHT in the gradual quietness that follows closing time.

Lot Curphey was on his way home from Ballaroddan village, not quite solid on his feet, and with little crumbs of song still coming out of his mouth; too cheerful to swear at the faintness of the starlight.

He was a small man, chiefly from shortness of the legs, with a tufty hairiness about the face. Warm, now, inside a huge old yellow coat given to him by John James Quilleash, his employer. Under its long skirts his left leg limped from an injury by a ploughshare years before; now and then the thick cloth dipped in the dust.

About half a mile from his cottage he was chilled by the night air and beginning to notice things.

He felt that he was being followed.

He stopped and turned. There was no sound but a sheep's cough far away on his right. He scraped his foot sharply in the loose surface.

A few yards away something slithered. Curphey could see a black patch against the lighter darkness of the road. Too small for a dog.

'Shoo, cat!' he said loudly. For a second his back tingled at the odd stillness of it. Possible horrors bobbed in his mind.

He stamped towards it with a hollow-feeling foot. The thing moved; and as it moved, it flapped. And spoke unmistakably.

'Quaa!'

That was how Lot Curphey met the duck.

It followed him along the road, stopped when he did, shuffling along behind at a respectful number of small paces. Twice he tried to chase it home, taking it to be a stray from the yard of old Skillicorn, who was unpleasantly litigious. Each time it scuttled close again as soon as he turned his back.

He came to the cottage where he lived alone, and went straight in and lit the oil lamp.

An eye glittered in the flare, low down on the threshold. He stooped, lamp in hand, and the duck grew clear.

The creature was amazingly ugly.

It stood on the rough slate step boldly, but with its right leg oddly twisted, like a bored corner boy. One eye looked in his face; the other was closed and hollow. Its feathers lay many ways; in patches there were none. Those that remained were a shiny black.

After a moment he picked it up, careful about where he touched it, and it was quiet in his hands. Thin, with skin loose in his fingers. A glance by the lamp showed the damage to its leg was old, and no treatment needed. And it was too skinny to eat.

He tossed it outside and clapped his hands loudly. A little later the door was opened once more, for a green crust to follow it.

In the half-light of the next morning, Curphey found the black duck among the seedlings in his front garden patch. He shouted and flung his hat at it. Having to clamber sleepily after his hat, he trod on three brussels sprouts. He swore, loud in the clammy air, tried to restore them, and swore again; threw a handful of gravel at the duck with seeming effect, and set off up the side path that pointed to Quilleash's farm.

The duck came behind, running crookedly. It trailed him as determinedly as in the darkness, using its wings when the man gained.

Curphey came into the farm street hurriedly, ready to be embarrassed, with a glance behind and a nervous dab at his hat. At his limping heel scrambled the duck. It ignored the other birds that watched curiously from the midden.

'It's taken a fancy to me,' said Curphey to the rest of the hands. He felt more comfortable when their laughter turned safely on to the duck. 'Mus' think I'm a – a charity for oul' twisty ducks!'

That day it followed him everywhere. When he went on the plough, a black head bobbed down the furrows a couple of yards behind, puzzling the hovering gulls and crows. He was uneasy. His mind ran vaguely on catnip and aniseed, and once, feeling uncomfortably traitorous to Quilleash, on the properties of his yellow coat; he stood, in a quiet moment, among the farmer's fat, preening Aylesburys to try its effect on them. But they seemed immune.

During the break he gave the creature a half bun that had fallen in a puddle. At dinner time it waited outside the kitchen door, menaced by a striped cat. It accompanied him to the stables and pigsties, and was chased by a dog as ragged as itself. And in due time, it trailed Curphey home.

By the end of the second day he had come to accept it as a whim of his own invention. He had also been made familiar, to the point of exasperation, with the habits of Mary's Little Lamb.

People would come to cottage doors as they passed, grinning slowly. He discovered small audiences at crossroads. Boys sniggered on the hedges. A carter reined in his horse and raised his hat ironically as the ugly bird twitched along the roadside. Some were alarmed: an old woman pulled a shawl over her head, and hid in a field clutching a charm-herb, till they passed; a pair of small girls on a garden patch were pulled suddenly indoors. Dogs barked. Nobody claimed the duck.

Lot Curphey found a habit of waving his yellow-coated arm broadly, with a certain fluttering of the fingers and jerk of the thumb; meant to convey a bright humour, rich with enjoyment of the situation, and the duck as a witless butt. A new, exciting self-consciousness ran through him. His limping foot felt as if it danced.

On the evening of the fourth day, the duck went with him to the village pub.

It was timid among the houses, and used its wings to keep a safer, crooked course; but never far behind.

At the door he stopped, winking and waving to the sunlit loungers. He stooped over the bird, picked it up, and went into the pub with a conscious air of making an entrance.

Inside, he stood, duck in hand.

The place was bright, with smoke deadening the mellow beeriness. The bar had half a dozen round it. One turned, wiping his frothy moustache pleasurably.

'Well, it's himself! An' will ye look what's at him!'

They swung round. Bit Moughtin the smith prodded a too-absorbed drinker. 'Take y'r face out o' that! The man's brought his duck!'

Curphey approached, pleased.

'Is that the one they're all on about?'

Kermit Kermode, behind the bar, drew Curphey a pint on the house and screwed up his eyes.

'It's an ugly devil. Did ye hatch it out of a bad egg or what? Come on, stick it down here an' let's have a sight.'

And the duck stood among the wet rings left by glasses, leaning on its crooked leg, the one eye fixed on Lot Curphey.

'I had a book of ducks' illnesses,' said little red-faced Quirk, looking round the bar. 'By the look of it, she hasn't left many out, eh?'

'Who are you, insultin' me prize bird!' said Curphey.

Amused, they treated him to a second pint, then another, and he warmed inside the yellow coat. The room grew still brighter. The others watched him, letting their interest ripen.

'Did ye train her up,' said big Moughtin, 'to follow ye? In the place of a dog, like?'

'Hardly at all,' said Curphey, and winked. 'The power o' the human eye, it was. Me havin' two, an' her only one, give me a natural advantage.' He stretched out a hand and chucked the bird's black bill. It scarcely moved.

'Aw, it's the funniest thing y' ever seen,' he said, 'when it gets goin'.' He giggled.

He put the duck on the floor and let it follow him round the room, jerking among the iron table legs, past the spittoon. Moughtin began to laugh, slowly at first, then deeper and more painfully, without stopping. Round and round they went, Curphey twisting and dodging, and urging the duck on. He was beginning to enjoy the act. In a tiny, false voice he called, 'Come on, then! Who's an ugly funny bird, then? Come to daddy an' have y'r oul' neck screwed! Where's the pie dish, then?' He began to pull faces.

Quirk gave little amused barks. Moughtin was shaking.

Curphey went faster, glass in hand. He pretended anger at the duck's performance, and spoke furiously and hoarsely, knowing it would have no effect. 'Put a move on! Ye one-eyed insect! Left, right, left, right! Don't ye know which is y'r left? Me handsome man-eater disgracin' me!'

Moughtin had tried to drink, and was being thumped on the back.

'Halt!' Curphey thrust his head out at the duck. It stared at him without expression. 'What are ye lookin' at me that way for? Eh? O-o-oh, I see! Well, I'm sorry, but I can't do it. Ye see' – a stage whisper – 'y're not really strong enough to be killed. An' I haven't the time just at the present, though I'm sorry to disappoint ye!'

He turned to the bar, and from his pocket brought a handful of ripe corn, rattling on the varnished wood.

'Will ye dip some o' this in a drop o'gin, Kermit?'

Big Moughtin, grasping the idea, sighed with expectation.

The duck was replaced among the glasses. In front of it was the doctored corn. Curphey offered a few grains in his hand. After a moment's hesitation, they went quickly.

'Aw, she's used to it!' said somebody.

The duck was nuzzling after the grains among the slopped beer.

'A bit more, Kermit! An' I'll have another pint meself.'

They placed the duck on the floor again. It waddled a few steps after Curphey, then staggered on its sound foot.

There was a howl of delight.

'Whassa marrer?' Curphey shouted at it, with a sham hiccup. 'You shay I wash drunk?'

The duck's bill opened and shut. Its eye blinked. One wing drooped. A grey foot groped, slipped back to safety. It could not walk.

Curphey grabbed it by the neck and swept it high. 'By yer leave, Kermit!' he giggled, and stuck its head into his own beer mug.

After a moment there came a quiet guzzling.

They clustered round to watch, laughing. Two or three fresh customers stood in puzzlement. 'Drinks for both of them on me, Kermit!' shouted Moughtin. 'The bird can down it like a right fella!'

For the rest of the evening, Lot Curphey tormented his duck.

It was soon helplessly drunk. Set on the bar counter, it

could only gaze into his eyes with a lovelorn fixity, while its head swayed and its legs slid.

For a long time he addressed it in monologues, pretending sometimes to listen and to receive offensive answers.

'What did you say? Did you say that? Ye wicked ungrateful creature, I wonder ye can look me in th' eye! Stand up straight when ye speak to y'r elders, will ye! Now, as I was sayin', strong drink is detrimental to the soul an' the linin' of the gizzard —'

They treated him again and again, keeping him going.

'Ye sorry fowl! I know why y're follerin' me all around — I can read ye like a book. Ye want me to learn y' how to swim.' More laughter. 'So I will, so I will, have no fear! Ask, and it shall be given unto... Wait a minute, though!' A doubtful scratch at his chin. 'Ye might drown.'

The audience responded.

Curphey frowned at the ceiling through the bottom of his glass. He swung round with a secret whisper. 'I'll tell ye what! Didn't y'r mothers once tell ye about th' Ugly Duckling?' A nod at the dozing duck. 'This must be himself! He's passed the time to change into a swan an' he wants help — forgotten how to do it! Here, give me strength, Kermit. Fill up!'

Gradually the sense went out of his talk.

'Aw, y've had enough,' said Kermode, at last, 'or ye'll never get home tonight, man.'

'Li'l duck,' murmured Curphey. 'Whad say? Now — listen, li'l duck —'

'Ye'd better take y'r clever duck away now, Lot!' said Kermode, loudly in his ear. 'Let her sleep it off. It's hard on closin' time.'

The comedian brought him into focus.

'I will, Kermit, I will.' He picked up the duck and buttoned it inside his coat. Once again, Moughtin began to laugh, wheezily now, at the two heads looking muzzily out of the yellow coat.

'Night, boys!' said Curphey, and moved unsteadily towards the door.

It was then that big Moughtin did a tactless thing. He named the cause of all their laughter.

'Look at it!' he said. 'The thing is; he − he's the bloody spittin' image o' the duck!' And wheezed enormously. His own joke pleased him most of any during the evening.

Curphey stopped, suddenly quiet. There came a stillness in every part of the room. Only Moughtin's wheezing.

Curphey looked round the bar. His lips made a movement, then closed. He turned, and went from the pub, leaving the door swinging.

His steps were quick and unsteady in the darkness.

He went faster, hot-faced and limping. In a few minutes he was above the village. His breath came tightly. Against his chest he felt the warmth of the duck.

Curphey stopped, dragged it savagely from his coat. Its bill gave a little guttural sound. 'By God!' said Curphey. He shook it.

In a sudden fury he flung it from him. Its wings opened before it hit the road, and it fluttered crazily in the darkness. He raised his foot to kick.

It dodged drunkenly.

He began to chase it. First in clumsy, set rushes, then snatching here and there; tripping over the heavy wings of his coat, swearing and growling. He could not see it, and listened for its pattering. Once he trod on it, and it cried out and flapped away.

In the first weak moonlight, they came to where the hedge was low.

In a frenzy, the duck scrambled aside over ditch and hedge, into rough open turf. Curphey splashed after it, clawing fiercely.

He could see it in the dimness, exhausted.

As he sprang, his foot gave under him. With a great, smacking squelch, he fell flat on his face.

He lay quietly on the boggy earth. The bird crouched, still, in a patch of reeds; until the tiny bubbling and sucking noises ceased.

The moon rose higher, and whitened the stone that had stunned him. His face lay in a puddle of brown mountain water, so shallow that it barely covered his nostrils.

When he did not appear for work next day, Quilleash sent to his cottage and found it locked.

Searching down the road to the village, they sighted his boots among the rushes not far away on the other side of the hedge. They turned him over, and were shocked, and curious at the manner of his death. 'Found drowned, it'll have to be,' said one.

Presently he was wrapped in two grey blankets and carried to the road. A handcart waited to take him down to the village. It set off, soaked blankets flapping heavily in the smart spring wind.

A short distance down the road ahead, something moved at the ditch's edge. 'There it is!' said a man.

The duck looked up as they came near; leaning sideways. Its black eye ignored the cart and stared past, up the empty road.

When they were far down the hill, one glanced back.

A tiny shape, the duck was still standing there. Its head seemed to jerk from side to side, looking for something.

The day after the inquest, it was stabbed with a long-handled pitchfork, by the son of the old woman who gathered charm-herbs. He wore a bunch round his neck.

The Terrible Thing
I Have Done

IRANAMET! I'VE GOT TO speak to you, no matter what! Please, it's terribly important!

Never mind your list of dishes – it won't be needed! I know what I'm talking about. Iranamet, there's hardly any time left – quickly, into this room here!

No, I'm not fussing; that you'll soon see. I've hardly ever asked a favour of you before, come to think; and after this –

I think I'll sit down. Feeling a bit rocky. Oh, don't fret; for once people aren't going to mind Pharaoh's taster taking it easy in an anteroom. Somehow I don't think they'll notice.

Let the clock flow a little farther, and they'll have other things on their minds.

Iranamet! I want to ask you something that worries me very much. Give me your hand.

I want you to promise me that when I'm dead – oh, never mind reassuring me! – when they take me down river to the embalming place, promise me you'll see that my copy of the Book of the Dead is a good one, with all the instructions. I know the embalmers often slip a dud scroll into the burial equipment, with mistakes in it, and pieces left out.

When I'm on the other side, you see, I'm going to have

157

difficulty enough in passing all the tests, without being misled by wrong instructions.

What's that – somebody coming down the passage? No, I don't hear anyone, yet; it isn't time. I'll have to talk quickly; and I know my words are tumbling over each other already.

Iranamet, I've done a terrible thing. Terrible.

I think I'll have time to explain, just briefly. Perhaps you've noticed that I've been on edge lately? Perhaps not; come to think of it, I'm not a person people notice a great deal.

Yet it's been the way that Pharaoh – may I be forgiven! I mean the Good God – the way he's been watching me that's upset me.

You – you remember the time his father died? Not so very long ago, was it? And you know what they gave out; that he was killed by falling downstairs from the loggia? Well, it wasn't strictly true. He wasn't the sort of person to tumble about the place. He only fell that time because –

I mustn't tell, because I'm under an oath. Perhaps I can say he – he drank something. And when he reached the stairs it was just taking effect. I mean, when people found his head smashed in, they thought that the fall had killed him. But a few minutes later, wherever he'd gone, and whatever he'd done, he'd have been found –

But I can't say that. I can't say who did it, either; or who instigated the plot.

Oh, no, it wasn't the present Pharoah – oh, again! I mean, the Good God! He doesn't know a thing about it. I suppose they didn't trust him because – may I be forgiven! – because he's weak. Or so that he wouldn't be able to use it against them if he fell out with them.

But they told me.

Oh, how I wish they hadn't! I'm only a servant; but they said I ought to know because of my position. That was when

I became the royal taster. Taster to the new Pharaoh – the Good God.

But I wasn't to tell anyone, not even the Good God. They made me kneel down and swear an oath that I wouldn't. It frightens me to think about that oath! It was more of a horrible prayer; that when I should die, I should have no trial by the gods, but be taken straight by the Eater of the Dead and drawn on his claws, and ground under his weight, and then crunched in his crimson teeth on every third day for ever! And that my screams and my pain should gradually take form and settle beside me in dreadful shapes!

If I broke my word.

It's so frightening! I do hope I haven't let anything slip.

You know I'm only a quiet man. Certainly I could never have done what – was done. Intentionally. But they insisted on telling me about it, and the knowledge tortured me.

I wondered if I might talk in my sleep. I began to avoid people, and to walk alone. I started counting to five before I spoke, in case I – I should say too much or the wrong thing. I had nightmares and beat my head on my wooden pillow when I couldn't sleep. I slopped wine on the holy garments.

And the Good God saw there was something wrong with me.

He would watch me out of the side of his eye when I handed him his food and wine after tasting it. He took me unawares with sharp remarks. Once he came up behind me among the red pillars, and whispered, 'What's the secret?' and I shook like a reed because I hadn't heard him coming. I must have looked guilty blushing and stammering there. But he went away.

So afterwards I wondered if I could drop a hint to him; perhaps do something that wouldn't break my oath, and yet let him know the secret. Then he would trust me again.

Excuse me belching. That's one of the first signs, I think.

But just now — just now in the breakfast room, the Good God was speaking to the vizier; called him in suddenly, in fact. And they both began to whisper together. Then they looked at me, Iranamet!

And the Good God nodded to the vizier. C-coldly, with his lips pressed tight. I knew what that meant! I've seen it happen before. I could almost feel the foot-twister working on me. Oh, I couldn't stand torture, Iranamet! I — I'm not strong really, and I'd break after a time, and tell.

And then, when it was all over, the Eater of the Dead would take me, and — and —

I thought of running away. But they always find you. And besides, there was something I wanted to do, in the palace. I wanted to let the Good God know the secret. That's right, isn't it? He should know everything.

The vizier went out; I could guess where he was going. And I was desperate.

Suddenly I knew exactly what to do. I brought out the old wine cup with the gold lion heads on it. You'll know the one.

I won't tell you anything more than just what happened then, and that won't be breaking my oath, will it? When I'd filled the cup to the brim with wine, I set it down, and very carefully twisted and pressed the right eye of the right-hand lion in a certain way. A little pale stream of something flowed into the wine, down inside the cup. Only for an instant, then it dissolved. But I knew what that meant, because I'd been told about it.

That isn't saying too much, eh?

I stepped up in front of — of the Good God, and raised the cup to my lips. Of course, nobody took any special notice, because it was the natural thing for the taster to do.

But I didn't just taste, this time. I drank, and drank, and felt like stone inside as I did so.

Because I knew I was going to die!

Remember the personage I told you about; the high personage who fell downstairs? That isn't revealing anything either.

When I'd drunk rather less than half the cup, I lowered it, because that was enough. It hadn't been easy to make myself drink even that much.

I meant to tell the Good God – just what I've told you. And in proof of it, he'd see me – see me die. If he was suspicious about anything, about a certain person falling down steps, I mean, he might have some instruction by it. And for me, it was the best way; I would dodge the torture.

Then my heart seemed to heave inside me; I suppose I was afraid. Little thoughts of the silliest things kept running through my head, and I seemed to forget where I was.

And through them, my eyes noted that Phar – the Good God was holding out his hand for the cup.

And Iranamet – I gave it to him!

I swear I didn't know what I was doing; I swear it! I would never have done that. It must have been force of habit.

When I came to myself, I saw him drinking – draining the cup. And I just stood there like a jug, not saying a word. I must have been stupid with different kinds of fear. Then I – it's no use trying to drop hints to a God who'll soon be dead himself, is it?

I've poisoned him. I've done a terrible thing, haven't I?

So I just – I just came out of the room, just wandered along here, and I met you. I had to tell somebody about it.

I've got so much to answer for on the other side. Quite apart from the oath. How can I stand in the Hall of the Two Truths and make the declaration of righteousness to the God of Death, and say I am pure?

When I've poisoned Pharaoh.

So please – make sure my Book of the Dead is right, at least. Sorry, I can't hold myself steady. I'm beginning to feel I don't belong to myself, just gradually.

What? Can you hear him? Groaning. Shouting. I suppose it's taking him first because he had more than I did. Or perhaps he isn't as strong as me. As if I were!

That people running? Yes, I can hear; sounds like a river. All running and howling and crying. River. Remember about – embalming.

Your face dim, 'Ranamet. Now – here it comes! Sudden! Sudden, isn't it? Feel I'm slipping and I want to roar an' shout!

But – before I can't help myself – promise about – Book of Dead – because I done – terrible thing.

Now! Hold me, 'Ranamet!

Quiet Mr. Evans

HE FOUND THAT A double quantity of raw chips sent into the fryer, hissing and crackling, would drown the whispers at the back of the shop for a time. He had peace then. Every so often during the evening he had caught phrases as clearly as if they were meant for him to hear.

'Poor old Evans! Failing.'

'Think he's human, that he can't see what's going on?'

'Maybe too faint-hearted to do anything about it.'

'Ach, practisin' to run one of those houses in Cardiff, he is!' That had brought a snigger.

He had been alone at the counter for some time, serving a crowded shop single-handed, when Mrs. Powell's turn came and she handed her blue flowered basin across. His face was burning and he knew it.

'The usual, if you please, Mr. Evans. Fish and eight. And no little dreg ones from the corners, look you!'

He stirred the fat. Chips swam quickly to the surface in their first pale skins. There were still whispers behind him, but now the gossip had become too deep and secret for him to catch any of it.

Mrs. Powell leaned across the counter and flicked the

greasy black hair from her eyes. 'Busy tonight, Mr. Evans?'

He did not turn from the fryer. 'Busy enough.'

Mrs. Powell's big eyes and gold tooth twinkled, missing nothing and full of malice. 'Back room full again, I see. Curtains drawn and everything. Very particular customers, too, the way Mrs. Evans is not to be seen for ten minutes at a time!'

A faint hiss of indrawn breath ran through the customers and broke the quietness. Two dishes clacked together. A child complained, 'When'll they be done?'

Mrs. Powell sensed the drama she had made and enjoyed it. 'Same last night, wasn't it? And before that too? Just one very particular customer?'

He stood with his back to her, looking down at the sizzling fat.

'Oh, be quiet, Mrs. Powell,' said a woman.

'I don't like people whispering,' snapped Mrs. Powell. 'P'raps I'm a very peculiar person, but I happen to believe in straight talking! And everybody here knows about the disgraceful business anyway, except the very one who ought to, seemingly. It's a nice thing in a village like this, I must –'

He turned suddenly, startling Mrs. Powell's bony elbows from the counter; one of them knocked the salt canister to the floor.

He stood facing them.

'All right then! I know about all the whispering!' The pale gaslight made his glistening face haggard.

'Now you can all get out of my shop!' His voice crackled. 'Go on! Take your nasty busy little minds home to feed you, instead of my chips!'

'Don't forget your old dish!' He pushed the chipped china across the counter to Mrs. Powell.

He stood and watched while they made their way to the door and out into the darkness, mumbling and shocked. As the door closed he heard one or two laughing in an embarrassed way outside. He felt surprised that they had all taken him at his word. They might almost have known what it was in his mind to do.

He stayed behind the counter until their voices died away and there was only the sound of the simmering fat and a distant murmur from the back dining room.

He was trembling now. His hands started doing things while his brain seemed to go to sleep. They scooped all the cooked chips from the fryer and covered them; damped the fire; led him to the door, limping on his crooked leg, to shut it softly; wiped the sweat from his face with his grease-spotted apron, which they threw under the counter; then knotted themselves until the veins stood out.

He went to the passage that led to the back room. Odd how quickly his brain had cleared now this cold resignation was on him.

'Megan!' he called. 'Megan!'

The murmur in the back room stopped, and after a moment there were slow footsteps in the passage. The gaslight shone on his young wife's face and showed its high colour. You couldn't call Megan a beauty, but she was pretty enough.

'I was just coming, Owen,' she said. 'Oh − closing time already, is it? I was just saying to John Phillips how quiet it had gone... Why, Owen, what's the matter?'

He swallowed and said nothing.

'So strange you look! Oh − and I left you single-handed again! That what's upset you?'

His mouth opened and he spoke huskily. 'Megan, I want you to go upstairs now. And stay there till I come.'

'Owen!' She frowned. 'Are you sick?'

'No, not sick at all.'

'What has got into you?' Her voice sharpened.

'Go. Please. I'm just going to tidy up for the night.'

She looked towards the back dining room with the curtain across the doorway. Different thoughts were going through her eyes. She said, 'I'll just tell John Phillips that it's time –'

'No. Just go upstairs.'

Her body stiffened and he watched her colour rise. 'Owen, what's the matter with you tonight? This isn't like you a bit.'

Her breath caught with a sudden shocked understanding; he felt angry with himself for not being able to tell whether it was genuine. 'Oh – I see it now! You been hearing things – some old cat chin-wagging over her sixpenceworth, just because John Phillips and me was talking out there!' There was pity in her face that might have been honestly felt. 'Oh, terrible lots of harm in a bit of talk, isn't there! Nothing to stop you or anybody else coming out to the back room, of course, but...'

'Megan!'

Her voice was a furious whisper. 'Theirs is the talk you want to watch! You'd let them gossip you into suspecting your own wife – I know you, Owen Evans! What are you made of? Even now you don't speak out like a man and say just –'

'I trust you, Megan.'

It must have been the way he said it that affected her. Genuinely this time, it seemed. Before her eyes dropped, he saw tears in them.

'Tired you look, girl. To bed now.'

She took a step to the stairway door, then turned and caught his arm. 'You're so different! Owen, if you start trouble in there because you've misunderstood something, I'll – I'll not forgive you.'

He smiled. 'Old Evans fight? Battling for the honour of the chip-shop lady, eh? Sir Owen Evans, the stainless nickel-plated knight?'

She gave a little sigh. 'That's your old self again. You be up soon?'

'Soon. I'll just see if John Phillips wants any more to eat – and then I'll come.'

She went through the doorway. When he heard her reach the landing above, he closed the door and locked it quietly.

He went back to the fryer and took out the big wire basket, heavy with chips. Enough for a dozen hungry people there were, at a long sitting.

The tread of his crooked leg echoed in the stone passage. He hesitated a moment in the darkness, then pushed aside the heavy curtain, its wooden rings clicking together. He stood blinking in the brightness of the small inner room, holding the sieve before his body. A thin stream of oily fat dripped from it.

The only occupant was a young man, good-looking in a brilliantined, self-conscious way. He was jerking his overcoat on with a great show of making ready to leave, grunting and sighing. It struck Evans that he had waited for him to appear.

'Oh – hallo, Mr. Evans. Didn't realise it was so late.' The worried look on the young man's face changed to a smile. A gap showed between his front upper teeth. 'Hope I haven't kept you.'

'No,' said Evans.

Phillips breathed a laugh. 'Your chips are dripping a bit there. Didn't realise it was so late till I heard you and Mrs. Evans talking down the passage and I looked at my watch. You haven't brought those for me, have you?'

At the door there was silence.

'Oh – I think I've had a feast tonight already. Be getting fat, I will! So I hope you didn't bring them for me – did you?' He was puzzled. He stood under the flowery lamp, hands in his coat pockets. Only a boy he was, and poorly built.

'My wife has gone to bed,' Evans said. 'I've locked up shop.

167

P'raps you'll have a little bite with me now?'

Phillips swallowed. 'Well, I don't – I –'

'Yes, of course you will, good man!' Evans closed the door with the out-of-date dance advertisement hanging on it. He put down the basket of chips on the glass-topped table. His face relaxed as he looked at the other man; a little smile came on it.

'Extra good chips I got tonight. And nobody to eat them. Pity, isn't it? Let's have your plate now. Can't be full you are, young fellow like you!'

Phillips sat down doubtfully. He watched the big man pick up a fork and fill the plate from the basket. It was a huge helping. Higher and higher the plate was heaped, until chips scattered over the edge and fell on to the table and floor. He was uneasy.

'Steady on!' he said. He had an idea. 'Look here, I'm short of money tonight. Honest, I just can't afford them.'

'On the house, man!' Evans growled.

'No – I really think I should be getting on my way, Mr. Evans.'

'But I want you to stay, Mr. Phillips.' The bleak feeling seemed to sharpen and brighten in him. He sat on the table.

Phillips twisted in his chair. His voice was hoarse suddenly. 'You aren't trying to threaten me, are you? I only come quite peaceful as a customer, and now I'm going!'

A fat hand settled heavily on his shoulder. 'You like lots of hospitality, don't you, John Phillips? And I like to see customers. And I like to see them enjoy their food. Eat these while they're hot now, that's a good man.'

Phillips wriggled. The hand was on the back of his neck.

'Let me go! Let me go, then, or how can I eat any –?'

'Come along!'

Phillips suddenly giggled as if he had realised it was all a joke, and took two chips on his fork. He had given in.

'That's it now! Don't let good food go to waste.' The hand pressed more heavily. 'All kinds of vitamins in chips, particularly in the fat.'

'Why – why don't you eat some yourself?'

Evans leaned across to the basket and picked one out. 'Those on the plate are all yours.'

The younger man twisted. 'Let go of my neck! You're hurting me!' The hand moved back to his shoulder. Evans swallowed his mouthful.

'You know, it's a distraction to have an eye for letters in this business,' Evans said. 'Always a terrible one for reading, I am. And a heap of cut-up newspapers is temptation indeed – Put some salt on it, man, or you lose half the flavour!'

'I was standing there at the fryer tonight, and my eye was forever wandering to a bit of a Sunday scandal sheet. Fine for wrapping, those Sunday papers; so many pages they have.'

Phillips protested. 'I'm full up! It's time! – oh!'

'Listen, now. My eye was on a sad case. A man with a young wife, it appeared – don't waste time looking at me, Mr. Phillips; they're getting cold – and she let another man come after her. Silly thing to do, but she was flattered by it all, even though she didn't take him serious.

'And do you know, Mr. Phillips, for a long time the husband didn't do a thing. Thought it didn't really matter. Kept blinkers on his eyes so he didn't see the other man's carrying-on, and refused to listen to a word of the whispers that were going round. But he had too much trust in his wife, d'you see? He left it too late and he lost her. That's what makes it a different case –'

'Different?' Phillips pulled sideways. 'Let go of my collar! What are you playing at? Lemme go!' He knocked the half-empty plate to the floor and grabbed at Evans to twist himself free.

'Now! That was – stupid!' Evans moved with the speed

and strength of a wrestler. The young man suddenly found both his wrists locked in a huge hand; he was forced backwards over the chair. 'Smashed a good plate!'

'If you try to – keep me here – I'll get the police!'

'I was telling you a little story while you were eating, man. You need feeding up – look how helpless you are. If you won't eat, I shall have to assist you – like this!'

A long golden chip was dangled before Phillips' eyes. Then it was being squashed into his mouth, through the gap in his teeth, even though his lips tried to refuse it. His feet scraped on the floor. Evans seemed to be everywhere.

'Chew quickly now, Mr. Phillips! Quicker than that! Don't try to shout or you'll choke yourself, indeed you will!'

Phillips kicked. The table skidded a yard away but did not fall. Chip fragments tumbled down the front of his jacket. He turned his eyes up and saw a round, tense face with lips stretched apart.

'More, Mr. Phillips, more! You like them so much you come here every night!' A handful of greasy potato spread itself over the neat moustache. 'And now you suddenly lost your appetite!'

Phillips' breath began to whoop painfully. A fragment of chip had stuck. Tears and trickles of grease ran together down his cheeks. He stopped struggling.

Evans gave a hiss and snatched up the wire basket. He spun it over. Warm, sticky slices scattered over Phillips' hair; tumbled down inside the collar of his jacket; wedged under his spotted tie.

'Salt and vinegar, Mr. Phillips?'

A white shower dusted like hoar-frost over the greasy face. A brown stream of vinegar stung his eyes and trickled coldly inside his clothes. Salt grains sprang up his nose and drew the last breath out of him in an agonising sneeze.

'Ou – aatch!'

Evans relaxed his grip. He stood watching for a moment, then seized the loose overcoat and jerked the gasping body to its feet. The flowery lampshade swung past Phillips in a sea of watery vinegar. His feet dragged as he was almost carried along the stone passage, hiccuping, and across the floor of the shop.

Evans supported him while he unlocked the door with his free hand. Phillips still groaned and wheezed. Then a cold gust swept round him and he was shot forward into the darkness.

He tottered a few steps. Tripped and fell blindly in the road.

Evans slammed the door. His chest heaved.

After a moment something picked itself up slowly outside, feet scraping. It coughed and sobbed.

It was moving away.

Along the street a voice exclaimed. There was a laugh. Then other voices. In a little while they were silent again.

Owen Evans gave a long sigh. He ran a handkerchief slowly over his face and neck, and rolled down his shirt-sleeves. Opening the stairway door, he stood and listened, trying to breathe more quietly.

'Megan,' he called. 'Megan, my dear.'

He waited again but no reply came down the dark stairs.

On tiptoe he went up, pulling on the banister to take the weight off his leg. There was no gas burning on the landing. Their bedroom door was closed.

He stood outside.

'I suppose you heard, Megan,' he said. 'Us down there, I mean.'

There was no answer.

'He played the coward, Meg. I knew he would. I – I only done it because of you, Megan.' In the silence he heard a tap dripping in the bathroom along the passage.

He turned the bedroom knob and pushed gently. The room was lit only by the low moon.

'Megan!' A cold draught rose in his head.

There was no one in the room. Her coat had gone from behind the door. Drawers stood open.

He stumped back along the passage. 'Megan!' he shouted. 'Where are you, Megan?'

The boards creaked as he hurried down the back stairs. The door leading into the yard was unlatched; so was the little gate beside the ashpit. He ran out into the moonlight shining on the potato patch across the lane. White haulms shone there like an untidy graveyard. The wind hummed in the wire fence.

He talked to himself to keep steady. 'Maybe she is gone along to Mrs. Hughes for the night. Or p'raps she's walking over to the mother's. Miles that is, though, and late now –'

A long mechanical whistling was blown from the other side of the hill. Funny how nice it was to hear ordinary sounds when things like this were happening. That would be the last train coming in.

His face froze as he looked up at the moon.

The last train!

Immediately he was crunching along the cinder path. The crooked foot slowed him by slipping sometimes or striking protruding stones, so that he staggered low, though never allowing himself to fall.

Eyes staring, he reached the road and clattered past the dead hills of crumbled stone from the mines. His breath was tightening.

A rat slipped across the road in front of him into the old workings. As he ran over the bridge, he heard the river far below and thought at first that the sound was of blood pulsing in his own head.

Then his thoughts cleared. Panting up the hill, he found his brain detached, like a floating compass.

If he looked to the left, he remembered, he would see the rough path leading up past the pines to the wild spaces of heather and bracken; where he used to walk with her before they married. Farther on, he passed under the great dead tree with clutching arms. 'Makes me want to run so it won't catch me!' she had said once.

He stumbled in a gravelly patch as he came to the red brick railway station. He nearly fell. She had done the same thing the day they ran to begin their honeymoon. 'Stupid people dropping peel about!' she had said, but her face was hurt, until he laughed and threw his arm round her waist.

His knees seemed to soften on the last few yards. He could see no lights that might belong to a train. Very slowly he ran into the entrance.

He stood, chest aching.

There was no train. It must have been pulling out when he heard it.

He found old Thomas, the stationmaster, checking his books in the ticket office when he lowered his hot face to the grille. He stammered, 'Last – last train gone?'

The stationmaster nodded over his reading glasses. 'Five minutes ago, Mr. Evans.' But he did not turn back to his fire and books and ignore the inquirer as usual. He came slowly across, watching Evans hard, till his head was framed in the little horseshoe of light. He nodded at the floor directly beneath.

Evans looked down. On the rough wood lay two chips.

Old Thomas spoke gravely. 'Those fell out of his clothes when he went to pay for the tickets. Like confetti. She never let go of his arm.'

He gave a dry cough. 'You're better rid of her,' he said, 'if she would go like that.'

Evans went stiffly to the window that looked down on the platform, arms hanging. He stared along the empty lines, shining pale blue, and his head shook slowly.

'Megan,' he said. 'Megan's my girl.'

Tootie and the Cat Licences

I WAS STRUCK IMMEDIATELY by the number of cats in the village.

It was one of the hottest afternoons of the year, and I was carrying most of my clothes, so doubtless they were equally curious about me. Every wall seemed to have a fat tabby spread over it: a gateway would show two or three. They lifted a furry eyelid, or paused to glare over a raised hind leg as I passed; if they moved at all.

The street was almost deserted. By a shallow greenish pool that lay at the roadside, a man was working. A low, fat man, erecting with red-faced energy a narrow signboard. There was no lettering on it yet.

I found the pub little cooler, and the beer was flat.

The only other customer was an old man, as silent and watchful as the cats.

Presently we were drinking. Halfway down the glass he spoke. 'The hay is comin' on nice,' he said.

'It is indeed,' I said. 'The countryside looks very healthy round here.'

I had gone too far. He looked at me coldly. 'Fair. Considerin' everythin'.'

There was a long pause.

At last he spoke again. 'The turnips now, though, isn't what ye might –'

The door opened.

It was the man I had seen working by the duck pond. He seemed annoyed. Close behind him followed a tall lean person with an expressionless face and hair like string. He was arguing: 'You know what ye said to me. You promised –'

'Yes, I know!' The little fat man certainly was annoyed. He turned to the bar. 'Ye'd better give this character a pint, too,' he said, and drinks were put before both. He paid, drank his off without enjoyment, nodded briefly round the room and went out.

'Well!' said the old man. 'Well! Ye'd think he hadn't time to be civil. What ye been doin' to him, Tootie?'

The blank-faced man swung round. After a moment he smiled like a sheep. 'I dunno,' he said; 'I dunno,' and reached for his glass again.

'How's the cat licences, Tootie?' called the old man. Tootie turned from his glass so quickly that beer ran down his chin, and swallowed. 'Eh? Aw, we – we're leavin' that.' He sniggered. 'Cats!' he said, and sniggered again. Catching my foreign eye, he blinked and was quiet.

As soon as he went, a few minutes later, I ordered more drinks for myself and the old man. 'I noticed you have a – a number of cats in the village,' I suggested.

But there was no need to make openings. As I caught his eye, I saw it had unfrozen.

'That fella that just went out,' he said, 'they call him Tootie Taggart.' He pointed to his forehead. 'A touch clicky is poor Tootie. Poor fella! An' th' other fella was Dicky-Dan Watterson.' His manner became slightly furtive. 'This is a kind of a private story. Ye'll not let on about it?'

'No,' I said. (I have changed the names, anyway.) 'I believe I saw – Dicky-Dan at work down the street a little while ago.

176

Putting up a notice.'

'Was he? Aw, he – he's a terrible responsible fella is Dicky-Dan. Always worryin' about the village here, an' puttin' things straight. But he's not so bad as he was. Little notices an' things doesn't bother anybody, now; but some while back – a year ago, maybe – Dicky-Dan made a tremendous splutter in the village, in a way. Mind you, he was in the right of it.

'It begun here in this very room.

'There was a big fella they called Gob Kelly too, a big squash-ear Irishman, with an ugly snarl on him, an' the marks of a dozen kinds of fights. It was just as well for the police that there is none of thim hereabouts: he would bust in here when he was passin' through, an' commit all the kinds of wickedness he could screw his mind round to. Insultin' an' fightin' an' desthroyin'. The women wasn' safe either. Fayle's daughter – but that one is fit to say anythin': no matter. The thing was: decent men were in dread to come for a single drink at all, in case they would find him choppin' at their throats with half a green bottle. Fearful it was.

'So one night here, when th' Irish fella was gone off screetchin' drunk an' they was clearin' up the broken glass, Dicky-Dan Watterson held a meetin'. Fellas was beginnin' for to come back one by one, peepin' about.

'"Now listen here," says Dicky-Dan, as big as bull-beef now the coast was clear, "somethin's got to be done about this village. It's a disgrace to th' Isle o' Man," he says. "Two things – this drunken fella an' the cats – is the worst of all. Now, let's take the first –"

'Well, talkin' bold about big Kelly was soon gettin' Dicky-Dan a whole lot of agreement in principle, as they say, but nobody was terrible eager to actually do anythin'.

'"All right then," he says, "we'll make a start with the cats!" Now – that's the way he is, is Dicky-Dan, scramblin' from one feed to another like Parr's pig. Augh, an' terrible vague with it. Terrible vague!

'"But the women likes cats," says some backslider, "an' another thing: who else would have the knack to catch the mice?" "Aw, there's too many altogether!" says Dicky-Dan, louder. "The craythurs is runnin' savage. Oul' Craine's widder has upward of two dozen slitherin' about the house! An' the squeals at night is fearful!"

'So, they got to considerin' how to get shut o' some o' the cats. Drownin' would be slow, for fully-grown fellas, an' the cruelty men might get wind of it. At last Dicky-Dan had a big idea. "Go an' fetch Tootie Taggart," he says.

'They found poor oul' Tootie at some caper like fishin' without bait, an' brought him along.

'"Tootie," says Dicky-Dan, comin' all over serious. "Y're just the man t' help me." Tootie just stands dribblin' an' lookin' seventeen diff'rent ways. "Ye know how dogs has got t' have dog licences on their collars?" says Dicky-Dan. Tootie thinks a bit, an' nods. "Well," says Dicky, lookin' dreadful innocent, "now they're puttin' out a law for cats to have licences too. They've made me th' inspector for this district, an' I want you for t' help me, good man." He goes over to oul' Tootie, that hadn't the smell of a notion what it was all about, an' gives him a little card he had wrote: 'Licence Inspector Taggart,' or some nonsense. "Don't show this to a livin' soul," he says. "It's secret work. Now this is what ye've got to do: scout round at night with a big sack, an' any cat that hasn't got a collar an' a licence on it, shove him inside."

'The first thing Tootie says, of course, when he gets it straight is, "How much wages?" Dicky-Dan was up to that one. "Well, we're not exactly on a wage," he says. "It's an honorary – I mean, ye do it because it makes y' important. Look, I – I'll treat ye to a drink now an' then for th' help ye'll give me – that's a promise! Will it do ye?"

'Tootie cheered up to hear that, for he never has a halfpenny. Then he says, "All right. What'll we do with th' oul' cats?" Now – Dicky-Dan had never thought as far as that; I tould ye how he is. All he had clear and certain was to chuck the cat-stealin' on to Tootie Taggart. "Oh!" he says, "for the Lord's sake don't distract me! We'll – take thim off some place, set thim adrift on the hills; or sell the skins – just try y'r hand in first, Tootie, an' don't fuss! Has anybody got a sack?"'

The old man set his fist to another glass of warm beer. 'Y'r health!' he said.

He wiped his moustache. 'Well, by this time Dicky-Dan was in his element. He was feelin' dreadful wise. "We'll plan against that Kelly fella now," he says. "I've got it all clear in me head. Listen now, all of youse: tomorrow's pay-night: he'll be in here an' raisin' twenty divils out of every pint – crazy drunk before a man could draw breath. Now one or two of us has got to look in for the sake of things seemin' usual, but for the rest –" An' he begun to sort out his big plan.

'About a quarter of a mile up the road ye'll have seen a dark turn in a little patch o' trees? The last few nights Gob Kelly'd headed up through there to sleep it off in the fields. So it was yonder spot that Dicky-Dan Watterson picked on, the next night. He laid a rope across the road with th' other end fast to a tree. An' there was eight or a dozen other fellas, with handkerchiefs hidin' their faces. I was there meself – just to watch the fun. Dicky-Dan was postin' thim like a gen'ral. He had men in every bush, an' two in the branches above.

'Well, for a long time we heard nothin' but cats carryin' on down by the houses. Once a fella on a bike come by, an' rid over the rope; he must've scented mischief, 'cos he went strainin' up the hill full git, fit to do himself an injury.

'At last there was a madhouse din down beyond. Gob Kelly makin' to sing. An' a splatter of glass when he'd of put his fist through somethin'. Then all was like the tomb again. 'Augh, he's gone th' other way,' whispers somebody after a bit.

'"Hould y'r hush!" says Dicky-Dan, "an' listen!"'

'So we did. There come a tiny indigestible rumblin' kind of a noise, an' it went on, an' got louder; an' it was big Kelly singin' gentle to himself. Everybody got excited. The bushes were fair quiverin'.

'At last we seen him, ramblin' an' sthaagerin'. Every now an' then he would clutch out at the hedge an' the singin' would go down the wrong way. Sometimes he cussed at the things his feet was doin'. But he kept on.

'All of a slap Dicky-Dan hauled on the rope. Big Kelly let a roar an' hit the road a dreadful shudder.

'"Laid him stretched!" shouts Dicky-Dan. "Go for him, boys!"

'There was a terrible commotion. Legs flyin', an' screetches, an' bodies crunchin' on the road. Even in the state he was in Kelly was a terror. He took all the bitin'-teeth out of young Kinley; an' lamed Gell the Slaughter; an' Corteen's wife was kept washin' blood out of his clothes for days after. It was a wonder of a fight. But they clang on like dogs.

'"Tie his hands tighter," says Dicky-Dan, makin' his voice squeaky, for disguise, "an' stuff his gob!" Gaggin' the big fella nearly lost Thomas Gawne two fingers.

'They larruped him a bit more, for the pleasure of it, an' then little Alfie Mylrea says, "What'll we do with him now?"

'It was a queer thing then.

'One by one they went quiet, till they were all glarin' at Dicky-Dan "It's the same as y'r big cat idea," says Alfie. "Ye never have any finish to thim!"

'There they stood in a bunch, colloguin' low so Kelly couldn't hear who they were, an' himself trussed an' wrigglin' on the crown of the road. They hadn't a ha'porth o' notion what to do with the fella. "Turn him loose anywhere at all, an' he'll come back at us," says one. "It wouldn't do to fling him in a quarry?" says another. "The police wouldn't thank ye for the gift of a wild fella like this!"

'They were carryin' on somethin' shockin' at poor oul' Dicky-Dan when all of a sudden a little low grey thing went whiskin' through thim. Under Alfie's legs.

'"Begod, what was that!" he says.

'A figure come runnin' up the road. It was Tootie Taggart, pantin' like a long dog. In his hands was a big sack, houldin' it before him at th' end of his arms like a child's sweetie-bag. An' at every jump Tootie made, there was a kind of a grizzy squawk out of it.

'When he seen us he nearly dropped dead. "Shh! An' come here!" says Dicky-Dan.

'"I'm just chasin' an oul' – an oul' tom-cat," says Tootie, when he got over the fright. "He hadn' any collar on, Dicky-Dan. I havn' foun' any that has got collars, Dicky-Dan."

'"Less o' the Dicky-Dan!" says Watterson, with one eye on th' Irishman. "Show me what ye got in the bag."

'Tootie held on tight. "They'll jump out!" he says. "There's two grey fellas, an' a black one, an' some more that hasn' got any tails. The no-tail fellas is awful hard to catch –"

'"It'll do!" says Dicky-Dan. "An inspiration's come!" His eyes was shinin' somethin' shockin' in the light of the moon. "Come on, boys, shove his head in the sack!"

'They had to turn th' Irishman bottomside-up an' edge him in bit by bit, squirmin' like sin. Then they got the sack pulled along an' tied it round his chest, an' stood him up. A wonderful funny creation he looked. With a huge big head, like, that was bulgin' seventeen diff'rent ways from the commotion of the cats.

'"Go on now," squeaks out Dicky-Dan. "Out of it, the whole bad bunch of ye!" An' fetches th' ugly fella a thump to set him on the right road. He went careerin' away somethin' desperate, trippin' an' clamberin'. Not a word out of him, of course, with the gag all over his face. But there was no gags on the cats. An' they was cussin' him loud an' clear.

'The fellas laughed till they had to lean on trees!'

The old man smiled.

'Would it surprise ye to know he never come back? Would it now? Well, "tread on the divil's tail an' he'll eat ye: laugh at his horns an' he'll cry," as the man said before now.

'He showed up in one o' the towns with a face like a junction of the railways. The cats had cleaned most of the red hair off him, too. He wasn't a quarter of the lady-killer that he had been. Aw, we'll see no more of him.

'But by an' by there was a splutter among the women over the cats that'd gone missin' – though Tootie stole no more, not havin' any sack. Then one or two of the craythurs began to find their way home.

'An' I think a foolish dread started to come over Dicky-Dan, now all the glory was gone cold; that the big Irish fella might get wind of who started it all, an' come howlin' for his blood.

'None of us would ever let on, of course. But the fly in th' ointment is oul' Tootie. These clicky fellas sees as far through a brick wall as anybody. Once Dicky caught him on the way to the dog-licence office with a box of kittens. "Leave that off now," he says mighty quick. "They're changin' the law about cats."'

'So often ye'll see him buyin' Tootie a drink; with bad grace enough sometimes. But for the sake of keepin' oul' times in their proper place.'

As I left the village, I saw Dicky-Dan Watterson again. He was finishing the notice by the duck pond, drawing a red 'R' on 'DANGER.'

A duck stood in the middle of the drying slime, watching him; the water came halfway up the bird's legs.

But perhaps in winter, it was deep.

Peg

'HALLO,' PEG SAID TO a nice boy with curly hair. 'Like to take me for a walk?'

He walked past her. She ran and caught him up and patted his arm but he didn't see her.

Peg sighed. He hadn't looked like he was thinking, or going any place in particular: he might have seen her.

Two women passed. They looked right through her.

'I give up! I give up!' said Peg. She shouted, 'I can see you all. Why won't you see me? I don't get it!' An old guy selling fruit off a barrow never even looked up from his oranges. Oranges! That's something you didn't see in the blitz. Only the Joes sometimes had one in their pocket.

'Hi, soldier,' she said. But the soldier had gone while she was putting her best smile on. Only a limey soldier, anyway, in his little sissy berry, yah! yah!

It was like a picture she once went to see with Lola. About some guy that was invisible. He could see people, but they couldn't see him; they could hear him though.

She yelled, 'Then why don't somebody hear me? Folks do hear ghosts, don't they?' The words froze her; she must be in one of her crazy moods tonight, or she wouldn't have said it out like that: crazy to be seen by somebody.

She ran, swinging her handbag. It was just getting dark, and the shop windows were popping out bright patches on the sidewalk. Her bag hit an old guy right in the kisser, but he didn't notice; he just kept right on walking. She dodged between the figures. If they walked sort of through you, it made you feel funny.

She passed a broken shop, boarded up ever since the blitz. It was an old friend. There was nothing inside but burnt woodwork and rats. She had had a look.

'Hey, you cop!' A policeman stood on a corner, and Peg ran up to him and danced up and down, waggling her hips. 'Why don't ya pinch me? I ain't got no identity card!' The policeman was watching a car across the road. She banged his chest and screamed, 'Lousy bum! Call yaself a cop?' but it didn't even disturb a tiny fluffy blob of dust that had settled on the blue cloth.

She looked at the faces. Nearly all civvies. Jeeze, what a corny mob! The women had long dresses. That was crazy! Why, you couldn't see even a bit of their knees any more.

'I got nice knees. Hey, Mister, ain't I got nice knees?'

Aw, does your momma know you're out!

Years and years it must be. They'd pulled down the shelters; she'd sat and talked to the men while they worked, but they didn't hear her. The old black-out was gone, the lovely, cuddly, crazy black-out. And the guns and the searchlights and the balloons.

Hardly ever a sailor, and no Joes.

Funny! It must be a long time, but you never noticed it. When you didn't have to eat and drink, it was like everything happened at once.

Jeeze, it could make you feel funny in the head! Only a minute ago, sort of, there was dark everywhere and those son-of-a-bitches with the white helmets standing in their twos on the sidewalk, watching the Joes. And the Joes were everywhere, and up the side alleys you'd find them, chewing, a bit high, and smoking lovely smelling cigars; with their caps sideways and pockets full of gum and money.

'Lady,' Peg said, 'why don't you get wise to things? Your old man ain't coming home tonight – he's going to be my poppa!'

The woman went on waiting for her bus.

Old pig-face! She hadn't got a fur coat. Peg's was nice thick fur. She liked the feel of nice things. And that was a raw deal, too! She didn't exactly feel things now. She did. And at the same time, she didn't. Crazy!

She came to the Electric Park and went in.

Yow! Boy, this was the place! She always climbed on a pin-table to get out of the crush and see everything. Boy! The old jukebox singing, and the coloured lights! It was just the same! The girls had boys, and there was rifle-shooting and prizes, and showing off and throwing money away! That was great!

She sighed.

The boys were only kids. Kids with prissy hair and their little shoulders padded to look tough. Why, you bet they felt big if they got just to kissing a girl.

These girls looked lousy anyway.

They didn't know anything; couldn't act the way a guy would want them. A lot of dough-faces.

The Joes would have raised the roof. They'd feed pennies into the machines for her and ask her name. She always told them a good one. Dolores or Sandra or Josephine. Never Peg. One night when she was a bit high she said Lola, and the Joes got the two girls mixed up. Lola was mad.

Listen to that music, will you! She stepped it out on the glass of the pin-tables, kicking her high heels in the solemn faces that stared at the numbers and the little chromium balls. 'Hey, look!' She danced over the barrels of the little toy rifles, and along the counter of the soda-bar, kicking at the hands and glasses. 'This is how we used to do it in the dance halls!' Her arms jerked. 'When the Joes was here!' Nobody saw. She got hep and danced great and nobody saw.

Outside, she was angry. You couldn't cry. You can't cry without tears.

She kicked at a piece of paper, and made it dance along the gutter. Really the wind was blowing it, but she pretended.

There was the chemist's where she used to get lipstick. Nice stuff that you wiped off and it left a lovely stain behind. Drug store, not chemist's. Drug store. Crazy little duck behind the counter must have mistaken her for somebody else. 'Mother well?' he used to say every time. Like she was on an errand.

There was the milk bar with its big open front. Hardly any customers. An old guy with whiskers drinking pink stuff out of a glass. Pugh! And the big flash pub on the corner. They'd gotten wise to her after a bit, and it was no more gin for baby there. The Joes brought it out in bottles.

Two big guys got out of a car and went in through the chromium and glass door; it used to be plywood in the blitz days. Big dirty guys in swell overcoats. In some racket.

'Hallo. Got a match?' No luck. Another man went past without a look. You didn't really expect anybody to answer. It was just a game.

She stood watching the cars and buses and taxis.

Ever since she was little, she liked to talk to people. She was quick; at school they all said she was. Just read things a couple of times, and she could say them by heart. Funny, she loved to talk so much and now nobody heard.

She looked across the road and saw – it couldn't be!

A Joe! A real live G.I.

Genuine upturned stripes on his sleeve, and the little round U.S. badges on his lapels shining in the shop lights.

She ran through the traffic. 'Hey, Joe!' she shouted. She felt she would burst, she was so happy. 'Joe! Joe! Oh, I felt so lonesome, Joe! And all the time I knew there must be somebody else the same way I am!'

She reached him.

He hadn't turned. He was looking into a shop window, cigarette between his lips. A Lucky.

It was no good. She knew it suddenly.

She screamed into his face, 'Joe! Look at me! You must be like me – you must! Answer! Answer!'

She hit at him and scratched the back of his tunic as he went.

'Goddam you! Oh – no! Joe! Come back!'

He stopped a few yards away and she saw him ask a man the way. So he must be a living Joe, after all. They couldn't all have gone.

She came to the bare place they'd cleared after the blockbusters. The empty space where the kids came to play. A little ball of dirty straw was being bowled over it by the wind. A rag of newspaper flapped.

It was where she had lived with Lola in the blitz; where she had been asleep the night the house caught it. The whole block had gone west in a few minutes. She often wondered where Lola was. Maybe she'd been in the house too.

Little bits of iron and brick stuck out of the ground. Once, before it was trodden flat, she saw a brooch in the dirt where kids were playing. 'Look there!' she had said to them. 'It's genuine rolled gold.' A Joe had won it for her from a crane-machine in the Electric Park; it took him seventeen tries. But they didn't see the brooch, and now it had gone.

She stood and thought. There was no need to sit, because she never got tired.

These stupid kids would go on growing; she saw them. And they would get old and creep round with grandchildren. But she would always be just fourteen.

Zachary Crebbin's Angel

HE WAS THE SORT OF old man you only saw going away.

You might glimpse him taking a short cut through a thistly field in the dusk, or vanishing over the skyline of a little hill among the gorse. But if anyone in the village had been able to draw, and they had been asked to sketch the old man's face from memory, the result would have been blank paper and a frown.

Then it got about that Zachary Crebbin had seen an angel.

They buzzed like black flies up to his cottage on the back road. If the story had come from wandering Mally Skillicorn, or Killey the Louse, who had hardly walked steadily in licensed hours since his infancy, it would, of course, have been different. But as it was –

He sat near the open fireplace among the squashed cushions of an old rocking chair. The shadowy skin round his eyes moved; his hands opened and shut, and there was wonder in his face at the way his house had changed. There were strangers in it.

It was easy to see the place held only one. Everywhere there were tables; loaded with dishes, underclothing, empty plant pots, candles, tools and shavings, a half-completed bird–

cage. A track led through the furniture from door to fireplace. There was an odd, compound smell.

'No more, now! No more!' somebody shouted, and they pressed the door shut. It was February, which kills old men.

The six or seven inside squeezed for room. No women, because it might prove a serious business.

The old man's fingers were dabbing slowly at his chin, as if to push back the white bristles that spiked out like dead reeds. Next to him, the short, shiny red-cheeked person who had been the first there, turned to the others.

'He says it was las' night!'

A murmur of wonder ran round, as each remembered what he had been doing then, to understand the matter more clearly.

The old man nodded, encouraged. 'Jus' after I let the lamp an' set the chimney back on it,' he said.

A heavy fellow by the door breathed noisily and said, 'What was it?'

The rosy first-comer chattered back officiously with the incredible, 'An angel! He says he seen –'

'Shut up, Quirk!' The heavy man looked past him. 'What was it, Mr. Crebbin?'

One of the old man's hands fingered the knuckles of the other. 'That's right,' he agreed. 'It was like he said.'

'An – angel?'

'Yes.'

There was a little silence.

'I was ready for t'have me supper,' said Zachary Crebbin. 'Two soda scones an' a bit of left-over cheese. I heard a kind of a noise outside. Like – like rooks settlin' for to roost. An' a minute later come a knock at the door. I thought, "That's queer!" – because there's not such a tremendous lot of people comes to see me.'

He flicked a glance over those who sat among his possessions.

The heavy man cleared his throat. 'What did ye do?'

'I says, "Come on in; it's not locked." An' the door opens. An' there –'

'Go on! What like was he?' said little Quirk.

Crebbin considered very seriously.

'Kind of a big shape. Not fat, mind you, but high. He had to dodge a bit through the door.'

There was another murmur. A voice was heard asking whether the figure had been shining.

The old man seemed worried, licking his lips. 'Well, not in so many words he wasn't. I made strange of him at the first. There was a – look, it was the way he had lost his edges; that was it, his edges was gone. An' he wasn't white. A yellowy kind of a colour.'

The heavy man snorted and muttered, 'By Heaven, there's some fools –!'

There was a gasp from the rest. A young man with large ears stood up and said loudly, 'Talk some other way about Heaven here, John James Quilleash! If ye've only come for to –! You can just mind yourself!' He swallowed. Quilleash had come noisily to his feet. 'I'm gettin' out! Think I'm stayin' here with – with' – he steadied himself and glared at each in turn – 'superstitious idolaters!'

Angry protests rose. Old Crebbin turned an expressionless face.

Halfway out of the door, Quilleash added, 'Yellowy! Augh!' He slammed it behind him. They were relieved to see him go.

'Now that we're shut of him,' said Quirk, 'ye'll be able to tell us the rest of it, Mr. Crebbin. Ah, you were on about his clo'es?'

The old man nodded. 'A long robe thing. A long, lovely robe. But ye could see it was real good stuff. Warm.' Daugherty the weaver murmured in self-conscious approval.

'Was there – wings?' asked the youth delicately.

Old Crebbin hesitated. 'In a way there was. I – couldn' get a proper sight of his back, an' the lamp is poor; I've been meanin' for months back to get another, but I haven' been in town at all. But I think he had them.'

'Did he speak to ye?'

The old man nodded hard. 'Oh, he did.' The chair rocked quickly a few times, creaking. 'He talked a lot.'

'Mr. Crebbin,' said Quirk seriously, 'would ye tell us just what happened? Y' see – it's hard to find what questions t'ask.'

There was almost perfect stillness. The old man wiped his lips, nodded to himself. 'I sort of bent down when I seen him. The first thing he said was, "Straighten up out of that, Mr. Crebbin; ye'll take a cramp." He had a wise sort of a face, not clever; an' eyes, ye could see them thinkin' but ye couldn' know what. He sat himself down on the shiny table. Jus' where you are now –'

He pointed to Gorry the smith. Long Gorry half rose, became conscious again of his doubts, and sat once more, smiling with embarrassment.

'Now, while I'm rememberin' – we'll just have a little sup of tea, all.' In spite of protests, the old man filled the kettle slowly from a pail with a tin dipper. 'The well-water is not the way it was.' He picked something from the surface and flicked it away; eased himself up slowly, to press the kettle among the coals.

'Ah. He talked so plain. "Are ye lookin' forward to comin' to Heaven?" he says. It sounded queer, that "comin'" instead of always "goin'".' I was sat down in this very chair. "Well, I am now," I says, an' then I says, "Could ye tell – but I suppose that's against the rules."

'"What?" he says. "Tellin' what it's like?" An' he smiles, an' I have to smile too, an' the next minute him an' me is laughin'. Laughin' like sin. "Ye know what that did to the cat!" he says. Curiosity, he meant. Then he goes quiet. "But th'age is there," he says. "This is your eighty-second year, is it not, now? And so ye'll often find yourself thinkin' about comin' up; it's natural," he says.

"'Is it – I mean, could ye just say is it a tremendous lot different?" I asked him then.

'He smiles again. "Well," he says, "that's a big thing now. It depends. But in the main th' answer is no. Queer how many people only fancies they want somethin'. You're a big gardenin' man," he says – he must have been round the back of the house for a sight before he come in – "so ye'll be easy fitted," he says. "There's flowers up in our place the beat of them was never dreamt of; you'll see. No frosts an' blight either. An' no wireworm nor caterpillars nor them dirts." "Say so?" I answers him. "That's a sensible idea." An' makin' bold, to keep him goin' on the subject, I says; "I suppose ye'll not need such stuff as manure at all?" He says, "Of a kind, yes. Accordin' to whether ye have a nose for the goodness of it; like half of life itself, eh?

"'Ever have a wife, Zachary?" he says, sudden. And I nod, "Long before now, I had." "Ay, I know," he says, "I was just wantin' to see what sort of look would come in your eye. I'd not be givin' ye too much grief with sayin' – that's all arranged?"

'That set me head off in a queer, sweaty, faintly way. I – I – Ye'll not remember. She was – a good, lovely woman.

'I know I shouted out somethin' soft, about havin' tea made ready, I think. He puts out his hand towards me. Me arm tingles, though he doesn't touch me; like pins'n'needles. "I haven't much of a thirst on, thank y' all the same," he says. An' of course I seen our tea wouldn' be suitable, even the dear kind. An' then I caught his eye. An' I knew it was all right.'

The old man rubbed his gums together, looking out of the window.

'What happened then?' said Gorry.

Zachary turned on him, eyes like a stranger's. 'Oh, he – he

went. "I just dropped in," he said to me. A strange sort of a smile he had.'

Little Quirk turned his head slowly till his eyes met Gorry's. 'Ah,' he said. 'It's wonderful, that.'

Old Crebbin was searching out cups one by one, and a damp cloth to wipe the dust out of them. The silence continued until they were gently sucking the top off their tea.

'I lay you were glad of a cup after that one had gone?' fished Gorry. Old Crebbin smiled.

'Oh, it restores a man!' Quirk's cheeks shone with the beam he put there as he sipped again, holding the spoon firmly down with his thumb.

'Was there – did he leave any kind of a mark, say?' Gorry went on. 'I mean – it would be a fine thing to shove in front of a doubter, an' say, "Look at this then!" Eh?'

The old man's face came up from his tea and fixed him. 'Do ye not believe what I been tellin', then?' He sounded incredulous.

They nodded, and shifted feet for emphasis.

'Yes, yes!'

'Ah, surely, Mr. Crebbin!'

'What else, indeed?'

The old man considered them, watching each face.

'Well then – look at this.'

He made his way between the tables to where a huge leather-backed Bible lay. He grasped it by the fat spine and tilted it, picked up something from underneath.

The palm he held out to the watching men quivered, from the stiffening of his body.

'He give ye them two flowers?' said Quirk.

The things were quite flat. Questioning with his eyes, Gorry took one. It felt as dry, perhaps, as autumn grass. But the colours were there. None of them could remember such a flower: big, with strangely brilliant, spotted tints. Delicate blues, a red that was dark and dazzling together.

Zachary Crebbin said nothing. His eyes were tightly shut in the direction of the flower he held. His lips moved wordlessly, like a baby's. His breath sharpened.

And then several of them became believers. For an unexplainable moment, they felt it distinctly.

The man seemed young.

And as it ended, he took the other flower from Gorry, and dropped both of them down into the fire. There was a flare of flame. Then it was a very old man who stood swaying before the fireplace.

They were just in time to put down their cups and catch him.

Three days later Zachary Crebbin died. It was expected. There were people in his house to the end, listening for further words, but he added nothing.

After the funeral, which many attended, if you include those who watched over hedges, and at which the minister disappointingly ignored the whole story, little Quirk visited the cottage "to shut everythin' up safe." He took away a number of articles by a round-about route. They included the half-finished birdcage, which he later completed and put round a linnet, and the great Bible; a family book with the birth-dates of old Crebbin and his family on the printed space inside the cover. Five children, all dead.

It was in this Bible that Quirk's wife made certain discoveries. She showed him.

Flattened, half stuck to the pages with a faint halo of long dried juice, they were; scented sweetleaf; dog-roses; foxgloves; honeysuckle; and occasionally, strange among the murky engravings and dark chronicles, large bright flowers they did not recognise. Quirk frowned, and presently he was sure that none were quite like the two that the old man had shown. So

195

they said nothing. It would have been embarrassing to do anything else.

The cottage fell into the hands of lawyers, who pretended to search for relatives. People carried away a table now and then as they needed one. Collapse set in. Zachary Crebbin's home became four low bare walls round a patch of nettles and long-legged ground spiders; like so many others on the island.

It is so today. Half-remembering, the villagers call it the Wizard's House, and children run past it with round, side-glancing eyes.

Bini and Bettine

THEY WERE IN THE same seaside pavilion show as me; that's how I met them.

Bini was a midget, two feet ten inches high. At least they claimed that; he always seemed bigger to me. He was an ugly little creature at first sight.

His partner, though, was something to look at. Bettine. She was at her best in those days, drowsy-eyed and very beautiful in that heavy, sexy way that doesn't last. She had a superb figure, taller than average – which made a useful dramatic contrast with Bini.

They did a mother-and-child juggling act; and that was a surprise. With her looks, you'd have expected her to lay on the glamour in some kind of solo. But she seemed quite content. She knew she had a first-rate partner, however small.

I remember their turn started with her wheeling Bini on stage in a pram; he was dressed as a baby, in frills and blue ribbons, and looked remarkably like the real thing. When they got about halfway across, talking comic dialogue, he would throw a big celluloid rattle out on to the stage. She would toss it back. And then, in a moment it seemed, the air would be filled with those celluloid rattles. She would take him out of the pram and seat him on her shoulder, and between them they would keep what looked like hundreds of rattles, rubber feeding-bottles, teething rings and woolly balls flying all round them. Then came the neatest part. Bini would begin to make all this stuff disappear – he was an expert at sleight of hand – bit by bit, into those frilly petticoats and bibs of his. Bettine played up to this, registering every kind of comic emotion, and when the last object had gone, she would shake him upside down over the pram till the whole lot came pouring out of his clothes.

They did acrobatics too, and a short dance routine. Clever, but not important. It was the way Bini vanished the juggling gear into that little outline of his that always got the audience; I was the next turn on and I heard the applause.

I used to see quite a lot of Bini and Bettine off stage too.

Bini never talked much, even about himself; I wish I could say as much for some other midgets I've met since. He was about twenty-five years old at that time, intelligent, reserved instead of vain, and with a streak of natural pathos in that creased little face. He never bitched about other acts in conversation, which is rare anywhere in show business. I've sometimes wished since that he had opened his mouth more; he must have had things in that small round head that would have been illuminating.

But it wasn't him I was interested in, backstage.

Bettine and I were married twelve days after the show opened, and we lived together until the end of the season.

The first week it was wonderful.

The second, it was pretty good.

After that we found we didn't get along so well.

There was a combination of reasons, with faults on both sides. We really knew nothing about each other, and it was a crazy idea – at least, getting married was. I've never been able to understand why we did it. Full church wedding with trimmings, and the whole company in attendance. The management were enthusiastic, of course, with a greedy eye on the publicity. 'Whirlwind Romance in New Pier Revue.' 'Stage Mother Becomes Bride.' The locals are supposed to love that sort of thing.

We became used to being pointed out on the beach as the happy couple. And all the time we knew things were cracking up.

There was a lot more to Bettine than the audience ever saw. For one thing, she had a cruel streak. She could locate a person's sensitive spot in a second, and she would probe gently. I know; I've seen her do it to other people too. Men found it interesting, at first.

My own weak point was my act – a straight song-and-patter. I know now it was bad, and I was beginning to realise it then. It was not until later that I found a more original line, and got somewhere.

She always chose her time. A night when I couldn't sleep, I'd hear her voice beside me in the dark. 'I shouldn't worry over that act; I've seen plenty worse. You take yourself too seriously, Sammy.' Pause. 'Did you notice how Bini held the laughs tonight? That midge is good!' Or perhaps on a rainy Sunday she would turn on a long-distance look and say, 'Sammy. You try too hard. You know about people who try hard? Oh, forget it!' Once I suggested she should come into my act with me – it seemed natural enough – and she laughed softly and kindly. I nearly struck her.

Perhaps these little items shouldn't have meant so much, but it was a non-stop drip. And there were other things; I'm not perfect. We had a flare-up and we were both glad when it came. For a long time things between us had been like a boil that won't burst.

At the end of it, she looked at me with an expression I'd not seen on her face before. It was openly and contemptuously vicious.

'All right,' she said. 'Just as you say; separate. No, I want nothing – I'll be all right! I've still got the midge, haven't I? And a good act. A *good* act!'

I got along without her.

I believe she had done something for me, though. Or perhaps it was disappointment that set me working harder on the rebound. I began to improve my act, and get results. Better-class bookings came along; the big circuits.

In the first months after we separated, I heard an occasional mention of Bini and Bettine, but soon lost all touch even with their names. I met other women, of course, but never actually needed a divorce, so I forgot about Bettine.

It was years later when I ran into her again.

During the war; I was touring with an ENSA show, visiting army camps. One day I happened to be buying a few things in a nearby market town.

It was about the middle of the morning, when the place was at its busiest. I was just leaving a stationer's in the main street – I'd been buying a fountain pen, I remember – when I heard voices raised in argument, and there I saw a huddle of shoppers, mostly women; a small aimless crowd that was dissolving as fast as it formed, as if there was nothing much to bother about.

I stepped across for a look. Two women were at the middle of it, each with a pram.

One of them was Bettine!

I just stood at the edge of the crowd, peering, trying to make sure I wasn't mistaken, and not wanting her to see me. Her face had changed. It was lumpy and folded now, and she needed a lot more paint. All the beauty of the pier pavilion days had gone.

She seemed to be involved in a dramatic argument with the second woman. They were both tense and angry. The other woman was evidently conscious of having the upper hand, and playing to the bystanders; she was complaining loudly; something about keeping children under control.

'I know mine wouldn't touch a thing belonging to another child!' she was saying. 'That's one thing I really have taught her –'

Then Bettine caught my eye. I cursed the crowd for opening just as she turned back to her pram.

Without the smallest hesitation she said coolly, 'Here's my husband.'

She was still looking at me, but I didn't take it in for a moment. She meant me. As if I'd left her only five minutes before, not five years.

I pushed slowly towards her. There was nothing else to do. 'Hallo, Bettine,' I said.

I saw now she was shabby too.

'Sam – this lady is apparently under the impression that baby stole her little girl's silk pram-cover, while both she and I were away shopping. I expect he wanted to look at it – you know what tiny children are!' She had taken my arm tightly in hers. Now she let her face crinkle miserably and a tear ran down her face. She must have known in a second that she had the sympathy of the onlookers. The other woman realised it too.

I tried to glance into Bettine's perambulator, but it had an enormous fringed hood, and all I could see inside was a huddle of blanket.

I felt a wave of understanding. Like a cartoon character with an exclamation sign drawn above his head. The weather was warm; and there was so much more blanket than there need have been.

'You got it back?' I said to the other woman.

She nodded, still heated, but submitting; I must have looked a sufficiently solid citizen to end the argument. She wheeled her child away, scolding it instead, and grumbling to herself. The crowd melted.

'Let's move out of here!' Bettine said. She turned the pram

in the opposite direction to the woman. I could see it was heavy by the way it handled.

I waited until we were in a quiet road.

'Well,' I said, 'd'you make much out of this – little racket?' I could see she didn't, so I tried not to sound harsh.

'You knew?' she said. Her eyes were all over my face; they were harder eyes than I had known.

I tapped my fingers on the worn grey skin of the hood.

'Bini always had a lot of talent with his hands. How do you do it? Run the pram alongside another when the mother's away, and leave him to grab what he can?' I imagined him inside, reddening. Bini had always been a simple soul.

'Yes,' she said. 'We move from town to town, and that's what we do.' Her voice was very soft and she was smiling as if she were proud.

I felt almost guilty for a second. 'If you'd only let me know –'

'I didn't want you,' she said, casually. Her voice grew hard again. 'It isn't only prams; they would scarcely pay. He gets handbags now and then; and in hotels there are other things. When we use the pram he has the stuff hidden in an instant; there's a false bottom, of course. He's very quick.'

'What do you call the act these days?' I said. I laughed. I put my hand on the pram-rail and stopped it. 'Poor old Bini, time you had a breath of fresh air,' I said. I tipped the hood over towards the foot of the pram.

A small face looked up.

It wasn't Bini. It wasn't any midget, but a normal child of four or five, far too old to be strapped in there among the pillows and fluffy clothes. He cringed for a moment; then he was staring me out, like a little cornered animal.

'Whose is he?' I said. But I knew.

And she still wore that smile.

The Stocking

On the day before Christmas, the sun came through the window so low that it lit the highest broken patch on the wall.

It was very cold when Ma came home, and she put an extra cover on his cot; the cover from their bed with the paper stuffing. A corner of paper stuck out with a picture of a lady on it.

She gave him a piece of bread and fat while she made the tea.

'Ma,' he said.

Ma looked hard and said, 'Yes?'

'Will you hang up a stocking for me tonight?'

Ma laughed and said, 'All right.'

'I got a big bag of sweets in it last year,' he said. 'Daddy Christmas is kind, isn't he, Ma?'

Ma laughed again and afterwards he heard her counting the money in her purse.

'Maybe Daddy Christmas'll come and maybe he won't,' she said, 'but Pa'll hang a stocking up for you.'

When Pa had finished his soup in the evening, he brought a chair and fastened an old one of Ma's long stockings to the wooden beam that ran across the room above the cot, a little below the ceiling.

Pa leaned on the cot as he stepped down, and it creaked and swayed. 'That'll never do,' said Pa, and he knocked four nails into the cot to hold it more firmly to the wall; it had no legs.

Plaster crumbled into his eyes as Pa hammered, and Pa leaned into the cot and rubbed away some of the grit with his sleeve. Ma said, 'Turn over, silly creature.'

He pulled himself on to his face until the hammering was over. 'That'll keep it fast,' said Pa, and his mouth twitched at Ma as he jerked his head at the places where the Minkeys lived.

Ma nodded and she said in the little voice he was not meant to hear, 'He doesn't mind the rats.'

Loudly, she said, 'You don't mind the Mickey Mouses, love. You're too big to be afraid of them.'

He smiled at Ma, though the plaster was still hurting his eyes. She meant the Minkeys.

They lived high up and they had fur on their bodies and long tails. And when the dark came and Ma and Pa went to bed, the Minkeys ran about inside the ceiling; sometimes they scratched on the floor below the cot. But when it was light they never came.

'There's plenty of room in that stocking,' said Pa and he laughed.

Ma laughed too, and then she said to Pa, 'Coming now?' and Pa said, 'Yes, the usual?'

Ma counted her money again and smiled. 'We can celebrate tonight.'

'He'll have the house to himself,' said Pa.

'Why aren't there any other people now?' he asked from the cot.

Pa laughed. 'They thought there were too many Mickey Mouses.'

'Oh, it'll be closing time before you come!' Ma shouted.

When they had gone, everything was still, only the candle flickering softly.

He looked up at the stocking, hanging straight from the beam; it might have a bulge in it by morning.

He sang to himself in the cot, faintly, a little song that turned out to be about the Minkeys; their strange ways, their quietness and their scuttling walk.

He listened to the noise of ships on the distant river, and wondered why his legs would not move, although he was five.

He wondered about Christmas, and why it was not in the summer.

He wondered about many things, and shivered and tried to screw himself up.

There was a tiny sound in the ceiling; a faint scraping noise as if somebody very small was shifting their feet. That would be a Minkey.

There came another little sound, and another, and presently a soft slither as if something had jumped on to the beam above. The Minkeys were coming out.

He looked up towards the dark ceiling, and saw the green glimmer of two tiny eyes, and then two more and then others.

The ceiling was full of a rustling and scuttling, as it always was when the house became still.

Minkeys didn't like you to see them.

A loose nail tumbled from above and clattered on the floor.

He saw that the whole wide beam was bulging on each side, and that the bulges were moving and changing; often a long tail twitched and curled.

Everywhere was a scratching and the little squeaky sound of Minkeys' talk, like the talk of the yellow bird that died, only quicker and sharper.

Suddenly it stopped.

He looked upwards again, and the flickering eyes peeped down from the beam. He saw that the long Daddy Christmas stocking was moving, swaying from side to side, and jerking. It seemed to have thickened at the place Pa had tied it to the beam; then it had thickened lower down, and lower.

And there was a Minkey, clinging to the stocking, and slowly dropping. Its eyes twinkled as it swung and its head shot this way and that.

He could smell the dark smell of the Minkey very close.

When the furry body had reached the end of the stocking, it hung curled upside down; and its tail twisted here and there, feeling the folds in the stocking. He started with the quickness of the Minkey's jump. For all at once the stocking was tossing empty, and the Minkey crouched on the foot of the cot, watching him.

But when he looked back at the stocking there were three more Minkeys climbing down, swinging like the first one. Yet there was no noise at all.

The Minkeys jumped on to the edge of the cot, one by one; and others took their place at the top of the stocking. They climbed down quickly, and many more bodies bobbed along the beam above.

The first Minkey crouched, and jumped into the cot.

He could feel its weight gently pressing the bedclothes down, and at the same time there was a small, cold feeling inside his head. But he was not afraid of furry Minkeys.

He held out his hand gently towards the first one. It did not move. Then suddenly there was a little sharp pain in his finger and he pulled it back.

The Minkey stared at him, with black, round eyes like the end of Ma's hatpin.

There was a tiny red bead on his finger that was salt when he tasted it.

And everywhere was full of Minkeys and strange with

the smell and warmth of them. All the whiskers and eyes and pointed faces moved together. They went 'Now – now – now,' like the bumping of the heart inside his chest.

There was a gentle weight on him.

He looked down. The first Minkey sat on his chest, watching his eyes with its own.

His hands were as log-heavy as his legs.

He saw its mouth open, narrow and sharp and pale; it gave one shrill cry of Minkey talk.

And instantly the whole room turned to hot, leaping fur. Squealing and tearing and chattering and biting.

Who – Me, Signor?

SIGNOR, NO MORE NEED be said! I shall tell everything – I insist! And the other gentleman shall take it down in writing, shall he not?

You understand my position, signor. When the collapse, I mean – when the day of liberation came, things were hard for all of us. I had not been without some small authority... under the Duce. But my minor position in the Party went for nothing, after so many years. And I had given so much money.

Yes, I should like to sit down – thank you, signor.

Alas! I was but a simple creature, God pity me, and in those days unable to recognise my folly. Now it is so clear...

Yes, I know – please, I know! That's nothing to do with this inquiry. We must get on. Ah!

It began with my friend Giuseppe Cavallini – at least, strictly, of course, he is not my friend, only an acquaintance: a big, brutal fellow, and always fiercely for the Duce, even when I began to see the light – he suggested taking advantage of the... unusual situation. I was misled into agreeing – but only to the extent of raising funds for the necessities of life.

There were several possibilities. Now, of course, I see how

wrong they were, but at the time they seemed ingenious to a superficial mind. For instance: the municipal services go astray. So if one arranges the blocking of certain underground pipes, one causes a demand for antiseptics or unobtainable water, according to the contents of the pipe obstructed. You see? One simply buys up all the water-carts or disinfectant first, and states one's terms. I was proud of this plan, but there was no time –

May I correct that, please? I have given a wrong impression. It was Giuseppe's idea, not mine. How confused!

Not to the point? Signor, my humble apologies! Henceforward no word shall leave my lips that is not specifically directed to the subject matter at present under discussion.

Yes. The matter of the paper notices. I must admit my fault. I understand several individuals are prepared to identify me as him who glued them upon the walls. Though I believed that at such an hour –

It was very wrong, I agree, that they should seem to be signed by the Allied Military Governor. But – oh, you have no idea how overbearing is this Cavallini – he threatened me when I protested at the deception. And stupid. 'You cannot post up a notice to blind men,' I had to say, 'because they will not be able to read it. Make it 'To the Relatives of All Blind Male Persons.'

Yes, it is true. We promised free food and clothing to the sightless.

But read, signor, what it says: 'The benevolent policy of the Allied Military Government proposes special concessions to the disabled, and accordingly arrangements have been made...' And so on. Benevolent policy! Special concessions! Why, what result? Popularity of your administration, surely? With all the people seeing those notices? No? No.

It was Giuseppe who procured the premises. They are a

disused hat shop that belongs to his uncle's mistress. That is where the notices told the blind ones to report. Very early, one single morning.

'Be there the night before,' Giuseppe instructed me. 'Bring a sweeping brush to clean the dust into the corners.' Ridiculous! For blind men! I took no brush.

When I got to the shop, Cavallini was already there. He wore a uniform of many kinds. Some of it was English, I may tell you: it bore the badge of a part of the liberation forces called Salvation Army; I saw the English lettering. He had also a postman's trousers and a cap that was a souvenir from the Spanish war. When I entered, he was doing something to his moustache. Combing it out into two fluffy bars. Similar to your own, signor – pardon! Giuseppe's was much inferior, dirty and stringy, you understand.

'I am the English Colonel Smit,' says Giuseppe, greasing his hair down flat and bulging his eyes. 'You are my collaborat –' – that is, assistant – 'and you must say little when the time comes, but do as I order.' So he rehearses me in his fraudulent scheme. Simple fool am I!

And then I try to sleep on some sacking. The night is filled with the crooning and gossip of cats in the back alley – horrible! I twist and turn! Plaster trickles down the back of my neck! When I stand up with the early light, I feel my face puffy and my hair dry.

We breakfast on a roll and a trifle of Parmesan, with some wine that Giuseppe has brought.

And as we eat, we hear outside a sort of mumbling and shuffling and a tapping of sticks.

'The sheep are falling in,' says Colonel Smit, and toasts the last of the cheese over his cigarette lighter till it runs and splutters and fumes. The whole place fills with a rich aroma.

He tightens his black belt. He bulges his eyes. He opens the front door of the shop.

Waiting noisily is a crowd of people. They are mostly men, old and young, with walking-sticks. Some wear dark spectacles; others cloth patches; yet others have nothing over their eyes, and they stare at nothing. And with them are women and small infants and a number of dogs, who have led the blind men to this place.

Then Giuseppe talks to them.

What a mimic is this despicable Cavallini! Just the very English officer! – I beg your pardon. But you should have heard him, signor. Oh, you should have heard him!

'I am Colonel Smit of the Allied Military Government,' says he in his ludicrous accent. 'We are going to give all you poor blind persons a completely new outfit of clothing and then portions of wholesome food. Such are the orders. My assistant will conduct you to the interior. Do not hurry, please.'

Then all the blind men start in a pitiable rush. What numbers! Have I seen so many staring blank faces anywhere? Never! As they stumble and clutch, I feel cynically that greed crowds out the pathos of their deficiency.

All the relatives press forward also. Giuseppe orders them back. 'Only the unfortunate sufferers, please!'

But still there are the dogs. They occur in infinite variety, signor, fierce and persistent. We must of necessity admit these creatures with their masters. However, while the next-of-kin remain outside, we are content. The windows are whitened so that no one can see in.

Giuseppe locks the door and places the sightless ones in a long double line. The fellows' heads are turning this way and that.

'There is a fine savoury smell,' says one, and then all are licking their lips and grinning as they sniff Cavallini's toasted cheese.

'Now,' says Giuseppe. 'It is necessary that you be reclothed. As the first stage in the replacement, please take off your hats.

My assistant will collect them.'

That is the way it was done, signor. I put their hats into a sack, excepting those which were too worn or dirty to sell again.

Then I took their jackets. Groping, they held them out. The dogs kept growling and gnashing their teeth. Signor, it was a frightful task! And I was so sorry for the blind men!

The jackets filled three sacks, all those fit for the unofficial market. I dropped them through the back window into a waiting donkey-cart while Cavallini talked to his victims.

Signor, my cheeks burned! He harangued about the mission of democracy; about the fall of tyranny; about the glorious future of free Italy – he who kept two uniforms of the late regime under his mattress.

Then I came back and took their boots and shoes. Some of those weren't so bad, either. We had agreed, Giuseppe and I, to keep on with the process down to their underclothes, or until they became suspicious. You see the idea? Not so stupid, was it?

'In the new era,' cries Cavallini, while I collect their socks – that was not pleasant – 'there shall be abundance for all nations, a place for all in every country! Freedom from fear, freedom from want, freed –!'

'Please,' says one of the sightless, 'I shall have sciatica from standing here in the cold, please. I take twenty-five centimetre socks...'

'Silence!' orders Giuseppe like thunder; but he winks at me. 'You will all be fitted in a few minutes! I am obeying orders.'

The time has come to get out. He crosses to where I am stuffing the sack, and jerks his thumb.

Then there is a most horrible thing, signor.

I see two of the blind men look at each other!

So!

As I at you, signor, straight in the eye! And they break the line. Shouting.

And then there is no line anywhere. Only running men. And yowling dogs. What rascals! Revolting! They were no more blind than I am a... They were not blind!

Signor, there was exactly one who was genuinely afflicted! He clung to the neck of his dog on the floor as the others trampled over him with their bare feet.

My nerves, signor, will never recover! Never! How my heart beat – cattuck–cattuck–cattuck! Oh!

To the window we fly. I hurl out the sack.

And – believe it? – this ten-million-cursed Cavallini thrusts me violently aside with his leprous paw! He springs out.

The last thing I am properly conscious of is seeing him whipping the donkey away down the alley like the abominable fiend. May his marrow fester!

And I? Those ravening pantaloons have me fast by the toe – hanging half out of the window!

They are tearing at me fit to kill! They gouge. They spit. They scratch. Their eyes flash behind the dark spectacles. My nose bleeds. Limb from limb – ah! My teeth scatter. My clothes are in strips – fabric flies like bats! I lose hair. I am bitten and gnawed by the dogs in twenty places. See? And kicked.

Signor, I am a humble, simple man. I do not make wild accusations. But those foul, dissembling monstrosities should be your victims at this inquiry!

I have suffered much. I have touched the depths of shame.

To escape with my life – how did I do it? – was to begin a plunge through lanes and alleys dressed in half a shirt and one sock.

Signor, think of it and take pity. I have hidden in a fishmonger's bin!

Hidden! Ah, not from my pursuers, but from my decent fellow-citizens! I am hunted down streets by the wholly proper; crowds cry for my blood. Finally I am arrested. 'Insufficiently clothed.'

Signor – I am thankful I was taken into custody. It has been a great privilege to speak to at least one intelligent and understanding person, and to explain my sufferings and perplexities.

Life is difficult, signor.

So often for the innocent it is a thorny maze without an exit. Delusion, deception leer on every side.

I have told – everything. I admit all, I confess, I am a wiped slate. My soul is purged. I am as a child who looks upon the world for the first time, with dewy eyes.

Signor, where must I sign? To be let out?

The Pond

IT WAS DEEPLY SCOOPED from a corner of the field, a green stagnant hollow with thorn bushes on its banks.

From time to time, something moved cautiously beneath the prickly branches that were laden with red autumn berries. It whistled and murmured coaxingly.

'Come, come, come, come,' it whispered. An old man, squatting frog-like on the bank. His words were no louder than the rustling of the dry leaves above his head. 'Come now. Sssst – ssst! Little dear – here's a bit of meat for thee.' He tossed a tiny scrap of something into the pool. The weed rippled sluggishly.

The old man sighed and shifted his position. He was crouching on his haunches because the bank was damp.

He froze.

The green slime had parted on the far side of the pool. The disturbance travelled to the bank opposite, and a large frog drew itself half out of the water. It stayed quite still, watching; then with a swift crawl it was clear of the water. Its yellow throat throbbed.

'Oh! – little dear,' breathed the old man. He did not move.

He waited, letting the frog grow accustomed to the air

and slippery earth. When he judged the moment to be right, he made a low grating noise in his throat.

He saw the frog listen.

The sound was subtly like the call of its own kind. The old man paused, then made it again.

This time the frog answered. It sprang into the pool, sending the green weed slopping, and swam strongly. Only its eyes showed above the water. It crawled out a few feet distant from the old man and looked up the bank, as if eager to find the frog it had heard.

The old man waited patiently. The frog hopped twice, up the bank.

His hand was moving, so slowly that it did not seem to move, towards the handle of the light net at his side. He gripped it, watching the still frog.

Suddenly he struck.

A sweep of the net, and its wire frame whacked the ground about the frog. It leaped frantically, but was helpless in the green mesh.

'Dear! Oh, my dear!' said the old man delightedly.

He stood with much difficulty and pain, his foot on the thin rod. His joints had stiffened and it was some minutes before he could go to the net. The frog was still struggling desperately. He closed the net round its body and picked both up together.

'Ah, big beauty!' he said. 'Pretty. Handsome fellow, you!'

He took a darning needle from his coat lapel and carefully killed the creature through the mouth, so that its skin would not be damaged; then put it in his pocket.

It was the last frog in the pond.

He lashed the water with the handle, and the weed swirled and bobbed: there was no sign of life now but the little flies that flitted on the surface.

He went across the empty field with the net across his

shoulder, shivering a little, feeling that the warmth had gone out of his body during the long wait. He climbed a stile, throwing the net over in front of him, to leave his hands free. In the next field, by the road, was his cottage.

Hobbling through the grass with the sun striking a long shadow from him, he felt the weight of the dead frog in his pocket, and was glad.

'Big beauty!' he murmured again.

The cottage was small and dry, and ugly and very old. Its windows gave little light, and they had coloured panels, dark-blue and green, that gave the rooms the appearance of being under the sea.

The old man lit a lamp, for the sun had set; and the light became more cheerful. He put the frog on a plate, and poked the fire, and when he was warm again, took off his coat.

He settled down close beside the lamp and took a sharp knife from the drawer of the table. With great care and patience, he began to skin the frog.

From time to time, he took off his spectacles and rubbed his eyes. The work was tiring; also the heat from the lamp made them sore. He would speak aloud to the dead creature, coaxing and cajoling it when he found his task difficult. But in time he had the skin neatly removed, a little heap of tumbled, slippery film. He dropped the stiff, stripped body into a pan of boiling water on the fire, and sat again, humming and fingering the limp skin.

'Pretty,' he said. 'You'll be so handsome.'

There was a stump of black soap in the drawer and he took it out to rub the skin, with the slow, over-careful motion that showed the age in his hand. The little mottled thing began to stiffen under the curing action. He left it at last, and brewed himself a pot of tea, lifting the lid of the simmering pan occasionally to make sure that the tiny skull and bones were being boiled clean without damage.

Sipping his tea, he crossed the narrow living room. Well away from the fire stood a high table, its top covered by a square of dark cloth supported on a frame. There was a faint smell of decay.

'How are you, little dears?' said the old man.

He lifted the covering with shaky scrupulousness. Beneath the wire support were dozens of stuffed frogs.

All had been posed in human attitudes; dressed in tiny coats and breeches to the fashion of an earlier time. There were ladies and gentlemen and bowing flunkeys. One, with lace at his yellow, waxen throat, held a wooden wine cup. To the dried forepaw of its neighbour was stitched a tiny glassless monocle, raised to a black button eye. A third had a midget pipe pressed into its jaws, with a wisp of wool for smoke. The same coarse wool, cleaned and shaped, served the ladies for their miniature wigs; they wore long skirts and carried fans.

The old man looked proudly over the stiff little figures.

'You, my lord – what are you doing, with your mouth so glum?' His fingers prised open the jaws of a round-bellied frog dressed in satins; shrinkage must have closed them. 'Now you can sing again, and drink up!'

His eyes searched the banqueting, motionless party.

'Where now –? Ah!'

In the middle of the table, three of the creatures were fixed in the attitudes of a dance.

The old man spoke to them. 'Soon we'll have a partner for the lady there. He'll be the handsomest of the whole company, my dear, so don't forget to smile at him and look your prettiest!'

He hurried back to the fireplace and lifted the pan; poured off the steaming water into a bucket.

'Fine, shapely brain-box you have.' He picked with his knife, cleaning the tiny skull. 'Easy does it.' He put it down on the table, admiringly; it was like a transparent flake of ivory. One by one, he found the delicate bones in the pan, knowing each for what it was.

'Now, little duke, we have all of them that we need,' he said at last. 'We can make you into a picture indeed. The beau of the ball. And such an object of jealousy for the lovely ladies!'

With wire and thread he fashioned a stiff little skeleton, binding in the bones to preserve the proportions. At the top went the skull.

The frog's skin had lost its earlier flaccidness. He threaded a needle, eyeing it close to the lamp. From the table drawer he now brought a loose wad of wool. Like a doctor reassuring his patient by describing his methods, he began to talk.

'This wool is coarse, I know, little friend. A poor substitute to fill that skin of yours, you may say: wool from the hedges, snatched by the thorns from a sheep's back.' He was pulling the wad into tufts of the size he required. 'But you'll find it gives you such a springiness that you'll thank me for it. Now, carefully does it −'

With perfect concentration he worked his needle through the skin, drawing it together round the wool with almost untraceable stitches.

'A piece of lace in your left hand, or shall it be a quizzing-glass?' With tiny scissors he trimmed away a fragment of skin. 'But wait − it's a dance and it is your right hand that we must see, guiding the lady.'

He worked the skin precisely into place round the skull. He would attend to the empty eye-holes later.

Suddenly he lowered his needle.

He listened.

Puzzled, he put down the half-stuffed skin and went to the door and opened it.

The sky was dark now. He heard the sound more clearly. He knew it was coming from the pond. A far-off, harsh croaking, as of a great many frogs.

He frowned.

In the wall cupboard he found a lantern ready trimmed, and lit it with a flickering splinter. He put on an overcoat and hat, remembering his earlier chill. Lastly he took his net.

He went very cautiously. His eyes saw nothing at first, after working so close to the lamp. Then, as the croaking came to him more clearly and he grew accustomed to the darkness, he hurried.

He climbed the stile as before, throwing the net ahead. This time, however, he had to search for it in the darkness, tantalised by the sounds from the pond. When it was in his hand again, he began to move stealthily.

About twenty yards from the pool, he stopped and listened.

There was no wind and the noise astonished him. Hundreds of frogs must have travelled through the fields to this spot; from other water where danger had arisen, perhaps, or drought. He had heard of such instances.

Almost on tiptoe he crept towards the pond. He could see nothing yet. There was no moon, and the thorn bushes hid the surface of the water.

He was a few paces from the pond when, without warning, every sound ceased.

He froze again. There was absolute silence. Not even a watery plop or splashing told that one frog out of all those hundreds had dived for shelter into the weed. It was strange.

He stepped forward, and heard his boots brushing the grass.

He brought the net up across his chest, ready to strike if he saw anything move. He came to the thorn bushes, and still heard no sound. Yet, to judge by the noise they had made, they should be hopping in dozens from beneath his feet.

Peering, he made the throaty noise which had called the frog that afternoon. The hush continued.

He looked down at where the water must be. The surface of the pond, shadowed by the bushes, was too dark to be seen. He shivered, and waited.

Gradually, as he stood, he became aware of a smell.

It was wholly unpleasant. Seemingly it came from the weed, yet mixed with the vegetable odour was one of another kind of decay. A soft, oozy bubbling accompanied it. Gases must be rising from the mud at the bottom. It would not do to stay in this place and risk his health.

He stooped, still puzzled by the disappearance of the frogs, and stared once more at the dark surface. Pulling his net to a ready position, he tried the throaty call for the last time.

Instantly he threw himself backwards with a cry.

A vast, belching bubble of foul air shot from the pool. Another gushed up past his head; then another. Great patches of slimy weed were flung high among the thorn branches.

The whole pond seemed to boil.

He turned blindly to escape, and stepped into the thorns. He was in agony. A dreadful slobbering deafened his ears: the stench overcame his senses. He felt the net whipped from his hand. The icy weeds were wet on his face. Reeds lashed him.

Then he was in the midst of an immense, pulsating softness that yielded and received and held him. He knew he was shrieking. He knew there was no one to hear him.

An hour after the sun had risen, the rain slackened to a light drizzle.

A policeman cycled slowly on the road that ran by the cottage, shaking out his cape with one hand, and half-expecting the old man to appear and call out a comment on the weather. Then he caught sight of the lamp, still burning feebly in the kitchen, and dismounted. He found the door ajar, and wondered if something was wrong.

He called to the old man. He saw the uncommon handiwork lying on the table as if it had been suddenly dropped; and the unused bed.

For half an hour the policeman searched in the neighbourhood of the cottage, calling out the old man's name at intervals, before remembering the pond. He turned towards the stile.

Climbing over it, he frowned and began to hurry. He was disturbed by what he saw.

On the bank of the pond crouched a naked figure.

The policeman went closer. He saw it was the old man, on his haunches; his arms were straight; the hands resting between his feet. He did not move as the policeman approached.

'Hallo, there!' said the policeman. He ducked to avoid the thorn bushes catching his helmet. 'This won't do, you know. You can get into trouble –'

He saw green slime in the old man's beard, and the staring eyes. His spine chilled. With an unprofessional distaste, he quickly put out a hand and took the old man by the upper arm. It was cold. He shivered, and moved the arm gently.

Then he groaned and ran from the pond.

For the arm had come away at the shoulder: reeds and green water-plants and slime tumbled from the broken joint.

As the old man fell backwards, tiny green stitches glistened across his belly.

They're Scared,
Mr. Bradlaugh

WHEN SHE WAS DYING, I said, 'Auntie, you're a fool.'

I always talk straight. I wasn' going to stop because she was like that.

'Don't, oh don't,' she said in her little whispery voice. But I knew I had to be cruel to be kind.

I sat on the edge of the bed and brushed away a few feathers that had come out of the eiderdown. I hate mess.

'I didn't think it of you, Auntie,' I said. 'Not really.'

And she just looked because she didn't want to talk much.

'Haven't you got any pride, Auntie?' I said. 'And don't turn your head away, because you've got to listen.'

I saw her lips go, 'What, Ralph?' but they didn't make much noise.

'I heard you saying prayers in the night!' I said. The bed squeaked because I was sharp.

'Yes, Ralph,' her lips went, and there was that dopey look in her eyes that I just couldn't stand. Like a bloody cow.

'Listen, Auntie,' I said, 'there's not many would have the guts to talk to you like this.'

'Yes, Ralph?'

'You're dying and you know it,' I said, 'and I want you to die proper – properly.' She looked stupid.

'I've lived with you a long time,' I said, 'ever since before Uncle died, and I've talked to you seriously so long as I've been able to reason.'

And that's true. Even when I was at school I used to read her the best bits out of the weekly *Freethinker* I bought, while she cooked the Sunday dinner. To show her how to reason too.

People say they're too old to learn. That's humbug. It makes me mad.

'You never tried, Auntie,' I said. Like I was scolding her.

She just blinked her watery eyes and her lips didn't say anything.

'You never even took to simple free thought like Mr. Bradlaugh[1] had, Auntie,' I said. I always call him 'Mr.' to show I respect his writings.

'You're a good boy, Ralph,' she whispered. For a second I felt a bit silly. Like she wanted to kiss me. She said, 'I'm sorry.'

'Now look here,' I said, 'I've read stories about tough men being soft about their dear old mothers, sentimental. Well, I'll tell you what I think about them; I think those stories are loathsome, nonsensical, daft trash.' I felt strongly. 'And I'm not tough a bit. And I never had any mother to speak of, and you're only my Auntie, see?'

She whispered so I had to say 'What?' and bend my head low to hear. 'I remember... the day you got your first wages. You gave me every bit.' Water ran out of her eye.

'Yes,' I said, 'I've always tried to pay my way. Sponging is economically unsound, elementary principle.'

I gave her a sip of water because her face was getting bluer.

'Now listen, Auntie,' I said. 'You've got to stop being a coward. That's all it is, you know.'

I leaned over a bit to look her in the eyes. 'All this about angels and harps and goddalmighty with his fishmonger's scales! Why, it's so silly it makes me want to laugh!' And I laughed to show what I meant.

'When you die, you just stop, that's all. Pop goes the weasel. Nothing any more, see? Like a good sound sleep with no dreams. Anybody can see that, only dopey preachers. "Salvation, my brethren"!'

She was whispering again.

'You're not a very big man, Ralph. Not very strong. But I fed you the best I could, always.'

'Aren't you listening, Auntie?' I said. 'Never mind that! You've got to listen! Don't you see how it is – dishonest, stupid, cowardly – whatever you like to call it?'

'What, Ralph?'

'You're not going to die full of old nonsense, that's what, Auntie!' I said. 'Going to Heaven and all that mumbo. Like an old savage. It isn't brave.

'That's it, not brave! Don't you see how much finer it is to face up to just nothing? Than to die praying and grovelling to something that isn't there anyway?' The bed was squeaking like anything.

I could hear the breath coming in and out of her mouth. I thought she was thinking.

She looked at me and I was sad inside. I held my mouth sideways to cover it up.

Then she said, only about half of a whisper:

'Ralph. Get married, Ralph. Some nice girl, nice girl. That'll look after you.' And she sort of moved her head, supposed to be a nod.

I was mad. 'Look here, Auntie,' I said, 'you're not listening. I don't want to get married. I've got no time for girls and softness, you know that. I'm rational!'

Her eyebrows and her upper lip were moving funny.

'I'm not asking you to "believe". I don't hold with any belief stuff,' I said. 'I want you just to *know* and to die decent

– decently. You don't realise. You've got no self-respect.'

Just for a minute, I sort of wished it was me that was dying so that I could show her how. I honestly did.

I was trying to think of something that would make her see when all of a sudden she moved.

Sudden it was too.

She sat right up in bed and put her arms round me tight. I never knew her so strong.

'Rallie!' she shouted. Her voice was as big as when she used to shout across the street to Mrs. Pettifer for the lend of half a loaf.

'Oh, poor little Rallie!'

That was what they called me when I was just about a baby. I didn't like it.

'Now, look here – "Ralph" my name is,' I said. 'Why, you must be getting better –'

While I was talking, there was a sort of noise. Her hands slipped down. And all of a sudden she was heavy.

My Auntie was dead.

I was looking in her face. I'd never seen anybody die before. Only one or two that were dead already.

I saw her eyes go out. Queer. Then she flopped back across the pillow.

That was all.

After a moment I shook her hand, but it felt so horrible that I stopped. 'Auntie,' I said. 'Auntie!' Which wasn't reasonable, because I knew it was no good talking to her, and it made me angry with myself.

A bit of dust settled on one of her eyes.

She wouldn't ever look with them again, and open her mouth and say something soppy and loving.

But I must have sat there on the side of the bed a whole long time, feeling funny. Not even trying to reason it out. At last I found it had gone dark and I was feeling chilly. When I tried to move my Auntie's hand then, it was like cold white china.

Things were muddled after that. People came and fussed about, tidying up my Auntie. I didn't bother much. Silly conventions!

When I'd got her buried, it became difficult. I expect it was because there was nobody to reason with. You see, I've got to have something to work on, being an active person. Just cooking my own meals and sitting listening to the water gurgling in the pipes got me all grey inside.

Places where my Auntie used to be, I found myself watching as if I might see her again; even though I knew perfectly well she was dead. Her old chair with the seat squashed to fit her behind. And the worn-away kitchen knife she was fond of. One night I felt so miserable that I burnt – well, never mind. Besides, I bought a new copy anyway. Of Mr. Bradlaugh.

Then one day I thought how to do it. One day when I was reasoning with myself pretty efficiently.

You see, this is the weakness about people like my Auntie: they've got one-track minds. Wouldn't say a sensible, rational word right up to the last, now would she?

But listen.

I'm not like that. I'm broadminded. As I told myself, a man should be able to see other people's points of view.

I'm putting by money from my gardening job. And some day I'll be drawing out every penny we had in the savings bank, her and me; and going down the road to the stone-mason's.

She's going to have a sepulchre – if that's how they spell it – made of pure white marble. The biggest I can get. With Bible words, and a stone angel on top. Holy, holy, holy. It's only the cough I get bothered with that slows up the fund-collecting.

I bet it's just what she'd have wanted. Silly cow!

Note

1. Charles Bradlaugh (1833–1891) was an English political activist, MP, atheist and founder of the National Secular Society. His writings include 'A Plea for Atheism' (1864), *Half-Hours with the Freethinkers* (1857) and *The Freethinker's Text-Book* (1876).

The Calculation of N'Bambwe

'THAT WAS MOST INTERESTING,' said Mrs. Berrilee. 'Next week we shall read from the works of Mr. W. B. Yeats.'

'"I will arise and go now —"'quoted Miss Tandy.

'My dear!' they pleaded, 'not yet! We have not even had tea. Please stay, do!'

Miss Tandy explained, disgusted, and added, 'I should not wish to offend anyone, but there is a large thumb-mark on page twenty-two of my Golden Treasury.' They looked at Mrs. Churchman, who had been the only one to read a passage from so near the beginning. She blushed at the fire.

'I wash my hands after every meal,' said Miss Tandy.

Mrs. Berrilee shattered the embarrassment. 'I am the dirtiest creature God made,' she said cheerfully. 'And now I shall brew the tea and cut the cake.' She rose and straightened her dress.

Miss Morgan fingered the brooch at her throat. 'It really has been most enjoyable,' she said stiffly. 'I do hope we shall be able to meet often — if Mrs. Berrilee will suffer us. She is so very good.'

'Very kind! Most generous! Poor Mrs. Berrilee!' they cried. Their hostess beamed.

'I should like us to have "The Hound of Heaven" another time,' said Miss Tandy. 'It is a poem,' she explained to Mrs. Churchman.

A cold draught blew into the room as Mrs. Berrilee opened the door and went out.

'It is rather an odd one,' said Miss Morgan, 'and somewhat morbid as it were. But, as you say, Miss Tandy, it is of a superior kind and written by a great man: quite suitable for our attention.'

'I do not like ugly things,' murmured Mrs. Churchman stubbornly.

'This is not ugly at all,' said Miss Tandy.

Miss Morgan's lips were doubtful. 'They say that even ugliness may have a kind of beauty.'

'Mrs. Churchman may not – appreciate that as well as you do, my dear,' said Miss Tandy gently.

The resulting thoughtful silence continued until the lady of the house returned with the tea trolley.

'Now you must stop your intellectual conversation!' Mrs. Berrilee clattered cups into saucers. 'I have made some tea: I always make it either too strong or too weak.'

'That will be nice,' said Mrs. Churchman sincerely. 'Though we have no right to put you to such trouble.'

'"The cups that cheer but not inebriate..."' quoted Miss Tandy.

'So nice,' smiled Mrs. Churchman, waiting for a cup.

Miss Morgan adjusted her spectacles. 'We had been talking, Mrs. Berrilee, about unpleasant poetry.'

The hostess handed out the thinly steaming cups.

Miss Tandy spooned a fragment of stem from the surface of hers. 'Do you believe that gloom is incompatible with beauty, Mrs. Berrilee?'

'I simply dote on ghost stories, Miss Tandy, and I am quite hideous, so I suppose it may be. I like to go to sleep quaking with fright, so I read them whenever I can.'

Miss Tandy's eyes glistened with pity.

'I don't like ugly things,' said Mrs. Churchman politely, 'very much.'

'And that reminds me,' said Mrs. Berrilee. 'I have such a funny little story I must tell you.'

'Please do!' Miss Tandy licked crumbs from her mouth.

'My husband, you know, has a brother in Africa. Nairobi or Johannesburg or Freetown – some name I can't remember, and he's always moving about, anyway, with his work.

'Gerald – that's his name – writes such amusing letters to my husband. He tells about the things he sees and the people in such a funny way: what they say and do and their huts and wigwams and things. They must be a scream and their sense of humour is often terribly – broad.'

'Oh!' said Miss Morgan.

'I must read you some next time if I can find them. I simply howl at them.

'And yesterday – or was it the day before? – we had another, but my husband's got it, I think. There was a very odd story in it. Will you have some more tea, Mrs. Churchman?

'It seems Gerald met a witch-doctor. I think that would be most interesting, don't you?'

Miss Morgan nodded and Mrs. Churchman's eyes widened.

'He told us his name too. Mm – no, Nnn – bam – bambwe, or some such native expression. A very clever man, Gerald thought he was. He had been worrying at quite elaborate things – deductions and calculations – for years and years in his own way with only his own gadgets and methods. Gerald is an engineer and he thought they were quite ingenious.'

'A sort of black Einstein,' smiled Miss Tandy.

Mrs. Berrilee poised her cake. 'And do you know the latest thing he had worked out?'

There was only the bubbling sip of Mrs. Churchman's tea for answer.

'That time was going to stop!'

'Poor old thing!' said Miss Tandy.

'Fancy!' said Mrs. Churchman.

'I suppose the idea is quite advanced really,' said Miss Morgan, holding her brooch.

'For a coloured man,' Mrs. Churchman added.

Miss Tandy drained the last of her tea. 'Your brother-in-law should have given him some books to read. The Dunne theory, for example.'

'And a Bible,' said Mrs. Churchman.

'There is a currant in this piece of seed-cake,' Mrs. Berrilee announced. 'For a moment I thought it was a fly. I never know what I am doing when I bake – No, Gerald said the old man was quite sure about it. He talked to Gerald for a long time and told him exactly what – when it was going to happen.'

'When?' Mrs. Churchman's mouth stayed open.

'After the equinox, whenever that is. Seven days – or seventeen – it was one or the other, I am quite sure – after the equinox.'

Miss Tandy smiled and took an envelope and pencil from her handbag.

'You see,' said Mrs. Berrilee, 'it was something to do with the position of the planets.'

'He must have known the earth is round,' said Mrs. Churchman slowly.

Mrs. Berrilee placed her cup on the trolley. 'Gerald said he expected it to happen quite suddenly – the old man did, I mean. Just a few – vibrations, the way a ball bounces up and down when you drop it, and then stops. But he thought it would only vibrate one way – Gerald said – only forwards, because that's the way time is. If you can see what he meant. I can't.'

'It doesn't sound a bit convincing,' said Miss Morgan. 'Just that part of it alone. Action and reaction, you know.'

Miss Tandy lowered her pencil. 'As a matter of interest,' she announced, 'seven days from the equinox was a week last Sunday. So that, I think, is that.'

'Mrs. Berrilee did say it might have been seventeen days,' Miss Morgan reminded.

'Yes,' said Mrs. Berrilee. 'If I had the letter, I'd know.'

'Seventeen days, then.' The pencil jotted again. 'That would be – yesterday. No, today!'

'How funny!' cried Mrs. Berrilee. 'Well, it hasn't happened yet.'

'I don't like that sort of thing.' Mrs. Churchman blinked at the fire.

'He was probably trying to stir up trouble,' said Miss Tandy. 'Using it to frighten other natives and dancing round in necklaces of bones the rest of the time – that's what they do. And they could be so well occupied with irrigation or something.'

Miss Morgan handed her cup across. 'Anyway, Mrs. Bernice, it was quite interesting and quaint.'

The hostess smiled. 'Could anyone drink some more of this awful tea? Nobody?'

'No, thank you,' said Miss Tandy. 'But I admire your silver teapot very much. The ornament is beautiful.'

'It was a wedding present. I wonder the thing has survived,' said Mrs. Berrilee, 'the way I treat them.'

'Let's talk about something nice now,' suggested Mrs. Churchman, with eyes on the glowing coal.

'To round off the meeting.' Miss Morgan fingered the back of her head.

'I have something very special that I was keeping as a surprise,' said Mrs. Berrilee. She opened a cupboard and took out a small box. 'Chocolates! You can have one each for being good.'

'How delicious!' said Miss Morgan.

'Thank you very much,' said Mrs. Churchman.

'These are quite a subject for discussion,' said Miss Tandy.

Mrs. Berrilee beamed and bit into a large flat one. 'I could eat them like a pig.'

They smiled politely as she put away the half-empty box. 'Till next week.'

Their mouths moved together. Chewing.

'Let's talk about something nice now,' suggested Mrs. Churchman with eyes on the glowing coal.

'To round off the meeting.' Miss Morgan fingered the back of her head.

'I have something very special that I was keeping as a surprise,' said Mrs. Berrilee.

She opened a cupboard and took out a small box. 'Chocolates! You can have one each for being good.'

'How delicious!' said Miss Morgan.

'Thank you very much,' said Mrs. Churchman. 'These are quite a subject for discussion,' said Miss Tandy.

Mrs. Berrilee beamed and bit into a large flat one. 'I could eat them like a pig.'

They smiled politely as she put away the half-empty box. 'Till next week.'

Their mouths moved together. Chewing.

'How delicious!' said Miss Morgan.

'Thank you very much,' said Mrs. Churchman.

'These are quite a subject for discussion,' said Miss Tandy.

Mrs. Berrilee beamed and bit into a large flat one. 'I could eat them like a pig.'

They smiled politely as she put away the half-empty box. 'Till next week'

Their mouths moved together. Chewing.

They smiled politely as she put away the half-empty box.
'Till next week.'

Their mouths moved together. Chewing.

Chewing.

Chewing.

Nature Study

'THIS AFTERNOON,' MISS BUNNARY announced, 'we shall all go out to gather leaves.'

She looked round the class and her lip slid up from her two crossed teeth in the front: that showed she was preparing to be angry.

'Has everyone brought a paper bag to put them in?'

There was no movement.

She stood with her eyes on Albert Johnson in the third row. 'Albert!' said Miss Bunnary loudly. He rose: clothing quite good but untidy. 'Show me your paper bag!'

He reddened and after a moment began to fumble in his pockets.

'It's no use pretending!' cried Miss Bunnary. 'I overheard you say that you weren't going to bring one for "her"! I suppose you meant your teacher!'

She strode up the aisle and pushed him from his place with a hand behind his head. Her thin fingers rasped in his hair.

'You are six whole years old and you do nothing you are told! Turn round and face the class! What do you expect to be when you are sixteen? Or sixty?'

She took his right hand in hers, turned it over and smacked the knuckles three times with a flat ruler. 'The next time you refuse to do as I say, you shall go straight to the headmaster!'

Albert Johnson licked his hand. The others sat still. The headmaster was terrible.

'The oldest boy in the class and you set such a terrible example! Go to your place! If anyone behaves like that again,' said Miss Bunnary in a cold, quiet voice, 'we shall not have any more outings. And we shall keep no tadpoles in a bowl next spring, as all my other classes have done!'

She went slowly back to her desk and moved the globe to its place in the exact centre. There was a snivel somewhere.

'Imogen!' She glared across the room. 'Stop crying like a baby!'

The snivel ceased.

'Now,' said Miss Bunnary with a note of pleasure, 'that everything is quiet at last, we can go. But Albert has kept us in by the way he behaved. Probably we have missed the best of the day, and I certainly doubt whether we shall have time to find the prettiest leaves. I trust Albert is satisfied.'

Guided by Miss Bunnary, they rose, turned right and marched out through the dark cloakroom, where they collected coats and hats.

'Keep in to the side!' she called. 'Stop talking! Halt! Now be quiet and still while I get my coat!'

Presently they were moving off through the gate, down the hill towards the last houses; a double column of small figures.

'Look sharp, everybody!' said Miss Bunnary. 'Heads up and eyes wide open! Autumn is one of the most beautiful times of the year, you know, and you must watch for interesting things! Albert, do I see hands in pockets?'

When they reached the place where trees darkened the

road, she called a halt. 'You may gather round now, and together we shall search for leaves,' said Miss Bunnary. 'Doreen, leave your nose alone!'

A little farther along they came to a stile. 'This will take us into the wood. The only leaves on the road seem to be dirty and trodden, so we shall go over one by one. Be careful with the planks: they are not our property.'

The line struggled over the wooden bar and squelched into the soft mould beyond.

'Come, come, keep together now! Eyes this way, Bernard! Those are only sheep: surely you have seen sheep before?'

Miss Bunnary stopped and cleared her throat. 'Before we go any farther, I have something to say. I must find nobody picking up horse-chestnuts! I believe that some silly children, particularly the big boys, collect them to play with in the school yard, very roughly. You must all remember that this is lesson time, and it is not to be wasted. We are here to learn!'

Miss Bunnary turned to lead her class upwards and deeper into the wood.

At the top of the rise she paused, panting slightly, and waited for them to catch up. Her heart was pounding. She rooted with her fingers in the crisp, brown vegetation at her feet: they grazed something hard. 'What I said about horse-chestnuts also applies to fir-cones!' she called. 'Now, we shall scatter and try to find as many interesting leaves as we can. Do not pick up dirty or torn ones: only those that are brightly coloured. Put them in your bags, and I shall come round and see what you have.

'Start – now!'

The children deployed through the wood, eyes to the earth. Pale October sunlight filtered down through the branches on to their heads.

'Now, Freda, let me see what you have found!' A small hand submitted a specimen for her approval. 'That is an oak leaf.' Miss Bunnary frowned upwards. 'If you look at the trees,' she said clearly, 'you will see that most of them are oaks and birches. But there are also beeches, elms and firs. The oak leaves are a red-brown colour.' She handed the leaf back. 'You may put that in your bag, Freda.'

Deeper in the wood, birds were singing. A haze hung over the darkening undergrowth like rising dust. Everywhere was the sweet decay smell.

'Look, all of you! Pauline has discovered a leaf of the hornbeam tree!' Miss Bunnary waved a red flake high in the air. 'You can tell hornbeam leaves because they are hairy underneath!'

A momentary breeze stirred through the wood, and at once tiny winged things were fluttering downwards in swaying, undulating clouds.

'Flying angels!'

'That is what ignorant people call them,' Miss Bunnery corrected. 'They are sycamore seeds, and they have just been broken off the trees by the wind.'

She stooped, and rose again. 'Now in my hand are some beech leaves, which are the most interesting red and orange: your new reading books tell about them. No, no, you must find some for yourselves! Go along!' She passed from one to another, examining the collections, discarding the ill-looking discoveries and reproving the finders.

'Only clean ones, I said. It does not matter if that leaf is unusual: it is very wet and grimy! We are not here to make ourselves unpresentable.

'Hurry now, look sharp! I do not want to spend all afternoon in this damp place and —'

Miss Bunnary's voice faded, and she began to count her charges. '— Twenty, twenty-one, twenty-two. Stand still, all of you! Marjorie — still! Twenty-two. Turn this way and let me see your faces!'

Her lips twitched as she checked names over to herself.

'Albert Johnson. Imogen Crabtree. And – who is it? – Geoffrey. Where are those three?'

There was a terrible silence. A leaf fluttered down towards her. A beech leaf.

Miss Bunnary rustled back along what must have been the path. 'Albert! Albert!' Her cry rang among the bare trunks.

There was no reply. She turned again to the silently standing infants. 'Go on looking for leaves, all of you!'

She came to where the ground was cut away in a steep bank, thickly overgrown with dying bracken, and called, 'Are you there, Albert?' Tucking in her skirt, she clambered awkwardly down the bank, clutching at exposed roots for support when her heels slipped. She landed at the bottom in a flurry of dead plants.

'He's running away!' said a voice.

Miss Bunnary peered over a dense bramble bush. The missing children were crouching there as if watching something. A few feet beyond them, what looked like a ball of dried leaves and prickles was clumsily making its way through the yellow grass.

'Gone now,' said the girl. 'That noise frightened him. What was it?'

Miss Bunnary advanced through the undergrowth. She felt a briar ladder her stocking.

'So this is where you are! Hiding in dirty bushes! What do you think you are up to?'

Albert's face was guilty. 'We found a hedgehog,' he said. 'He was fast asleep.'

'A real live one!' Imogen said. She was clearly excited. 'He twitched his nose and then he woke up!' The third child said nothing: he stared at the ground.

Miss Bunnary sniffed and her crossed teeth showed. 'Go up there!' she ordered, 'and go quickly!'

'There is an easy way round,' Albert said.

Miss Bunnary clamped her mouth and reached for a root. 'Don't answer me back! Now, straight up!' she demanded.

Little showers of earth and stones fell while they climbed. Imogen's knee bled and she sniffed as they crawled over the edge. The rest of the class stood watching, bags in hand.

'Go forward!' gasped Miss Bunnary. They ploughed knee-deep through the leaves. 'Stand there!' 'Now!' she cried. 'Attend to me, everyone! Here are three wicked children! Quite deliberately, they left us to go wilfully walking on their own! And they have just caused their teacher great discomfort and effort to find them. They would not answer her calls!

'And do you know why they would not answer?' Her eyes flickered from face to face. 'Do you know?'

'Because they were watching an animal sleeping under a bush! A dirty hedgehog!' She was quivering with rage.

'All of you know how bad Albert Johnson was this afternoon. Now he shall certainly go to the headmaster; and I shall deal with the other two myself when we return! Time-wasters! Our outing has been totally spoiled!'

The watchers shuffled their feet. Some had screwed up the mouths of their paper bags, ready to leave.

Suddenly everyone was looking at Miss Bunnary.

There was a little moan from her, and the crossed teeth showed; but this time it was not in anger, and her eyes were shut. Stiffly her arm went round a lichenous trunk; tiny beads appeared on her pale forehead; her lips were blue; her knees bent. They watched her slide limply down beside the tree, and the grey hair rest against it.

'My heart!' whispered Miss Bunnary.

Nobody moved.

Her head turned weakly; the bone of her nose showed white through the stretched skin. 'Albert,' said a voice so tiny that it did not seem to belong to her, 'I want to speak to you.

Albert – dear. Please come here.'

A long silence was broken by rustling, and she closed her eyes more tightly as she waited for him to come and take her message.

But the noise became louder and louder, as of many feet; then gradually it died away. When she opened her eyes she could not see a single child.

The pressure in her chest was terrible. 'Albert!' she whimpered.

Far down the glade a voice shouted loudly: 'That's not a beech tree, naughty boy! Smack, smack, smack!' There was a burst of laughter.

A breeze stirred again through the trees that the sun had left. As she pressed her face into a patch of moss, she felt that the pain was easing.

Shadows flickered across the patches of sky: knobbed shadows that turned over and over as they fell.

'Oak leaves,' murmured Miss Bunnary.

The Patter of Tiny Feet

'HOLD ON A MOMENT. Don't knock,' Joe Banner said. 'Let me get a shot of the outside before the light goes.'

So I waited while he backed into the road with his Leica. No traffic, nobody about but an old man walking a dog in the distance. Joe stuck his cigarette behind one ear and prowled quickly to find the best angle on Number 47. It was what the address had suggested: a narrow suburban villa on a forgotten road, an old maid of a house with a skirt of garden drawn round it, keeping itself to itself among all its sad neighbours. The flower beds were full of dead stems and grass.

Joe's camera clicked twice. 'House of Usher's in the bag,' he said, and resumed the cigarette. 'Think the garden has any possibilities?'

'Come on! We can waste time later.'

Weather had bleached the green front door. There was a big iron knocker and I used it.

'It echoed hollowly through the empty house!' said Banner. He enjoys talking like that, though it bores everybody. In addition, he acts in character – aping the sort of small-town photographer who wears his hat on the back of his head and stinks out the local Rotarians with damp flash-powder – but he's one of the finest in the profession.

We heard rapid footsteps inside, the lock clicked and the door swung open, all in a hurry. And there appeared – yes, remembering those comic letters to the office, it could only be – our man.

'Mr. Hutchinson?'

'At your service, gentlemen!' He shot a look over Joe's camera and the suitcase full of equipment, and seemed pleased. A small pudding-face and a long nose that didn't match it, trimmed with a narrow line of moustache. He had the style of a shopwalker, I thought. 'Come inside, please. Can I lend you a hand with that? No? That's it – right along inside!'

It sounded as if the word 'sir' was trembling to join each phrase.

We went into the front room, where a fire was burning. The furniture was a familiar mixture: flimsy modern veneer jostling old pieces built like Noah's Ark and handed down, from in-laws. Gilt plaster dancers posed on the sideboard and the rug was worn through.

'My name is Staines,' I said, 'and this is Joe Banner, who's going to handle the pictures. I believe you've had a letter?'

'Yes, indeed,' said Hutchinson, shaking hands. 'Please take a seat, both of you – I know what a tiring journey it can be, all the way from London! Yes. I must say how extremely gratified I am that your paper has shown this interest!' His voice sounded distorted by years of ingratiating; it bubbled out of the front of his mouth like a comic radio character's. 'Have you... that is, I understand you have special experience in this field, Mr. Staines?' He seemed almost worried about it.

'Not exactly a trained investigator,' I admitted, 'but I've knocked out a few articles on the subject.'

'Oh... yes, indeed. I've read them with great interest.' He hadn't, of course, but he made it sound very respectful.

He asked if we had eaten, and when we reassured him he produced drinks from grandmother's sideboard. Banner settled down to his performance of the 'Hicks-in-the-Sticks Journal' photographer out on a blind.

'You – you seem to have brought a lot of equipment,' Hutchinson said quickly. 'I hope I made it clear there's no guarantee of anything... visible.'

'Guarantee? Why, then you *have* seen something?'

He sat forward on his chair, but immediately seemed to restrain himself and an artfully stiff smile appeared. 'Mr. Staines, let's understand each other: I am most anxious not to give you preconceived ideas. This is your investigation, not mine.' He administered this like a police caution, invitingly.

Joe put down his empty glass. 'We're not easily corrupted, Mr. Hutchinson.'

To scotch the mock-modesty, I said: 'We've read your letters and the local press-clipping. So what about the whole story, in your own way?' I took out my notebook, to encourage him.

Hutchinson blinked nervously and rose. He snapped the two standard lamps on, went to the window with hands clasped behind him. The sky was darkening. He drew the curtains and came back as if he had taken deep thought. His sigh was full of responsibility.

'I'm trying to take an impersonal view. This case is so unusual that I feel it must be examined... *pro bono publico*, as it were...' He gave a tight little laugh, all part of the act. 'I don't want you to get the idea I'm a seeker after publicity.'

This was too much. 'No, no,' I said, 'you don't have to explain yourself: we're interested. Facts, Mr. Hutchinson, please. Just facts.'

'For instance, what time do the noises start?' said Joe.

Hutchinson relaxed, too obviously gratified for the purity of his motives. He glanced at his watch brightly.

'Oh, it varies, Mr. Banner. After dark – any time at all after dark.' He frowned like an honest witness. 'I'm trying to think of any instance during daylight, but no. Sometimes it comes early, oftener near midnight, occasionally towards dawn: no rule about it, absolutely none. It can continue all night through.'

I caught him watching my pencil as I stopped writing; his eyes came upon me and Joe, alert as a confident examination-candidate's.

'Footsteps?'

Again, the arch smile. 'Mr. Staines, that's for you to judge. To me, it sounds like footsteps.'

'The witness knows the rules of evidence, boy!' Joe said, and winked at us both. Hutchinson took his glass.

'Fill it up for you, Mr. Banner? I'm far from an ideal observer, I fear; bar Sundays, I'm out every evening.'

'Business?'

'Yes, I'm assistant headwaiter in a restaurant. Tonight I was able to be excused.' He handed us refilled glasses. 'A strange feeling, you know, to come into the house late at night, and hear those sounds going on inside, in the dark.'

'Scare you?' Joe asked.

'Not now. Surprising, isn't it? But it seems one can get used to anything.'

I asked: 'Just what do you hear?'

Hutchinson considered, watching my pencil. He's got the answer all ready, I thought. 'A curious pattering, very erratic and light. A sort of... playing, if that conveys anything. Upstairs there's a small passage between the bedrooms, covered with linoleum: I'll show you presently. Well, it mostly occurs there, but it can travel down the stairs into the hallway below.'

'Ever hear –?' Joe began.

Hutchinson went on: 'It lasts between thirty and forty seconds. I've timed it. And in a single night I've known the whole thing to be repeated up to a dozen times.'

'– a rat in the ceiling, Mr. Hutchinson?' Joe finished. 'They can make a hell of a row.'

'Yes, I've heard rats. This is not one.'

I frowned at Joe: this was routine stuff. 'Mr. Hutchinson, we'll agree on that. Look, in your last letter you said you had a theory – of profound significance.'

'Yes.'

'Why don't we get on to that, then?'

He whipped round instantly, full of it. 'My idea is – well, it's a terribly unusual form of – the case – the case of a projection – how can I put it? It's more than a theory, Mr. Staines!' He had all the stops out at once. His hands trembled.

'Hold it!' Joe called, and reached for his Leica. 'I'll be making an odd shot now and then, Mr. Hutchinson. Show you telling the story, see?'

Hutchinson's fingers went to his tie.

'You were saying –?' I turned over a leaf of the notebook.

'Well, I can vouch for this house, you know. I've lived here for many years, and it came to me from my mother. There's absolutely no... history attached to it.'

I could believe that.

'Until about six years ago I lived alone – a woman came in to clean twice a week. And then... I married.' He said this impressively, watching to see that I noted it.

'A strange person, my wife. She was only nineteen when we married, and very... unworldly.' He drew a self-conscious breath. 'Distant cousin of mine actually, very religious people. That's her photograph on the mantelpiece.'

I took it down.

I had noticed it when first we entered the room; vignetted in its chromium-plated frame, too striking to be his daughter. It was a face of character, expressive beyond mere beauty: an attractive full-lipped mouth, eyes of exceptional vividness.

Surprisingly, her hair was shapeless and her dress dull. I passed the portrait to Joe, who whistled.

'Mr. Hutchinson! Where are you hiding the lady? Come on, let's get a picture of –'

Then he also guessed. This was not a house with a woman in it.

'She passed away seven months ago,' said Hutchinson, and held out his hand for the frame.

'I'm sorry,' I said. Banner nodded and muttered something.

Hutchinson was expressionless. 'Yes,' he said, 'I'm sorry too.' Which was an odd thing to say, as there was evidently no sarcasm in it. I wondered why she would have married him. There must have been twenty-five years between them, and a world of temperament.

'She was extremely... passionate,' Hutchinson said.

He spoke as if he were revealing something indecent. His voice was hushed, and his little moustache bristled over pursed lips. When his eyes dropped to the photograph in his hand, his face was quite blank.

Suddenly he said in an odd, curt way: 'She was surprisingly faithful to me. I mean, she was never anything else. Very religious, strictest ideas of her duty.' The flicker of a smile. 'Unworldly, as I said.'

I tried to be discreet. 'Then you were happy together?'

His fingers were unconsciously worrying at the picture frame, fidgeting with the strut.

'To be honest, we weren't. She wanted children.'

Neither Banner nor I moved.

'I told her I couldn't agree. I had to tell her often, because she worked herself up, and it all became ugly. She used to lose control and say things she didn't mean, and afterwards she was sorry, but you can't play fast and loose with people's finer feelings! I did my best. I'd forgive her and say: 'I only want you, my dear. You're all I need in the world,' to comfort her, you see. And she'd sob loudly and... she was unnecessarily emotional.'

His voice was thin, and tight. He rose and replaced the photograph on the mantelpiece. There was a long silence.

Joe fiddled with his camera. 'No children, then?' Cruel, that.

Hutchinson turned, and we saw that somehow he had managed to relax. The accommodating smirk was back.

'No, none. I had definite views on the subject. All quite rational. Wide disparity in the prospective parents' ages, for instance – psychologically dangerous for all parties: I don't know if you've studied the subject? There were other considerations, too – financial, medical: do you wish me to go into those? I have nothing to hide.'

It was blatant exhibitionism now: as if he were proffering a bill on a plate, with himself itemised in it.

'There's a limit even to journalists' curiosity,' I said.

Hutchinson was ahead of me, solemnly explaining. 'Now! This is my theory! You've heard of poltergeist phenomena, of course? Unexplainable knockings, scratchings, minor damage and so on. I've studied them in books – and they're always connected with development, violent emotional development, in young people. A sort of uncontrolled offshoot of the... personality. D'you follow?'

'Wait a minute,' Joe said. 'That's taking a lot for granted if you like!'

But I remembered reading such cases. One, investigated by psychical researchers, had involved a fifteen-year-old boy: ornaments had been thrown about by no visible agency. I took a glance at the unchipped gilt dancers on the sideboard before Hutchinson spoke again.

'No, my wife may not have been adolescent, but in some ways... she was... so to speak, retarded.'

He looked as pleased as if he had just been heavily tipped. If that was pure intellectual triumph, it was not good to see.

'Then... the sounds began,' Joe said, 'while she was still alive?'

Hutchinson shook his head emphatically.

'Not till three weeks after the funeral! That's the intriguing part, don't you see? They were faint and unidentifiable at first – naturally, I just put down traps for rats or mice. But by another month, they were taking on the present form.'

Joe gave a back-street sniff and rubbed a hand over his chin. 'Hell, you ask us to believe your poltergeist lies low until nearly a month after the – the –'

'After the medium, shall we say, is dead!' His cold-bloodedness was fascinating.

Joe looked across at me and raised his eyebrows.

'Gentlemen, perhaps I'm asking you to accept too much? Well, we shall see. Please remember that I am only too happy that you should form your own – your own –' Hutchinson's voice dropped to a whisper. He raised his hand. His eyes caught ours as he listened.

My spine chilled.

Somewhere above us in the house were faint sounds. A scuffling.

'That's it!'

I tiptoed to the door and got it open in time to hear a last scamper overhead. Yes, it could have been a kitten, I thought; but it had come so promptly on cue. I was on the stairs when Hutchinson called out, as if he were the thing's manager: 'No more for the present! You'll probably get another manifestation in forty minutes or so.'

Cue for the next performance, I thought.

I searched the staircase with my torch. At the top ran the little passage Hutchinson had described; open on one side, with bannisters, and on the other, a dark papered wall. The linoleum was bare. There was nothing to be seen, nor any open doors. The very dinginess of this narrow place was eerie.

Downstairs I found Joe feverishly unpacking his apparatus. Hutchinson was watching, delighted.

'Anything I can possibly do, Mr. Banner? Threads across the passage – oh, yes? How very ingenious! You've your own drawing-pins? – excellent! Can I carry that lamp for you?'

And he led the way upstairs.

We searched the shabby bedrooms first. Only one was in use, and we locked all of them and sealed the doors.

In half an hour, preparations were complete. Hair-thick threads were stretched across the passage at different levels; adhesive squares lay in patterns on the linoleum. Joe had four high-powered lamps ready to flood the place at the pressure of a silent contact. I took the Leica; he himself now carried an automatic miniature camera.

'Four shots a second with this toy,' he was telling Hutchinson, while I went to check a window outside the bathroom. I still favoured the idea of a cat: they so often make a habitual playground of other people's houses.

The window was secure. I was just sticking an additional seal across the join when I sniffed scent; for a moment I took it to be from soap in the bathroom. Sickly, warm, strangely familiar. Then it came almost overpoweringly.

I returned as quickly and quietly as I could to the stairhead.

'Smell it?' Joe breathed in the darkness.

'Yes, what d'you suppose –?'

'Ssh!'

There was a sound not four yards away, as I judged it: a tap on the linoleum. Huddled together, we all tensed. It came again, and then a scamper of feet – small and light, but unmistakable – feet in flat shoes. As if something had run across the far end of the passage. A pause – a slithering towards us – then that same shuffle we had heard earlier in the evening, clear now: it was the jigging, uneven stamp of an infant's attempt to dance! In that heavy, sweet darkness, the recognition of it came horribly.

Something brushed against me: Banner's elbow.

At the very next sound, he switched on all his lamps. The narrow place was flung into dazzling brightness – it was completely empty! My head went suddenly numb inside. Joe's camera clicked and buzzed, cutting across the baby footsteps that came hesitating towards us over the floor. We kept our positions, eyes straining down at nothing but the brown faded pattern of the linoleum. Within inches of us, the footsteps changed their direction in a quick swerve and clattered away to the far corner. We waited. Every vein in my head was banging.

The silence continued. It was over.

Banner drew a thick raucous breath. He lowered the camera, but his sweaty face remained screwed up as if he were still looking through the viewfinder. 'Not a sausage!' he whispered, panting. 'Not a bloody sausage!'

The threads glistened there unbroken; none of the sticky patches was out of place.

'It *was* a kiddie,' Joe said. He has two of his own. 'Hutchinson!'

'Yes?' The flabby face was white, but he seemed less shaken than we others.

'How the hell did you –?' Banner sagged against the wall and his camera dangled, swinging slowly on its safety strap. 'No – it was moving along the floor. I could have reached out and touched – My God, I need a drink!'

We went downstairs.

Hutchinson poured out. Joe drank three whiskies straight off but he still trembled. Desperate to reassure himself, he began to play the sceptic again immediately. As if with a personal grievance, he went for Hutchinson.

'Overdid that sickly smell, you know! Good trick – oh, yes, clever – particularly when we weren't expecting it!'

The waiter was quick with his denials: it had always accompanied the sounds, but he had wanted us to find out for ourselves; this time it had been stronger than usual.

'Take it easy, Joe – no violence!' I said. He pushed my hand off his arm.

'Oh, clever! That kind of talc, gripe-watery, general baby smell! But listen to this, Mr. Bloody Hutchinson: it should be more delicate, and you only get it quite that way with very tiny babies! Now this one was able to walk, seemingly. And the dancing – that comes at a different stage again. No, you lack experience, Mr. H.! This is no baby that ever was!'

I looked at Hutchinson.

He was nodding, evidently pleased. 'My theory exactly,' he said. 'Could we call it... a poltergeisted maternal impulse?'

Joe stared. The full enormity of the idea struck him.

'Christ... Almighty!' he said, and what grip he still had on himself went. He grabbed at his handkerchief just in time before he was sick.

When he felt better, I set about collecting the gear.

Hutchinson fussed and pleaded the whole time, persuasive as any door-to-door salesman in trying to make us stay for the next incident. He even produced a chart he had made, showing the frequency of the manifestations over the past three months, and began to quote books on the subject.

'Agreed, it's all most extraordinary,' I said. 'A unique case. You'll be hearing from us.' All I wanted was to be out of that house. 'Ready, Joe?'

'Yes, I'm all right now.'

Hutchinson was everywhere, like a dog wanting to be taken for a walk. 'I do hope I've been of some service! Is there anything more I can possibly –? I suppose you can't tell me when the publication date is likely to be?'

Nauseating. 'Not my department,' I said. 'You'll hear.'

Over his shoulder I could see the girl's face in her

chromium frame. She must have had a very great deal of life in her to look like that on a square of paper.

'Mr. Hutchinson,' I said. 'Just one last question.'

He grinned. 'Certainly, certainly. As the prosecution wishes.'

'What did your wife die of?'

For the first time he seemed genuinely put out. His voice, when it came, had for the moment lost its careful placing.

'As a matter of fact,' he said, 'she threw herself under a train.' He recovered himself. 'Oh, shocking business, showed how unbalanced the poor girl must have been all along. If you like, I can show you a full press report of the inquest – I've nothing to hide – absolutely nothing –'

I reported the assignment as a washout. In any case Banner's photographs showed nothing – except one which happened to include me, in such an attitude of horror as to be recognisable only by my clothing. I burnt that.

'Our Mr. Hutchinson's going to be disappointed.'

Joe's teeth set. 'What a mind that type must have! Publicity mania and the chance of a nice touch too, he thinks. So he rigs a spook out of the dirty linen!'

'Sure he rigged it?'

Joe hesitated. 'Positive.'

'For argument's sake, suppose he didn't; suppose it's all genuine. He manages to go on living with the thing, so he can't be afraid of it... and gradually... "new emotional depths"...' The idea suddenly struck me as having a ghastly humour. 'Of course, publicity's the only way he could do it!'

'What?'

'Banner, you ought to be sympathetic! Doesn't every father want to show off his child?'

Charlie Peace and the King

OGLETHORPE IS SO SMALL that people have been known to insult it by calling it a village. It looks as if it was lost at sometime in that remote corner of the North, and dug itself in and covered itself entirely with grey stone, prepared for the worst.

I was there looking for someone who turned out to have gone away. Rain came on – as it did most nights, they said – and I went to the cinema because in Oglethorpe, though nobody would admit it, there is nothing else to do.

This cinema is not ordinary. It has a special antiquity, for it has scarcely altered since the days when it used to be the big cart and carriage shed for the richest man in town. The front, of course, is called 'Cinema House' now, on a board above the entrance, and there is a ticket office inside. But the old walls are as they have always been, and should you not feel like paying, you can stand outside and listen to the soundtrack; people do. The single show starts at seven o'clock, to give everybody proper time for tea and a clean-up after working in the pickle factory.

The film would be one I had not seen for a long time; I bought a shilling ticket and found one of the less-worn seats.

The lights were still up. People were trickling in. A middle-aged couple sat down next to me and talked busily. Children poured into the front seats, whistling and shouting. At about quarter-past seven somebody must have decided there was a quorum, and switched on the panatrope behind the screen.

To my surprise, everybody stood up. It was playing 'God Save the King.' One verse, right through.

'You a stranger?' It was the man in the next seat. 'Tha didn't reckon on 'em to play t' King at start, eh?'

'Oh,' I said, 'I know it is sometimes done.'

'Ay, but Charlie plays 'im at th' end as well. That's when he really lets hissen go. This is just warming up, like.'

His wife leaned across. 'He means Charlie Peace, as runs this place. Half telling a thing!'

I must have looked surprised again.

'Yes, I know,' she said. 'Poor lad! To call him Charlie, t'wur downright wicked of the Peaces, but they say th' owd man wanted a daughter. Hallo, here we are!'

The lights snapped out. From the projection box at the rear, a beam shot out and fastened a little shakily on the screen: one of those droning American shorts about baseball aces. A howl of disappointment went up.

Conversation broke out strongly all over the 'Cinema House.' A hand thrust into the low beam made rabbits' heads on the screen. In every row people brought out bags of hot chips and passed them, crackling, to each other.

'Tha'd be interested in owd Charlie,' said my neighbour, above the din. 'Wouldn't he, luv? He's a character, is Charlie!'

'Don't bother people, Stan!' his wife whispered.

'Nay, Mother, but he couldn't help be interested.' He turned to me again, 'Ey, tha'st no idea the trouble Charlie's had wi' t' King. (Luk at those poor fools playing at kids' rounders yonder, thinking they've a game!) It's not that Oglethorpe folk aren't loyal – ba gum, any one of 'em would be right proud to shake t' King by th' hand! But, sithee, playing 'im at th' end of pictures is different, like, and only rightly to be dodged. So everybody thought, any road, and they got cute.

'Tha shouldst have been here in yon days. Folk'd rush out at th' end of picture as if Owd Scratch hissen wur on their tail, nigh trampling over each other to get free. Many a time when a picture's had a sudden end, I've marvelled they weren't plucking corpses from th' exits. Even after weepy tales, tha'd find 'em scamperin' out wi' hankies to their eyes, and bumping into each other. Tha'd see 'em strain in their seats whenever the picture looked like coming to a finish, fretting to be off. Sound of a drum roll 'ud send 'em frantic. For it wur counted no small disgrace to be caught by t' King and made to stand still wi' hat in hand halfway to t' door.

'Now Charlie, wi' it being his place, and a lad for dignity, wur upset by such behaviour. He took to clapping t' King on within the split instant of t' other finishing. "The End" never had a chance to grow on t' screen before Charlie'd banged th' head of t' King on top, and – "tarara, ta, tara!" – full speed and as loud as machine'd bear. Just to show folk, like.

'But they wur equal to 'im. Ey, they showed such cunning to scent out th' end o' pictures, it wur hardly worth while o' film men to finish 'em. Charlie'd see 'em stealing out, and he'd grind his teeth in th' operating box wi' t' King clutched hot in his hand. Once he went up on stage, and appealed to folk to be respectful. He tried switching off th' exit lights and leaving doors shut. It made no difference, but that a lad broke his nose. (Yon's a daft game, look. Dressed up wi' paws like great munkeys!)

'Now, some of t' lads wur on for a jest wi' owd Charlie. "Hast not heard," says one, "t' King's coming up this way next month – so council say." "Ay? Happen he'll look into thy cinema, Charlie," says another, "there being nowt else much to see, bar t' pickle factory." Charlie had read of t' King travelling north, and he took this into his head very deep.

'He sought out a new picture to show, special, and then got to work wi' a wonderful "God Save," the like of what nobody'd ever seen in t' world. He made it in his back room yonder, where he has snippets of owd films. King and t' family he had o' course, and guns and palaces. Soldiers, aeroplanes, boxing matches, jungles, dancing figures, dog shows, ghosts, soccer, weddings, dam-building, Roman gladiators, volcanoes, collisions, hunger strikes, murders an' all. Nowt wur missed. And then he cleaned up the place, even chewing gum from under t' seats. Ey, he must've believed in tale!

'O' course, t' King got no farther than Manchester when he came up this way. And Charlie had a great disappointment. He felt t' King had let him down proper.

'But he isn't a lad to lie down under such a thing when he'd put in so much time and trouble, isn't Charlie! He reckoned to be as crafty as t' rest o' folk, and he thought nowt o' their silly laffing – but set to hatching out a scheme.'

'This picture's ending,' said his wife. 'Tha'd best hurry up. Dost see,' she said to me, 'there's no dogs or racing to watch here in Oglethorpe, and folk need summit more lively than t' pools.'

'Ay, well!' Stan said. 'I'm telling. Owd Charlie reckoned that folk like a gamble – hallo!'

A scratched Donald Duck burst upon the house and further talk was impossible.

The main film was given a fair hearing in spite of savage cuts, and stoppages between reels, and a sly unfocusing on the part of the projector that brought yells of 'Charlie!'

At last it was over. I was interested to see what would happen. But – nobody moved. People rose attentively in their places.

'God Save the King' rolled out for the second time that evening. It completed a verse, to the accompaniment of pictures of the Royal Family, made many, many years before. I got ready to leave.

But it was going on. To a silent, motionless audience, two more full verses rumbled slowly from the panatrope. From what flickered across the screen, this was evidently Charlie Peace's special: the one Stan had mentioned. Every human and natural activity seemed to be there, in tiny eye-twisting flashes of colour and monochrome. Finally, after what seemed about ten minutes, the thing ended with shots of flamingoes and the Mint.

Still nobody stirred. And I recognised the feeling in the audience. It was not duty, but expectation.

I was turning to ask my neighbour what the next stage in the ceremony was to be, when something bright flashed on the screen. 'F 9' it said, scratched hurriedly on a black slide. A faint cheer rose somewhere in front.

'All right? Come round to the box after, then!' a voice shouted. Through the projection-slit apparently.

'That's Charlie,' said the man next to me. Everyone was beginning to move now. 'He draws seat numbers out of a hat after t' show. Whoever's sitting in the winner gets in free next time. He'll draw twice if first turns out to be empty. As Mother here said a while back, folk like a touch of try-your-luck.'

He grinned in a sort of admiration.

'And, ba gum, it keeps 'em quiet for t' King.'

Previously Uncollected

Billy Halloran

WITH A DRUNKEN MAN'S jerky singing outside for the only noise, they nodded under the tiny cold electric bulb, ratifying the drawn cards' choice.

'Take your time about it, Billy,' said Hearne then, with his thick boots perched on the next man's chair. 'Say, within the next two days. Don't rush and do something stupid.' Peter O'Donovan made to bang his fist on the table, and changed it into a slap of his knee. 'It's the case of a traitor, surely to God? You'll not leave him two days?' Hearne fixed him with a challenging lift of his eyebrows, and in the silence that came: 'A single shot, Billy. One noise in the night is nothing. Repeat it, and you've an object of curiosity.'

He took out the German automatic revolver that had the silencer, and gave it to Billy Halloran. It was received by a gentle hand.

The gentle hand opened the gun, and Billy's soft eye ran over the row of shining deaths in the clip. He listened, and heard his voices speaking to him in his mind. 'You've started, Halloran. They know you're the only man can do what they want. They're thankful the cards fell in with it. Every man has his opportunity, his start. This is yours, Halloran. Just a month now: in a month Hearne'll be whispering to you for all the advice you can give him. That's the way Halloran!'

'Billy,' said Hearne. 'Here's spare clips. You might need them.'

In the late afternoon Billy Halloran came to the scaly house where Edward Connor lived with his wife, and passed by on the other side.

His overcoat was buttoned high and both hands were in the pockets. His hat bent the tops of his ears outwards.

At the end of the street he turned and stroked the soft hairs of his little moustache. 'Halloran,' said his guiding voices, 'get back there and find out something. Action, Halloran!'

With a great unseen cunning, he tipped his hat back and went along with his coat flapping full open, frankly.

He knocked, yawning, at the tenement house where the Connors were: with a great, cheerful ignorance he said to the woman who opened the door to him: 'Is Mr. Ned Connor living here?'

The woman nodded, wheezing, a wet cloth dripping in her other hand. 'Back from work about seven. But lately I don't see when he comes in.'

As he turned away, she asked suddenly: 'Are ye a doctor, or what?'

Billy Halloran raved inside at his sudden fright, and his fingers closed on the gun. 'Ah – insurance,' he said. 'Just business. No importance at all. I'll see him again.' He went quickly.

He walked with long, savage strides and left the street to its slow traffic and spitting gossipers. He was angry.

No more scraping and peeping for him! Prying from washer-women like a broken-down divorce detective. For the sake of offal-scraps of information. It was all in his mind from now on.

Connor was a fool. Why hadn't he guessed?

In his big pocket Billy gripped the heavy cast butt.

People were 99 per cent fools. Credit a man with wits and he soon drove it home to you. The baubles of capitalist civilisation dressed up every sow's ear like an imitation silk purse...

'Halloran, soldier,' said the voices in his head, 'don't waste your time studying them.'

He stepped into a stuffy little tobacco shop and bought cigarettes to while away the waiting.

'A plan, Halloran,' the voices said, warm and nudging. 'Come on now, a plan! With the sure simplicity of genius. A general is a general in mind when he's only a private by rank. Halloran, what's it to be?'

He stopped. A match flared under his soft hat-brim. He puffed smoke into the still dusk, and walked.

Voices in his head. 'Throughout his brilliant, puzzling career, Generalissimo Halloran has been inspired in decisive action by spiritual messages, secret, occult....' Why be cynical about it? Cynics were bleary fools!

Voices in his head. Not strictly voices. Ideas came first, flashing, gorgeous ideas. And when words came into the ideas, they were about himself. What else was a voice? The words chattered richly inside him like a tiny, dodging, excited soul, a second William Halloran that was never on the birth register. They would come on to his lips softly. Voices enough.

Like the saints and mystics of the past, with their hypersensitive reflexes and vestigial instincts, Halloran was different.

He went hunched and slow beneath an archway, where water ran down the walls.

The world had been dark for hours. He watched the place where Connor made his home, waiting, guarding the rat-hole. He had seen the man enter: a thick, clumsy, brutish figure. His lip had slid up at the unconscious air of it.

Halloran had no plan. He was waiting now for the rushing inspiration of the moment. It would come.

There was always a purpose – he was being kept for something – when his mind was blank this way. Listen to determining reason, said the fools: the lucid, instructed voice of reason, said the beetle-heads. It was their shock-absorber. The glory of the mind was in its untaught, secret parts, scanning time and space for the creature that let them. The subtler processes were all muddled up with diseases, by the cough-mixture quacks with great pretended learning. They misunderstood the spiritual nature of what they called disease – wasn't Bonaparte epileptic? Half history's geniuses of action?

His fingers flexed over the thick steel angle in his pocket.

If it came to that, there was epilepsy in the Hallorans. Talk that was hushed up with a glance. An uncle gone queer and dying in a way that shocked the women. They feared it and crossed themselves in pale, quivering ignorance and fear. He did not, being a fatalist. Like looking down a long white rickety avenue, he saw himself, the infant Billy Halloran, being cuffed – beaten – by a school-teacher 'for trying to drive himself into a fit.' The liar! The ignorant bitch! He remembered queer feelings. A churning of the brain, followed by a blankness that set him goggle-eyed on the world. Poor, pitiful, innocent kid. As if he could have helped it! What but suffer, knowing no spiritual meaning to the horrors?

The butt was warm and terrible in his hand. His jaws tightened until the teeth trembled in sore sockets.

Now the world was going to squeal!

Halloran let the Mauser sag while he lit another cigarette. He could never help admiring the tigerish control in his hands.

'Billy's all right,' Hearne had said, thick-skinned;

pompously, heavily instructive. Big man, Hearne, big man in the Organisation. Big man! Mark one Halloran, Mr. Commandant Hearne.

After tonight.

His eyes burned at the house. A tingling ran like ants all over his body. The butt was warm and terrible in his hand.

'Why not go in and accost him, Captain Halloran?' prodded the voices. 'What does he know? – not much or he wouldn't be still there! Would he take you for a dear friend still, and be led out? But fools have a kind of a cunning. Watch now...'

Smoke drifted from his cigarette-glow into the lamplight.

'Ring him up, bogus? Would he respond? An appeal for help? Maybe if you –'

He saw the light brighten in the house. The front door opened and a man came out. He hurried down the steps.

Halloran peered, narrowing his eyes so that they could miss nothing.

It was Connor! Beyond a doubt, Edward Connor. He frowned.

The man was running, clattering in uneven paces along the opposite pavement. He drew level with Halloran; passed, hatless, through a cone of light.

'Halloran, for God's sake!' cried the voices. 'He's got wind of you! Your fat washer-woman of this afternoon – she's made him suspicious. You shouldn't – but no recriminations. He's running from you!'

He started, trotting in the shadow with his hand on the German gun.

His steps grew longer and quicker.

'He's running from you, boy! Oho, like a scuttering coney! Cold, shrieking fear in his belly!'

Halloran ran more lightly, terribly.

Past a pair of lovers he went. They did not seem to notice

him. A little late car whitened his legs with its headlamps. A cat scampered ghostlike.

'Man, you're on to him!'

Chief Halloran saw the dumpy, unsteady figure more closely. He felt himself flying, freed by the darkness. Above, the lights of houses passed like windows to another world. This one belonged to fear and Commandant Halloran.

The clatter of Connor's nailed boots stopped.

He crouched also.

The man in front had halted on a corner. His shirted chest was heaving so that it showed at that distance. He put a hand to his head, hesitating. Started round the high brick corner without a look behind.

A few seconds later, General Halloran went round the same. There was a smile on his face.

The fool didn't know he was being followed!

'See him, Halloran,' said the voices. 'No real idea where you are at all! Would you believe it? – but you saw then! Running from the fear of you!'

He suddenly and fiercely wanted to shout: 'Hi, there!' and watch Connor twitch round. Go up a bit closer – and a bit closer – suddenly pull off his hat. And shout: 'Go on – run now! It's me here!'

Halloran found his breath broken by something like laughter.

Funny! The funny mouse-fool! Funny he never looked behind. Halloran suddenly remembered a Punch and Judy show when he was little. While Punch bragged squeakily over the edge of the stall, a black varnished crocodile came up, clicking its wooden jaws. And all the children screamed: 'Look behind you! Look behind you!'

'Look-behind-you!' His mouth opened to pant.

The next street they came into was deserted. It was dark and made of high, windowless walls.

Halloran raced. Still the fugitive seemed to hear nothing. Holy Judas, the man might be stone deaf! Mere little yards between them.

A great nervous trembling took him, to say that the time was now. He bared the Mauser to the moving air.

He was fantastically close, out in the road.

The gun rose towards the trampling, blacker shadow on the wall. Its outline was clear enough. 'Look – look here –' He could say nothing more.

His finger squeezed.

Pointed flame lit up the street, and a white face. The explosion was loud, frightening. But they said it was no more than the whacking of a pillow, or a burst paper bag.

He peered, dazzled.

There was a red–black burning silence.

Then a noise that was something like a cough. A heavy, scraping slither that rang the pavement.

Connor the traitor was down!

Generalissimo Halloran looked to both blue ends of the street. Nothing stirred. 'Not even a policeman,' sniggered the voices.

His steps took the hot gun forward, raised ready for a sham. In the dimness he could hardly tell which end of the man was which. Then he saw the thick, shiny blackness that ran across the face. He could feel the warmth of the lying man.

A hand grabbed feebly. He felt a sudden touch on his suede shoe. But he stepped back with the dignified control of a leopard.

Connor whimpered. Small spitty sounds came from his mouth. 'Doctor,' he said. 'Doctor.'

'Ha, ha, ha!' the voices screamed, when they got over a moment's shock, 'Hear it? What does he think you did it for? A doctor!'

Halloran the conquering master looked down like a giant over the faint gleam of the barrel, and saw that Connor was the world.

'What do you snivel for?' he said. As if he was very, very curious.

Connor gave a little faltering sigh. 'For God's sake – get – get doctor –'

Emperor Halloran showed his small teeth in the darkness, glowing with power. Little fancies sang into his mind. A final word, now, a cunning word to crush the desire to live.

There was a bubbling, desperate noise at his feet. The man wriggled on the flagstones.

'The doctor.' Connor coughed helpless. His voice turned to an urgent, talking groan. 'Me wife – having – child!'

When he could move, little Billy Halloran jerked the gun away, clattering. Twitching from the feel of it, his hands sprang together for sympathy. His legs swung strangely. Then his fingers were scraping themselves on the coarse hardness of the wall.

'Never done it!' The breath rushed about in his body. 'I never done it! Holy Mother of God, it wasn't me!'

There were no voices in his head.

Nothing.

Not even the ghost of a soft whisper, as he ran in pattering suede feet with the world on top of him again.

For he was little.

Little and feared by no one.

It Doesn't Matter Now

THE RIGHT HONOURABLE EDWARD Francis, Baron Holburgh, O.B.E., formerly Judge of the King's Bench Division, looked at the envelopes. Some were coloured; some scented delicately; some bore engraved arms, and one the mark of royalty. This he opened first, when he had set the marker carefully in the Bible so that it indicated the exact verse he had reached in the Book of Job, wiped the water from his eyes, and put on his spectacles again.

Seventeen altogether the butler had laid before him. He went through them slowly, nodding, wrinkled lips and eyebrows moving in sympathy with the words. All congratulating him on being ninety years old. One or two of the younger writers were distantly facetious: 'Growing younger every day' – 'They'll have you back on the Bench yet – they certainly should!'

'Best wishes for the years to come.' Pleasant letters, but they would have to be answered. There was one from Vernon Wells: he was evidently failing. Vernon would be seventy-six, seventy-seven now.

Lord Holburgh wiped the water from his eyes again. How quickly the years went. He rang again – or perhaps he had not rung the first time – and soon there was his thick greatcoat, and the soft scarf being wound high round his throat, for the weather was uncertain.

'When I return, I shall be lunching alone, of course,' he said.

The sunlight outside hurt his eyes, and he pulled his hatbrim down, standing still and leaning upon his stick to do so. But there was almost no wind this morning. That was good, wind made his eyes water greatly. 'Yet I always insist on going out – even on windy days. So I cannot complain. As the maxim says: *volenti non – volenti non fit injuria.*'

'In possession of all his faculties,' they would be saying. 'Quite a remarkable age.' He noticed, when he came to it, that the gravelling of the highroad was completed, and that the surface was treacherous; heard that the telephone wires were faintly singing somewhere above his head – it was upsetting to look up; felt that his dry hands were cold inside his gloves, and his jaws were stiff. Yet lately law reports had proved most difficult reading, and their points strangely obscure. Things took on soft outlines and the details slipped away so easily.

He turned off at the little path that led to the clifftop. The sea air freshened one. Though but little until one was close enough to see the water. It was with the sight that the stimulation came.

Lord Holburgh's breath was straining as he came stiffly to the edge and looked far down at the tiny waves licking bald, black rocks. The sun glittered in across the water and made it a vast dazzle-surfaced green translucency. Nothing was so splendid. Perhaps it would be pleasant as a burial place, with that clear, shining colour about one for atmosphere. He stood with eyes to the horizon, breathing deeply.

'Calm, isn't it?', said a voice.

A few feet away was standing an old man, perhaps younger than himself; a working-class fellow in a cap and white stubble. Lord Holburgh's finger went absently to his own clean-shaven chin.

'I come here almost every day,' he said. 'I wish it were always like this.'

There was a little pause; a gull moaned far below them.

'A long time since I seen you before, sir.' The man came nearer.

Lord Holburgh looked at him, eyes watering. 'I'm afraid –'

'Since I met you, I should say. I've watched you come here often, from my cottage. I can't get out much, until summer, with my chest being bad. But I wanted to speak to you. It was so long ago p'raps you won't remember who I am?'

Blinking, Lord Holburgh saw his lined face was quietly intent.

'Birdie, my name is, James. James Roberts Birdie, sir. No?' He shook his head. 'It was Sheffield Assizes. May, nineteen oh eight.'

Lord Holburgh dropped his eyes and two little tears fell to the grass. 'Well – I – indeed...' he murmured.

'I remember you well, sir,' said Birdie.

Larval, memories stirred in the judge's mind. 'Was it some office you had? Or were you –?' He frowned.

'On trial, sir.' The other's white chin glistened in the sunlight. 'I was being tried on a murder charge. Went on nearly three days and then they brought in "Guilty". Even now I remember how I shouted when you gave the sentence.

'They commuted it to life. I been out a long time now.'

Lord Holburgh felt confused. He fumbled for something to say. 'Well, I – now it is all done with – I am glad to see you well – Birdie.' He stood stiffly, head fluttering a little, hands firm upon the walking-stick.

'You'll be cold, standing there, sir,' said the other old man. 'D'you mind if I should walk with you a bit?'

Oddly, Lord Holburgh seemed to himself suddenly frail.

He threw out his voice to make it sound strong. 'Very well.'

They went slowly along the clifftop path, Lord Holburgh's brass-tipped stick leaving a ragged row of pits in the clay as he pressed heavily upon it, Birdie's feet dragging occasionally.

'You see, sir, I never did – what they said I did.'

Lord Holburgh stiffened and his step paused. That was what they always said before trial; often they said it afterwards; some never stopped saying it. Forlorn perhaps, or something more obscure.

'But you had a fair trial – a fair hearing. At least, I hope so. I am sure I did all I could to see it was just.'

Birdie stopped and blew his nose carefully with a handkerchief held in both hands, before he spoke again.

'I suppose you did, sir. My bad luck that the evidence was – showing I did it.' The sunken corners of his mouth sharpened. 'But you know, sir, it was really you that made sure of my case.'

Lord Holburgh started. 'How was that?'

'I noticed it more because of me not having done it. You saw points, and ways of taking the evidence, that not even the lawyers didn't. And I had no alibi or anything. Of course I was there, when it happened.'

'I – I think I remember now,' said Lord Holburgh.

'We had quarrelled, and there was the knife. But it was queer.' Birdie's voice was quiet. 'Sort of suicide, and maybe accident – all mixed up. That's what I said, because I knew it was true, but I just couldn't make it sound right. They didn't think there was any doubt.

'I wish you hadn't spotted them points; it wasn't right they should be brought up against me. Then it might have been different.'

Cloudy stories that Lord Holburgh had heard came looming back on him. Judges being attacked by revengeful criminals. Several cases. Quite often, really. There had been Lord Justice _____.

'No. I didn't murder any man. I just couldn't have done it. But afterwards – it'd have frightened you if you knew how I hated you. When even the appeal was turned down, I knew I was made a murderer. I wanted to burst out of prison and kill you.'

Lord Holburgh realised he was on the outside – the cliff side – of the narrow path, and swallowed.

Birdie's knotted fingers plucked a tuft of grass from the low bank as he passed. 'I had plans and everything to escape. And track you down. But something always went wrong. One time I was shoved off to another prison; another time I was pinched. And – after a bit – I got to being faint-hearted about it. Prison sort of dries up your inside.'

He looked sideways at his companion. 'I know what you'll be thinking about that. But truly, I never killed anybody.'

They went a few paces in silence. Just ahead the path skirted a tiny hillock tufted with bracken and low bushes bunched against the wind.

'You know what it's like in those places, sir? I suppose you will, being a judge for them. I got nearly full remission, but I never took on any of their narky jobs. Other men, with my name being what it is, they used to make jokes about my wings.' He looked round defensively.

'But I think religion's a comfort when you're at this end. When you got a long time to think about – things, sometimes you get afraid. Now I never let a day go past but I read some.'

Lord Holburgh found himself nodding. 'So do I.'

'I come here to live about a year ago – funny, when you get out, you don't feel you belong; I don't, even yet – and when I found out who you were, I wanted to meet you.

'But you would have been frightened if you'd met me in them first days.'

A step or two further on, Birdie halted, shuffled round, on the path, looked up at the screening hillock above them. His face slowly became pale grey under the white sparkling bristle. His eyes went back to Lord Holburgh, then to the depths.

'What is the matter?' said Lord Holburgh.

The other old man's mouth worked as he stood blinking at the sea. His voice quavered tiredly. 'Don't you see? You – you and me all alone – up here on the cliff.'

Lord Holburgh moved away. A tremble ran through him. His knees were very weak.

Birdie's head went sideways like a half-comprehending dog. 'Sort of thing I had dreams about. Thirty years ago I'd have given every penny – I'd have given my soul for this here.

'To just have me and the judge alone at the edge of a cliff! And nobody able to see!'

He swung round and Lord Holburgh saw that his pale eyes with the yellow whites were blinking and twitching. He raised the walking-stick uncertainly. 'Keep back!' A thin squeak came from his mouth. 'Keep away from me!'

The distant rattling of the waves came up faintly to the two old men as they faced each other.

Suddenly, Birdie gave a long gushing sigh and tottered across the path against the cut-in bank. His knees buckled. He crouched there with weak, throaty noises. His cap lay on the path.

After a moment, Lord Holburgh approached him.

Birdie whispered to the clay: 'You needn't worry. I – I couldn't attack a man any more than I had done at the beginning of' – his head wobbled – 'of everything.'

Lord Holburgh was watching in silence. He bent forward stiffly, leaning on the stick. 'You'd better get up, then. It's all right.'

Birdie strained, hands discolouring with his weight upon

them. Then looked up. The older man took his arm and, struggling, raised him by supreme effort, swaying from side to side and clutching desperately at any hold. Bones cracked, lungs strained, knees trembled. 'Steady, now!' said Lord Holburgh. Birdie was on his feet.

'I'm sorry,' he said. His mouth slobbered. They leaned against the bank, panting. 'I made a – a show of myself.'

Lord Holburgh turned his head slowly to settle its odd internal motions. His eyes watered a great deal, yet there was no wind. His mouth opened and shut again. 'That takes something out of me,' he said at last to the shaking man.

'Yes,' said the other. 'I'm nearly eighty-one.'

Lord Holburgh remembered the morning's letters. 'I am ninety today. It is my birthday.'

Birdie's mouth was apologetic as he shook his head. Soon he said: 'We're both pretty old, eh?'

Balancing awkwardly, he picked up his cap and wiped it with care.

They walked together beyond the little mount, very weak in the legs. Beside the path they came on a family of baby rabbits playing in the sun, and stood to watch.

'Quick little creatures,' murmured Lord Holburgh.

A hand touched his arm.

'You know now – I never did it?' said Birdie. The young animals scampered away.

Lord Holburgh gave a slow little nod that had none of the decision of former days. His eyes were not on the path, and they were sad.

'Yesterday – no, this morning – I read in the Book of Job. Do you know it? I was trying to memorise a piece to keep my wits alive.

"But where shall wisdom be found? And where is the place of understanding? Men know – man knoweth not the price thereof: neither is it found in the land of the living." Have I it correctly? I shall have forgotten it tomorrow.' The cap nodded.

Lord Holburgh's stick continued its monopoded track along the clay as they approached the junction with the road. '"The depth saith: It is not in me: and the sea saith: It is not with me."'

The wrinkles about Birdie's eyes deepened when he smiled and finished: '"It cannot be got for gold, neither shall – shall silver be weighed for the price of it – the price thereof."'

He added, flatly: 'I suppose – perhaps what I was talking about – it doesn't matter now, really. At our age.'

Lord Holburgh blinked water at a tiny breeze, and touched his arm. 'There shall be lunch for two today at my house, if you do not mind coming.

'And afterwards we shall talk together. About' – he cleared his throat – 'about Job.'

The Old Woman with All the Cats

SHE KNEW WHEN SHE woke up and saw Lord Mompommon on top of the wardrobe that it was going to be the wrong sort of day. He was sprawling among the black plastic bags and vases as if he had a right to be up there.

'Get down!' shouted Mrs Parry. 'That's a NO place!' She clapped her hands together to make the noise they always respected, as if you were smacking them on the bottom, though being covered with fur it wouldn't make that sort of noise and anyway none of them had a bottom to speak of.

The cats round her on the bed shifted uneasily. Hibbs and Dodo, she noticed. Hooter, Crust, Nellie and Dippypaws. There had been others during the night but they must have left.

'Down, Lord Mompommon!'

The big black-and-white rose and stretched himself as if it was his own idea and he wasn't obeying her and might very well lie down again where he was. But she guessed what was in his mind. She quickly clapped her hands again. Lord Mompommon eased himself over the edge, pawing his way down the wardrobe door before dropping to the lino.

Mompommon was a boss cat. When he made for the door

the others went jumping from the bed to follow him.

'Go on, run after him!' shouted Mrs Parry. 'See if he'll make your breakfast for you, I don't think!'

She got up, feeling stiff. Her foot caught in the torn edge of her nightie and nearly tripped her. She sagged back on the edge of the bed. If she fell and hurt herself, who would come to find her? 'You wouldn't, not any of you,' she called. It wasn't quite true. Two or three of them might. Taggy and Badgerbits might. They were natural worriers, not just out of cupboard-love but their own kind of fussy concern. They liked to keep everything in order, like the time Badgerbits, with his vague terrors, kept following her out of the house and wailing loudly to stop her going off anywhere.

It was supposed to be different with dogs, which would lick people's faces to revive them in snow, or drag them to safety out of burning buildings. Dogs were noble, unselfish, smelly, toadying creeps.

She found three cats asleep in the bathroom. They had got the door of the airing cupboard open and were curled up among the towels. At least she had the use of the lavatory to herself, since Dido had disappeared. Dido had learned to squat on the seat's edge and perform like a human.

She dressed herself slowly. It was Pension Day, of course, but that wouldn't make her feel so ill-at-ease. It was just something not to forget. It felt as if anything could happen. Perhaps she had picked up the notion from them. They often knew things. She could hear them quarrelling downstairs but that was usual, because they wanted breakfast.

Everything she wore had threads pulled out. All along the shoulders where they would jump up and cling and rub their faces on hers. Skirts were clawed ragged. Stockings were a mass of ladders, hardly worth putting on, but she did her best with them as she was going out.

She went downstairs. They were waiting in their usual

places, Sir Tim and his followers in the hall, the rest in the kitchen. 'Good morning, good morning,' she said to them. Lord Mompommon was on the kitchen table with several others. He glared at her while she filled the kettle. He knew how strong he was, and he was the sort who might spring straight at you with all his claws. 'Good boy, Mompie,' she said to him. To make peace.

She went to the pantry to get bread and milk for them. She cut up a stale loaf, watched by all the anxious faces. Desperate, as if they couldn't believe she would really feed them. Beseeching paws patted her. Hisses and jealous snarls broke out.

'How now, what talk! Vanessa, behave yourself! And Hooter!'

Only old Pearl, who was twenty-three if she was a minute, showed no interest. She lay drowsing in her corner.

'Shall we have some milk on it?' she teased them. 'Shall we? Or don't you fancy any today?'

Frantic miowing, as if they believed her. Several of them leapt up on the draining-board beside her. She felt paws kneading her shoulder.

'All right, then.' She poured milk generously over the chopped-up bread, then warmed it with boiling water from the kettle. She stirred the steaming, softening mess and spooned it out onto their tin plates. The cats surged forward, spitting and sparring with each other as she put the plates on the floor.

She made tea.

She poured some out in bowls, cooled with much milk, for those cats that had a taste for it. Only Minna May enjoyed it as hot and sweet and strong as she did herself, and jumped up beside her to share her cup. Mrs Parry touched the gulping, purring throat, stroked the brindled coat and felt full breasts below.

'Where have you put your kitties, Minna May? They

aren't in the box. Where did you take them to?'

The cat had drunk enough. She scrambled down and made off. Mrs Parry finished the cup and poured herself another. The uneasy feeling persisted. The weather, perhaps, or some worrying dream she had forgotten. Then it occurred to her – this might be the day for a Visit.

'Oh no, please God!'

Her shout startled the cats. They cringed or glared, licking milky lips. She exclaimed more gently to them: 'If he comes here knocking at our door, we won't let him in! Not one inch! And if he starts his spying through the letterbox, you go for him! Tim and Mompie, scratch his eyes out – right out of his head!' She shouted down the hall, as if there really was somebody there: 'You come here looking for cruelty –well, now you've got some so run away!'

Her laugh went wrong on her, cracking and suddenly squeaking into that sound it never used to have. She grumphed it down.

'Mr Inspector,' she said when she could manage the right quiet dignity, 'we are all in good health here. Well fed. No sickness. Just a few scratches and split ears due to high spirits. Please leave us be.'

Holding it down like that made her shake. Hatred on the boil. The cats made little worried sounds because they could see she was talking to somebody that they knew wasn't there. 'Never mind,' she whispered. 'Don't you be upset. If he does come here, that's what we'll say.'

The thought of a Visit, now it had got in, wouldn't leave her. She picked up Bellameen and rubbed her face in the thick black fur for comfort. Bellameen purred, pleased to be chosen. Others showed immediate jealousy. Vanessa jumped down on her shoulder from her perch on the top of a door, and clung with claws that hurt. 'Oh, Vanessa!' she cried.

Visit after Visit. Mrs Parry, this can't go on, surely you see that? It's impossible for you to look after so many animals. You've got something like a population explosion here, it's insanitary, a noise nuisance, you could face prosecution for neglect. Yes, we know you do your best, we know you feed them and all that but it's not enough. This whole house stinks! I don't smell it, Inspector. We know you don't, Mrs Parry, but everybody else does. And it's simply no good asking us to find homes for the kittens, it's not our responsibility. Even putting them down costs time and money. We do it by injection. No, not drowning, you mustn't drown them, kittens don't drown easy I know that, Inspector, they squeal and struggle and you hold the sack down in the bucket but they won't give in, I tried, I tried! It's best done with a quick blow to the head, Mrs Parry, use a stick. If you're going to do it yourself, that is. But there's no need, the thing is to stop them breeding, don't you see that? Yes, doctored. We'll do it for you, yes, free. And I brought them Wilson and some others and they were done. And then I brought them beautiful Lowdy with the golden fur, to be spayed too. (I'm sorry, Mrs Parry, she's gone. What d'you mean, gone? Well, disposed of, wasn't that the idea? Sorry, sorry, a misunderstanding. She wouldn't have felt any pain, Mrs Parry.) Beautiful, perfect Lowdy! Well, you're not getting any more of them, none of my darlings or their babies either!

So it had to be the Stick. Kept out of sight beneath the scullery sink where they couldn't come across it and smell it and know it was for hitting kittens. It was easy enough after that first, bad, time. You got the knack. Over in an instant for the frail, blind things. Out of the world before they knew they were in it. Just leave one or two for the mother to suckle, and the rest were for the garden.

'How many of yours out there?' she whispered to Bellameen. Bellameen purred more quickly, as if she understood and approved. The batches of kittens were buried in the back garden, the graves unmarked. 'They didn't need names, there wasn't time to know them,' Mrs Parry said. Only the big cats, when they died, got 'Whisky' or 'Esmeralda' and the date, pencilled on garden labels. Those were everywhere now, and sometimes scratching paws dug them up, so they had to be put back carefully in the proper places. And when the pencil on the plant sticks faded, as if the names were trying to follow their owners into the earth, she marked them again carefully. Names were important.

But the strange thing about cats' names was you often had to change them as you got to know them better. Horace became Hooter from his caterwaul. Samantha turned into Mrs Taggy. Even Lord Mompommon had started as Moony and then Mumpie, before his full ferocity had developed.

'I had another name too,' she said to Bellameen. She turned to the rest. 'You didn't know that, did you? Before I was Mrs Parry, I was Miss Underhill. Miss Elizabeth Underhill. I was a girl.'

She giggled. Saying it like that, to them.

For once they didn't know what to make of it. She saw tongues halted between parted lips, in the middle of washing paws. Others were gripping their tails for the after-breakfast scrub, and staring at her. 'Oh, my dears,' she cried, 'my very own Bessie and Ginger Tib and little Simmie! Slippytoes, Bogo, Hooter, Bismarck, Mudgie!' Green eyes batted their lids at her, returning their love for the fond croon in her voice. 'Boyboy, Tim, Crust, Lord Mompommon dear, Pearl and Tomnoddy and Vanessa. Nibbs. Sniggler. Jessamine.'

She put on her coat and found her two big straw shopping-bags. She took the Pension Book out of her purse and showed it to them. 'See, I hadn't forgotten.' They would know. They could count the days of the week.

A few of them slid out of the front door with her. Boxer and fat Wilson, one of the black longhairs and a couple of tabbies. They never followed her far. After a hundred yards or so she looked round and saw Wilson sitting alone on the pavement. The others had gone back.

It was still the wrong sort of day. It felt heavy, as if there might be a thunderstorm to make people say that'll clear the air. But it wouldn't. You just got wet. Or you would meet rude children and only think afterwards of the things you should have said to them. That sort of day.

When she reached the shops she went first to the Post Office. There was the usual queue of pensioners. It always amazed her that they looked so old and she felt so young she must be cheating. The oldest-looking of all were women who had dyed and curled their white hair to look blonde. Above their wrinkled faces they had tresses like young girls, except that no real young girl would have had them like that, all frizzed and crimped. She hated those women.

When at last it was her turn at the counter she scribbled her name and pushed the book through.

'Why, what's this, Mrs Parry?'

It was the fussy one with the thin face sticking out of jowls. The nit-picker. Making a big thing of lifting the book up and staring at it.

'What's wrong?'

'That's not your name.'

The woman shoved the Pension Book back to her beneath the safety window. There it was, a plainly scribbled signature in her own writing: E. UNDERHILL. She could only stare at it herself.

'Well?'

'It was my maiden name.'

The woman made a tight smirk. Trying to think of something witty to say for the benefit of the queue behind. But she couldn't, so she fell back on Post Office rules. 'Just as well I know you, Mrs Parry, or I'd refuse to cash this. Sign again, please. Your correct signature.'

'Where?' Her face felt hot and stupid.

'There, just below.'

She picked up the scratchy pen, feeling so self-conscious she hardly knew what she was doing. It could come out as anything. But there it was: E. PARRY.

'That's better.'

Forgiving now. As the money was counted out she knew she had just been categorised – there, she could think of that odd word easily enough, categorised – in a different way. One of the batty ones, wits slipping, needs watching, only a matter of time.

'There we are, Mrs Parry.' She took the money. Two of the golden-haired ancients were primping and giving her looks as she passed them. She would have made their day.

She went on to the butcher's shop.

They had it put by for her, her usual large order. Lights, the great swelling masses of lung that nearly filled one of her bags. And beef heart, some pig's liver and a lot of chicken heads they didn't charge for. And all the tins she could carry.

'What about yourself, missus?'

'A couple of nice chops,' said Mrs Parry.

Not much else to buy after that. More stale bread, and she went to the pet shop for worm pills. She had given up flea powder because the fleas always got the upper hand and it was easier to scratch along with the rest of them. She was well used to it.

She started home with a heavy bag in each hand. The tins were the worst, being dead weight. Lights, in spite of their bulk, had a certain bounce in them.

Why on earth had she done that, getting her own name wrong!

Only Elizabeth Parry wasn't her real name, not what she started with. It was Frank who put Parry on her when he married her. Like changing the name of a cat. Cats didn't mind. Some people said cats never knew their names anyway, that they just listened to the tone of your voice when you called, finding tiny differences to mean this one or that one. And their names were nothing but people's fancy, to make them seem human.

'Oh that isn't true!' she said aloud, and pushed the thought away because it was a kind of treachery. Cats did know about words. They had their own language of sounds, not just miows but the chirrups and mutterings that were quite exact. If one greeted her in the dark she could always tell who it was. Perhaps they had named her too, in their own way. Had given her many names, one from each. And she hadn't known.

'Oh, my dears.'

She put the bags down to rest a moment, leaning them carefully against each other so that the contents didn't spill. Once she had chased a family-size tin across the pavement and into the road where it was squashed flat by a big truck before she could catch it.

She felt tired. Nothing inside her but a cup and a half of tea. She decided to take the short cut home.

A path ran across waste ground. It was a bumpy track you could easily trip on, and it led between clumps of bramble and other bushes. You never knew who you might, meet there. But her arms ached.

She walked carefully, watching for holes and stones. One of her heels was working loose, she knew. She ought to take it to be mended but that would cost money. When she was nearly at the end of the path and feeling relieved about it, she caught sight of something in the undergrowth.

Half hidden in the twitch-grass was an untidy bundle of newspaper.

Mrs Parry came to a stop. She peered closer. You often found rubbish dumped in places like this, but not always rubbish. Once she had found several packs of Chinese takeaway in the gutter, unopened. She had taken them home and the cats were ravenous for them. Or it might be something a thief had thrown away as he ran. Valuables. There might even be a reward.

She put her bags down and reached for it. She pulled it clear of the grass and opened the layers of crumpled newsprint. Inside there was a baby. A tiny human baby. It looked dead.

'Oh!' said Mrs Parry.

It was a very pale colour, as if all the blood had run out of it. A long umbilical cord trailed from its shrunken little belly and there were patches of soapy birthstuff still on it, though most had soaked off into the newspaper. The eyes were slightly open and quite lifeless. It was a girl baby.

She put out a hand and touched it. It was cold and stiff. Most likely born during the night. To some wretched girl who was ashamed, although nowadays... or perhaps just didn't know what was happening. Cats always knew. They would split the caul with their teeth to get the kitten out and then snip the cord through. Mrs Parry glanced about, nervous of finding another horror, the mother dead too, heavy white legs somewhere in the thrashed-down grass, and blood.

But of course, the newspaper. Whoever it was had managed to wrap it up and bring it here and hide it.

She wondered whether it had been still-born and just left to die. It was very small and withered-looking, perhaps premature. And the night had been cold.

'Poor you,' she said to the baby.

Or it might just have been left in the caul too long. There was no sign of a caul, though. Perhaps it was different with human babies.

'They threw you away.'

Better not get involved. There would only be questions and officials and more trouble about the cats. She tucked the newspaper round the body.

She tried not to touch it but it still made her shiver. And pushed it back where it had been. Visible enough for somebody else to find. Let them deal with it.

She picked up her shopping bags and made for home.

Wilson was still outside, waiting for her as he always did on meat days. He was one of the greediest of them. Being doctored seemed to have made him fat and stupid, and he had no conversation. Just squawks to indicate hunger.

As she let herself in others came clustering round, sniffing the bags and standing on their hind legs to see inside. But fewer than usual. 'Where are the others?' she asked them.

She kicked the front door shut and stood with her mind running different ways. Perhaps after all she should go to the police. Somewhere there was a guilty person, a woman who had bad reasons to hide her pregnancy or the silly, ignorant girl she had thought of before, perhaps not so ignorant but vicious and under the thumb of a lover who wanted her to get rid of it and she'd left it too late. A crime of some sort, anyway–

From the back of the house sounded a rending screech, enough to curdle the blood. Mrs Parry sighed.

It was a mating, of course. That's where they'd all gone. When she got to the kitchen she could see them in the garden, the toms gathered expectantly round the female who had just come into season. It was one of the tortoiseshells, Wendy, who had been looking broody for a day or two. Now Lord Mompommon was mounting her. He had the scruff of Wendy's neck firmly between his teeth and his hind feet trod hard on the ground as he made his thrusts. It was quickly over. As Mompommon disengaged himself Wendy shrieked with ecstasy and clawed at him, then rolled on her back. Next moment she was raising her ready rump again.

'Little slut,' said Mrs Parry.

This time it was Ginger Tib who threw himself at Wendy. The other toms sparred amongst themselves, impatient for their turn. Lord Mompommon sat washing himself. Whenever he wanted he would scatter them and exercise his boss cat's sexual rights again.

It could go on like that most of the day. The toms, normally the greedy ones, would have no interest in food beyond a quick snack to keep them going. but when Mrs Parry turned round she found she had other customers. The elderly and the neutered, the halfgrown and the nursing mothers, all there licking their lips. Scruffy old Pearl came dragging on her weak hindquarters from her nest in the corner of the kitchen, uttering her hoarse cries. She might be senile but she could still smell raw meat.

Mrs Parry tipped it all out on the table. Slapping down interfering paws, she cut off hunks of the spongy lights, strips of heart and liver. She chopped them small and scattered them in handfuls onto their plates, followed by a score of chicken heads. The cats flung themselves at the bloody stuff, spitting and snarling at each other. A few hung back, uninterested, the ones who would only eat it cooked. Bessie and Minna May and one or two more.

Mrs Parry got out the great pan she used for boiling lights, and tipped the rest in. Just the right amount of water and she sot it on the gas. Cooked, it would keep in the pantry for a couple of days.

More savage shrieks and yowls came from the garden. The brown tabby Crust was having his turn. This was the noise the neighbours had fussed about. 'I suppose you think it's rude?' she had retorted to them. 'Well, cats are rude sometimes and good luck to them!' Their fuss didn't get them anywhere, they being fifty yards away with the brick yard in between.

Just the same, she felt excluded at these times. If they looked in at her through the kitchen window; it was with a blank stare as if they had forgotten who she was. And if she went outside they would seem to hate her. A troop of wild animals about their secret business, and she must keep out of it.

Wendy was getting her fur in a mess. When she finally came in, probably not till night, it would be all caked with mud and misfires from the toms. And then, after nine weeks, kittens. Time to get out the Stick again.

The lights were on the boil, foaming and swelling in the pan as if they were trying to breathe again and do their duty to the beast they had belonged to. She stirred them and they sank down.

But the Stick. It might have been the same for that baby, it was possible. Put an end to. It was bigger than a kitten so it wouldn't be so easy, but just the same. She had seen no mark on it but it could have been smothered up with a pillow, just stopped from breathing if it had ever managed to start.

It might even have been the rejected one of a litter. People had twins often enough and nowadays three or four or even five were common. Just the same it wouldn't be right to take the one you didn't like and wrap it in newspaper and shove it under a bush. No more for a baby than for a kitten.

There was a dreadful shriek from the garden. Mompommon again, bowling that miserable little Wendy over and over, and she striking at him with all her claws and squealing.

They said it was ecstasy. Pain and pleasure all mixed up because the tomcats' cocks had bristles on them.

Frank's had no bristles or barbs or anything else. Nowadays you could buy all sorts of funny gadgets in the sex shops, just walk in and ask. 'Family Planning' was what they started calling themselves when the law got busy. A joke that, when it was all about not having families but just the fun. Frank wouldn't have gone into one of those shops anyway, he'd have felt demeaned. The idea that he needed titillation. He managed with what he bought at the barber's, his french letters. He went on with them far too long, though. She got to mocking him about it: Got your little rubbers, have you? We don't want any mistakes, do we? Because he wouldn't trust her to see to it, not once. And when he finally gave them up it was too late. She was a barren fig tree. Perhaps she had been all along and it had been a complete waste of time and money, him shoving all those little rubbers on himself. A bit of a joke that, except that it wasn't a joke at all. He switched right round. 'If you can't give me a kid, you're no good, you're not a woman at all!' he said once. He took to taking her by surprise, coming at her just anywhere, in the kitchen or the landing. He said it might make all the difference if she didn't expect it. Tearing the knickers off her and plunging his thing in any old how. He was clumsy on purpose, he told her so, as if hurting her might stir something. Perhaps if he'd gone to a sex shop and bought himself something with bristles to shove on his thing and make her screech like Wendy, that might have done it. But there weren't any sex shops, not then. He'd get in furious rages with her. He was trying to prove something about himself. And then he found the easier way and just went off her. He knocked up a woman on the other side of town. He boasted about it, even told her the name of the woman. It was Carol something, or Coral. And then he got himself killed outside that pub. Can I come in, Mrs Parry? Your hubby's had a bit of an accident. On his way home, they said, but it might not have been. A lot of nights he didn't come home, so he was more likely going to Coral or Carol, whichever she was. But it was herself and not that Coral or Carol who got the widow's pension. She wondered sometimes what happened to the kid. If there truly was one it would be grown up by now. Unless the woman did something else with it. She might not have let it get born. Even if it was, she might still have done something.

The lights were simmering now, collapsed. Mrs Parry added the rest of the meat, the heart and liver, to the pan. The toms would be angry because most of them liked it raw. Serve them right, then!

Wendy's screeches were growing fainter. They'll kill that poor thing yet, she thought. She rapped on the kitchen window. The whole lot turned and glared at her. Boyboy, who was trying to mount the tortoiseshell, was startled into falling off her. He spun round, hissing like a wildcat. Boyboy, that she had reared on the bottle when his mother died. He had been such a pretty kitten, a particular favourite, always ready to chase a bit of string and find artful ways to trap it.

'Boyboy!' she called.

The young cat did nothing but snarl at her. He even started a little run towards her. He looked so menacing that she was glad of the window between them. Hating her for upsetting his manhood in the middle of trampling Wendy. She saw his mouth open wide in a fierce cat's roar.

Not Boyboy or Wendy or Sniggler, none of those names belonged on them now. They knew who they were and it was their secret.

It came to her: perhaps names only hide the nature of things. They're a trick we have, to pretend we know what they are. If we had no words to label things with and make them seem small and say it's only a this, or only a that, then we should have to face what they really are. And we couldn't bear it.

Bessie and Hooter, Badgerbits and Wilson and Jessamine and Simmie and Minna May and Bellameen and Nellie, there on the floor, waiting again and watching, and you pretend you know them and have the power of the names that you put on them. But they aren't pretending.

She felt herself alone in a house full of animals.

Another bloodcurdling screech from the garden caught at her nerves. She moved about the kitchen quickly, for no reason. She trod on something, a tail or a toe, and a cat jumped aside with a squeal of offended rage. They always thought you did it on purpose. This time, though, she didn't beg forgiveness. Too many things were slipping into her mind. She shivered with excitement.

Perhaps it would still be there.

She turned off the gas. She covered the pan with a heavy

lid so they could not steal the meat. Some of them wouldn't mind scalding their mouths.

She put her coat on. She remembered to take one of the straw shopping-bags with her. Some of the cats ran after her but she stamped her foot at them and drove them back. She let herself out.

Crossing the road she caught sight of a dog in the distance. She shivered. If dogs had come.

She walked quickly to the path and made straight for the place. It was still there: the newspaper bundle just where she had left it, seemingly undisturbed.

She pulled it out. The paper was a *Daily Mirror*, she noticed now. She opened the crumpled pages and there it was again, the tiny body more dried out and shrunken. When she picked the bundle up she felt movement. She gasped and nearly dropped it. But the slitty eyes were just as dead. It must be the limbs softening, the rigor starting to wear off.

She placed it carefully in the bag with the newspaper covering it. She got to her feet. There was nobody about to have seen her.

She found it heavier than she thought. Comparing it with a weight she knew in the bag, lights say, she guessed it as over five pounds, maybe six. And that, she believed, was quite normal for them.

She started back to the house.

Perhaps it had been accidentally overlain. She had never known it happen to a single kitten, though, even born to an inexperienced young queen. More likely somebody smothered it.

When she reached the house she saw faces watching from the windows.

As soon as she was inside they were all round her, mewling. And there was Lord Mompommon, spraying on the wall and staring her out as he did it. He must have been driven indoors by hunger, or else he was spent. He ran to her and reached up to grab the bag with his claws. She lifted it high.

'Get away!' she cried.

He was sniffing. He knew it was something dead, so it must be meat. Next they were all doing it, squealing and demanding.

'It's not for you!'

With cats all round her ankles she ran and started frantically up the stairs. When she got to the top, panting, she saw they hadn't tried to follow. It was the way they would suddenly pass a thought round among themselves and change their tactics. They knew she would have to come down again.

She stumbled across the landing, her bad heel nearly bringing her down on the slippery lino. Cats watched her from the bathroom. Another came out of the bedroom and slid quickly past.

She slammed the bedroom door behind her, then threw it open again. There were cats on the bed. A grey and a long-haired black, turning brown with age, called Mudgie. Once a close confidant, not now. They were already on the move. She yelled at them: 'Out – get out!' They ran.

She was trembling all over.

She shut the door and put the shopping bag down on the bed. She was alone with the body. She unwrapped the Daily Mirror from it and sat down beside it.

It was hers.

Nobody else wanted it. She could do whatever she liked with it and nobody would know.

She felt a flush of the same bad excitement that had sent her out to find it. Like a long time ago, before Frank and his rubbers. With other men. Boys. I've got something to show you. Then show me, what are you up to, what d'you think you're trying to do? No, go on, go on, you cheeky. And it was nice sometimes, more than nice. But Frank. We don't want you up the spout, not yet, in the club, maybe some time, not yet though. And then all of a sudden, what's wrong with you, why can't you, it must be your tubes, I want a kid, if you can't you're not a woman, I want a kid!

I've got a kid, Frank. Look here.

It was softer now when she touched it. She was able to lift its hand. As small as one of their paws. Not claws but tiny perfect fingernails. And hair on its head. And ears. She ran her fingers down the face but she didn't close the eyes or anything, the way you were supposed to, because she liked them open a bit, as if it was just dropping off to sleep. Not it, she. A girl baby. She touched the slit between its legs, that was not going to grow up and have bad fun, or any fun at all.

Suddenly she picked it up, the cold creature, and held it to her as if she could warm it. She rocked it for a moment, the way you would a doll. But the limp feel of it sickened her and she dropped it back on the bed.

There was wet on her hand. As if it had managed to pee or she had squeezed something out of it. Then she felt a chill trickle on her cheek and a blur in her eyes, and knew it had come from there.

Another mad flush hit her. Without thinking, only giving in, she pulled her coat off and threw it aside. And then other clothes until there was nearly nothing on her. She grabbed the baby up and held it between her naked legs, just where the white hair grew. And panted and swayed about, and made believe for a moment that it had come out of her body. She cried out and clutched it to her and put the face of it to her bare breast, to the hanging nipple. She even took hold of her own flesh and pressed it between the icy bloodless lips.

'Can you not suck? Not at all? Oh, my baby!'

It was saying it that did it. The tears came splashing down on the body and on her own stomach and naked legs.

'My baby is dead.'

She laid the chill, floppy shape down at last, and dressed herself. There were practical things to be done and it was best to think only of those. Mrs Parry, can I come inside a minute? Don't mind my uniform, I'm afraid your hubby's had a bit of an accident.

She started searching in the drawers. Somewhere, she was sure, there was that old christening robe, long in the family. It had been used on herself. I name this child Elizabeth Underhill. She turned out whole armfuls of clothing, old woollies and vests that needed darning, even some socks that must have been Frank's. She heaved them all out on the floor.

She started up at a heavy crash somewhere in the house. It seemed to shake everything. They must have upset the pan of lights, that was it. Mompommon would have done it.

Reminded of their existence she remembered what had happened to the christening robe. She had torn it up years ago to make kittening nests. So it was gone.

Instead she found something she had knitted with her own hands, a half-finished cardigan. Cats had tormented her by playing with the balls of purple wool and she had given up. She laid it out on the bed. It had no sleeves and of course it was unworn, so it was clean. It looked right, though a bit gaudy. She placed the baby on it and wrapped it solemnly round. Then she put her coat on. It would be cold in the garden.

The kitchen was in the dreadful mess she expected. The big pan lay upside-down on the floor, which was awash with thin gravy. The cats were standing in it, crouched over lumps of meat. Some had dragged their spoils away and were growling fiercely. Others spat and sparred over smaller pieces. Younger, timider ones contented themselves with lapping gravy.

Some ran away guiltily as she came among them. Only Mompommon, grinding bits off the biggest lump of lung, showed any interest in what she held, in case it was something still tastier.

She picked up the spade on her way out.

In the garden there were only three toms still waiting by the fence, round the filthy, exhausted Wendy. 'Shoo!' she said to them, 'go on!' But none of them moved.

She laid the bundle down and plucked at the weeds to clear a space. Then she started to dig. She thought she had chosen an unused spot but when she was down a few inches the spade turned up small crumbling bones.

She made a fresh start nearby. The clay was harder here. Soon she was puffing. But she kept steadily on until the hole seemed deep enough, more than two feet.

When she turned she saw that a number of them had come out of the house. Leading them was Lord Mompommon, his tail held high and twitching as he advanced.

'No!' she screamed.

She picked up a stone and flung it as hard as she could. A cat squealed in pain. The rest stared at her, unable to believe it. She scrabbled up whole handfuls of gravel and soil and sent them flying at the cats. Pebbles. A half brick even. They understood now all right. They were shooting in all directions, some back into the house, some over the fence. Even the battered Wendy. In a moment the garden was clear of cats.

Mrs Parry went down on her stiff knees. She opened the bundle a little. 'I name you,' she whispered, 'I name you Mary Anne Underhill.' She pressed the slitty eyes shut now, and folded the purple woolly over it and put it down in the hole.

She pulled herself to her feet and used the spade again. Soon the hole was full. She dragged a piece of crazy-paving from the broken path and laid it on top. She had never seen a cat dig deep but that would make sure.

She knew the animals were watching her. They were all keeping out of her sight. Soon she would have to go in and clean up the mess they had made.

But first she would stay here for a while, imagining.

Note on this Edition

Tomato Cain and Other Stories was originally published in November 1949 by Collins in the UK, as a hardback edition comprising 28 stories. An American hardback edition, published by Knopf, followed in 1950, with two of the stories removed ('The Terrible Thing I Have Done', 'Charlie Peace and the King') and three extra stories added ('Essence of Strawberry', 'Mrs Mancini', 'The Patter of Tiny Feet'), taking the story count to 29. (A UK paperback was published by Collins imprint Fontana in 1961, following the updated Knopf line-up but omitting a further three stories – 'God and Daphne', 'Flo', 'Chains' – taking the total down to 26.)

This new Comma Press edition includes all 31 of the stories from across both the UK and US versions, plus three additional stories, the first two of which were contemporaneous with the collection: 'Billy Halloran', published in the August 1946 edition of *Tattoo*, and 'It Doesn't Matter Now', published in the August 1946 edition of *Britannia and Eve*. An unpublished, third story, 'The Old Woman With All the Cats' was discovered amongst Kneale's archival papers on the Isle of Man in

September 2022, and only included in this second print run of the Comma Press edition. Never previously published, it's unknown exactly when it was written, though it's most likely to date to some time around the late 1980s. (This dating is based on deductions made by Kneale's son Matthew, based on the typewriters he was using at the time, and by his daughter Tacy, based on similarities between Pearl and Wendy with their actual cats, Mog and Wienitz). With these three new stories, this edition is the closest thing we have to Kneale's complete short fiction.

Several of the *Tomato Cain* stories had a life beyond the anthology itself. Some, credited to the early pen-name 'Nigel Neale', were first published in story magazines – 'Lotus for Jamie' in the February 1944 edition of *Convoy*; 'The Calculation of N'Bambwe' in the March 1945 edition of *Strand*; 'Enderby and the Sleeping Beauty' in the February 1946 edition of *Argosy* (under the title 'The RAF and the Sleeping Beauty'). Others were republished elsewhere soon after the Collins collection – 'Minuke' in the February 1950 edition of *Argosy;* 'Jeremy in the Wind' in the April 1950 edition of *Argosy*; The Putting Away of Uncle Quaggin' and 'Oh, Mirror, Mirror' in the June 1950 edition of *Harper's*; 'Minuke' and 'Curphey's Follower' in the September 1950 edition of *Harper's*.

A few of the stories were read for BBC Radio, often prior to their publication. The titular 'Tomato Cain' was read by Kneale himself for the *Stories by Northern Authors* strand, broadcast on the Home Service Northern regional programme on 25 March 1946. 'Zachary Crebbin's Angel' was read by Kneale as the *Mid-Morning Story*, broadcast on the Light Programme on 19 May 1948 (and later repeated in the *Twice-told Tales* slot on the Home Service on 7 Sept 1950). A reading of 'Bini and Bettine' (reader unknown, but likely Kneale himself) was broadcast on the Home Service

Northern regional programme on 18 May 1949. (It was later read by George Parsons as Radio 4's *Morning Story* on 18 October 1988).

Subsequently, 'The Pond' was read by Meg Simmons as Radio 4's *Morning Story* on 5 April 1978, and again by George Parsons as Radio 4's *Morning Story* on 6 September 1988. 'Oh, Mirror, Mirror' was dramatised by the listener-funded Californian radio station KPFA for their *Black Mass* strand and broadcast on 16 October 1963. 'Essence of Strawberry' was read by Kneale for the Home Service Northern regional programme on 1 March 1950, and it was also dramatised for American television by Alvin Sapinsley as part of the CBS strand *The Web* on 17 January 1951. For British television, a filmed reading of 'The Photograph' by Tom Baker formed part of the *Late Night Story* strand and was broadcast on BBC 1 on December 23 1978.

A select handful of the more genre-flavoured *Tomato Cain* stories, including 'The Pond', 'Minuke' and 'The Photograph', were anthologised many times over the years, notably for the Fontana *Books of Great Horror Stories* and Pan *Books of Horror Stories*. In 2014 the Isle of Man's Manx Language Society, aka Yn Çheshaght Ghailckagh, published a truncated dual-language version of *Tomato Cain*, comprising seven of the original stories with a strong Isle of Man setting (namely 'Tomato Cain', 'The Tarroo-Ushtey', 'The Excursion', 'The Putting Away of Uncle Quaggin', 'Curphey's Follower', 'Tootie and the Cat Licences' and 'Zachary Crebbin's Angel'), in both English and Manx.

Andy Murray
Manchester, November 2022

Special Thanks

The publishers would like to thank Andy Murray for his tireless efforts in bringing this edition together; his familiarity with the life and work of Nigel Kneale has been instrumental in making this re-release happen. We would also like to thank Matthew and Tacy Kneale, Nigel's executors, for their heartfelt support throughout. Thanks are also due to Jon Dear, Toby Hadoke, Stephen Durbridge of The Agency and Norah Perkins of Curtis Brown Ltd., as well as Celia Phillips at the National Library of Scotland, Jesse Willis at SFFAudio and Raph Cormack for their sleuthing skills in tracking down two of the previously lost stories.